SE...
OF THE DEAD

"This book is a tense, moody white-knuckler sure to send a creeping chill up your spine."

PAUL TREMBLAY, *New York Times*-bestselling author of *Horror Movie* and *A Head Full of Ghosts*

"Lebbon's latest proves without question that he is a master at his craft… I will confess to being powerless to put this book down, and the final denouement will leave you breathless as only Tim Lebbon can."

RONALD MALFI, Bram Stoker Award® recipient and author of *Small Town Horror*

"*Secret Lives of the Dead* is a riveting, wholly absorbing crime-chiller rooted in trauma and friendship. Tim Lebbon is a true master of unrelenting suspense and he continues to shock me and impress me in equal measure with his dark literary powers book after book."

ERIC LAROCCA, author of *Things Have Gotten Worse Since We Last Spoke*

"A rocket-fueled, blood-soaked tale of cat and mouse with a witch's curse as its beating heart... *Secret Lives of the Dead* is a wholly original thriller."

CHRISTINA HENRY, author of
Alice and *The House that Horror Built*

"*Secret Lives of The Dead* is now my all-time favourite Lebbon book!"

NUZO ONOH, Bram Stoker Lifetime Achievement Award[*] recipient and author of *Where the Dead Brides Gather*

"If Britbox and Shudder wrote a book together, it might come out something like Tim Lebbon's genre-busting, dread-inducing crime horror novel *Secret Lives of the Dead*. Full of secrets, trauma, friendship, and curses, Lebbon's latest is a must-read!"

CHRISTOPHER GOLDEN, author of *The Night Birds*

"Tim Lebbon has hand-crafted a stunning hard-boiled artifact of horror noir, equal parts witchcraft and crime, blood and heartwood, serving as further testament to his supernatural abilities as one of contemporary speculative fiction's leading alchemists."

CLAY MCLEOD CHAPMAN,
author of *Wake Up* and *Open Your Eyes*

"Great characters, an unstoppable, implacable evil, and pacing that grabs you by the hand and doesn't let go make *Secret Lives of the Dead* the perfect horror thriller. It had me from page one!"

ALMA KATSU, author of *The Fervor*

"A propulsive, imaginative, page-turning heist-to-horror novel in which no one is safe. I absolutely burned through this book."

KEITH ROSSON, author of *Fever House*

"A horror novel so good it tangles itself in your bones."

LINDY RYAN, author of *Bless Your Heart*

"*Secret Lives of the Dead* is both an eerie and original slice of folk-horror and a riveting, relentless psychological thriller that will very likely keep you up all night. I couldn't put it down. It may be Lebbon's best yet, and that's saying a lot."

DANIEL CHURCH, author of *The Hollows*

*Also by Tim Lebbon
and available from Titan Books*

THE LAST STORM
EDEN
COLDBROOK
THE SILENCE
AMONG THE LIVING

THE RELICS TRILOGY
RELICS
THE FOLDED LAND
THE EDGE

THE RAGE WAR
PREDATOR: INCURSION
ALIEN: INVASION
ALIENS VS PREDATOR: ARMAGEDDON

THE CABIN IN THE WOODS: THE OFFICIAL MOVIE NOVELIZATION
ALIEN: OUT OF THE SHADOWS
KONG: SKULL ISLAND – THE OFFICIAL MOVIE NOVELIZATION
FIREFLY: GENERATIONS

SECRET LIVES OF THE DEAD

TIM LEBBON

TITAN BOOKS

Secret Lives of the Dead
Print edition ISBN: 9781835413555
E-book edition ISBN: 9781835413531

Published by Titan Books
A division of Titan Publishing Group Ltd
144 Southwark Street, London SE1 0UP
www.titanbooks.com

First edition: August 2025
10 9 8 7 6 5 4 3 2 1

This is a work of fiction. All of the characters, organizations, and events portrayed in this novel are either products of the author's imagination or are used fictitiously. Any resemblance to actual persons, living or dead (except for satirical purposes), is entirely coincidental.

© Tim Lebbon 2025.

Tim Lebbon asserts the moral right to be identified as the author of this work.

No part of this publication may be reproduced, stored in a retrieval system, or transmitted, in any form or by any means without the prior written permission of the publisher, nor be otherwise circulated in any form of binding or cover other than that in which it is published and without a similar condition being imposed on the subsequent purchaser.

A CIP catalogue record for this title is available from the British Library.

EU RP (for authorities only)
eucomply OÜ, Pärnu mnt. 139b-14, 11317 Tallinn, Estonia
hello@eucompliancepartner.com, +3375690241

Typeset by Rich Mason in Minion Pro.

Printed and bound by CPI Group (UK) Ltd, Croydon, CR0 4YY.

'A thing is not necessarily true because a man dies for it.'

OSCAR WILDE

SKELLINGTON

SEPTEMBER 2024

RURAL EXPLORING

BEYOND SUSPICION

BB

Jodi was setting her usual good pace, and although it was earlier than BB usually preferred to go running, he thought he might just get used to this. The chill morning was still and quiet. Mist hung in a low sheen, silvering the dew-speckled fields. The looming sunrise sculpted the line of low hills to the east, just silhouettes right now, but he could already see the pale ghosts of farmhouses beginning to emerge. To their left the sluggish river flowed with a comfortable murmur, calm beneath a hazy blanket. It was beautiful.

They crossed a low wooden bridge spanning a stream feeding into the river, their footsteps loud and then quiet again when they hit the grass on the other side. Once through a small gate and in the field beyond, BB put on a burst of speed so that he was running beside her.

"You've kept this all to yourself," he said.

"You're the one who prefers road running."

"I mean the early mornings. This is glorious."

"And you're the one who likes a lie-in."

"The river looks inviting, too. Fancy stripping off for a swim?"

She smiled sidelong at him, then switched direction straight across the field, no longer following the trodden footpath beside the river. BB slowed for a few seconds, then fell in behind her again, trying to match her footsteps through the tall wet grass. It was a game he'd played as a kid when he was out walking with his parents. Then, he'd had to stretch. Now, his footfalls were tight and fast. They ran in silence until they reached the far corner of the field, where she vaulted an overgrown stile and disappeared from view.

"Hey!" BB leaped the stile, caught his foot on a trailing bramble and almost spilled. He landed, caught his breath, and looked beyond the hedge. A narrow path wound uphill, and he just caught sight of her red running pack disappearing from view. "Jodi!"

She didn't answer. It didn't matter. They both knew where they were headed, and though BB hadn't run these trails before he often travelled the surrounding roads and lanes on his bike. He was familiar with the old, abandoned house on the hill, too, though he'd never paid it that much attention. Not until two weeks ago. Now, it was the only thing on his mind.

BB ran on, enjoying the silence and watching his footing. It wouldn't do to turn an ankle now. What the hell would Matt say to that? He glanced at his watch, though he had a pretty good idea of the time. Approaching seven in the morning. They were nearing a narrow road, and around the corner he slowed and came to a stop where Jodi was leaning against a fence. A potholed lane lay beyond, connecting one main road to another and providing access for several farms and a handful of isolated country homes. Unlike the house forefront in his mind, those other places were all inhabited. She took a swig from her water bottle and handed it to him.

"Matt'll be on his way," he said.

She nodded, breathing hard, and tapped two fingers against her forehead. "Mission going entirely according to plan, sir."

"Er, I think you're the boss of this operation."

"Shared ownership."

"I love it when a plan comes together," BB said.

She frowned.

"George Peppard. Hannibal Smith, *The A-Team*."

"Huh?"

"You're fucking kidding me."

"I thought that was Liam Neeson," Jodi said, bemused.

BB went to protest again, never quite sure when she was winding him up, when they heard a car engine. Jodi grabbed his arm and tugged him away from the fence, back towards the sheltering undergrowth.

"Hey, we're just two runners—" he said.

"But if we don't *have* to be seen, best we're not." She pulled him down behind a wild hedge and they saw the silvery flash of a van pass by.

He leaned in close and kissed her ear. "*Euch*! Sweat."

"You don't usually complain," she said. "Come on. Across the road then up the hill."

They moved on, and BB felt the familiar thrill of effort, made more complete by exercising with Jodi. They didn't do it together often enough. He preferred biking or running on the roads when the sun was up, her love was trail running pre-dawn or at dusk. She said she liked the peace and solitude, and it was a reflection of her general dislike of crowds, and other people in general. A perfect run for her was ten miles along the river or around the local hills without encountering another person. This morning he was really starting to understand the allure, and not only because of what they were doing. This felt good for the soul.

Or maybe it was the idea of an extra few grand in his bank that made it feel so good.

As they passed through a small woodland, something big took fright and disappeared into the shadows with a heavy rustle of undergrowth.

"What the hell was that?" he asked.

"Deer," Jodi said, slowing to a walk. "Maybe a tiger." They were at the edge of the small wooded area, halfway up a steep hillside, with the dawn landscape laid out before them.

"There are deer here?"

"You wouldn't see them on the bike. Connect with nature."

"I'm a townie."

"Yet I still hang around with you." Jodi stood with hands on her hips. "Just get a load of that."

"'Hang around' with me?"

She didn't answer. As he stood beside her he saw why. The view was gorgeous, and both of them breathed hard from exertion as they soaked it in. From higher up the whole countryside was bathed in morning mist, glowing pink from the dawn sun breaking over the distant hills. Copses of trees and rolls in the land peeked above the sun-touched mist, and in the distance a church spire and a windmill marked their place. The scene was still and quiet and incredibly peaceful, but BB's gaze was drawn closer. To the right, on top of the hill and visible behind old oaks and a scatter of younger trees, the pale façade of Morgan Manor caught the sunrise.

Jodi shrugged off her running pack and dug out a small pair of binoculars. She scanned the house, then handed them to BB.

He laughed. "Really?"

"What?"

"It's like we're professionals, or something."

"We've got to make sure. You know how careful we have to be, right?"

This time his laughter was nervous. Yeah, they'd talked about it, but this was a bit of an adventure, that was all. One with a possible payday, and that would suit him fine. Even Matt didn't know the extent of his remaining gambling debts from back in the day, and if things worked out here no one ever had to. At the very least, they'd have a couple of hours exploring this old place that had once featured heavily in local history and myth, but which over the last couple of decades had faded away in most peoples' memories. When they were kids, and BB was still just plain Sam King, he and Matt had once spent a day planning an excursion here because rumour had it a homeless guy had lived in the house for a while, and no one had seen him in months. Matt said maybe they'd find his skeleton. Except back then he'd said "skellington". BB had been keen to go. Then something else had grabbed their attention – he couldn't remember what now, only that it was Before Girls so was probably a new bike or a superhero TV series, or something – and their expedition had never made it off the page. He couldn't recall the last time he'd even looked up the hill at the partially hidden structure when he was cycling past.

Not until two weeks ago, anyway.

BB lifted the binoculars and scanned the house, the trees that partially shielded it from view and the surrounding hillside. The long driveway was hidden on the building's opposite side, where it curved downhill through fields given over to grazing cattle until it met the road half a mile distant. That was where Matt would arrive from, and once their recce was done they would make their way around the foot of the hill to meet him.

BB gasped and froze, looking at the house.

"What?" Jodi asked.

"It's *horrible*!" he said, and he almost dropped the binoculars as she shoved him against a tree.

"Dick." She grabbed the binoculars from him and shoved them in her backpack. He heard them clank against something else, and her eyes flickered to his and away again.

BB didn't think anything of it. Later, he'd have cause to remember that moment, and the strange look in Jodi's eyes. He was used to her being like that. They'd been together for just over a year, and he loved her like absolute fucking crazy, but a couple of months ago after a beer too many he'd told Matt that he really didn't think he knew her all that well. When Matt asked what he meant he'd spent a good minute or two thinking about it before saying, *It's like she's haunted.* Matt hadn't mocked him like he should have. BB lived life shallow and fast, and Matt wasn't used to seeing his friend so serious.

Jodi shouldered her backpack, clipped it on and glanced at her watch. "Come on. All looks good, and quiet. His Matt-ness will be on his way, and I want to be there to open the gate for him."

They left the cover of the woods and headed out into the dawn, skirting around the hillside and staying away from the old place they'd come to burgle. Just a young couple out for an early morning run.

JODI

Two weeks earlier, they are enjoying an afternoon in the pub garden. Jodi knows she has him when he stops talking and just stares at her over the top of his pint. He's only ever that quiet when he's thinking something through, and once he starts thinking about this, he'll be in. She's pretty, pretty certain of that. So she doesn't lay it on too thick. That would feel like overkill, and she doesn't want to appear too keen. It's just a loose, crazy idea after a few drinks in the sun. Let BB muse on it, perhaps even make it *his* idea, and he'll be more likely to take it seriously.

And once he commits, Matt will be along for the ride.

"So why hasn't anyone else gone there and taken it?" BB asks.

Jodi shrugs, takes a sip of wine and pretends not to care. She catches Matt's eye and he's giving her the smallest of smiles, and she knows that he knows what she's playing at here. He's sharper than BB, quieter, a little more dour. He can see right through her, or at least he thinks he can. Deeper than BB, at least. She raises one eyebrow at him in return. They get on really well, and that more than anything makes her feel so comfortable in the company of them both. Matt and BB have been friends since they were barely walking kids at Mariton's local nursery, and she loves the feeling of being accepted by Matt. She hasn't taken his friend away from him; rather, BB has brought Matt another friend. He's a good-looking guy but she doesn't fancy him, and that's because what they have is closer to brother and sister. Jodi always wished she'd had a sibling. And thinking that always makes her sad, because it brings her mum to mind, and her dad's violent death.

"How do *you* know about it?" BB asks.

"I told you, that would be telling."

"But you don't know what's there, so it could just be a box full of old cracked plates, or a treasure hoard of global significance."

"That's why it's an adventure. At the very least we get to take a look in that fucking spooky old place."

The garden in the King's Arms is buzzing. It's a Saturday evening in early September, and people are taking advantage of a stretch of warm weather. Families gather at bench tables, kids lark around the playground in the garden's corner, and Jodi has led them to the table closest to the river. It's away from the others, and she chose it partly so that she could plant the seed of her idea without anyone overhearing. It's also peaceful so close to the flowing water. One time a couple of months back they'd seen a kingfisher dipping in and taking its lunch.

"Supposed to be a curse over it, too," she mutters.

"Curse?" Matt and BB exchange a glance, and it carries the comfortable weight of decades of friendship. Perhaps that's what makes Jodi feel a little distanced, but she thinks not. She thinks it's because she's glossing over something that has troubled her for fifteen years. Whenever she thinks of her dad's final day it's all blood and fire and death.

"Just something stupid," she says. "Bad luck. That sort of crap."

BB chuckles. Matt sips his pint and rolls his eyes.

Then BB sits up straight and says, "We'll be rural exploring! You know, like urban exploring except—"

"Except rural." Matt glances around to make sure no one else is within earshot. Jodi is quiet – she's always careful to keep her head down, subdued even, when she's had a few drinks – but BB is getting louder. She knows very well that he's pretty daring, doesn't mind a bit of adventure, and loves the thrill of doing something a little off the chart. He alludes to a roguish past, but when she presses him on it he becomes a bit vague, as if the stories he has to tell belong to someone else. That's fair enough; she gives him the same. She likes to think they're beyond trying to impress each other, but she also knows she has to pitch this just right. It's far too important to risk fucking it up. She could do it on her own, sure. But with Matt and BB in with her, it was much more likely to go right.

That's why she's waited until they are three drinks in.

They drift away from the conversation, and Matt tells them about a new contract he's bid on that might take him away from town for a few weeks. It sounds like a good earner, but he doesn't like being away from home. BB calls him a pussy. Matt tells him it's his fucking round. BB goes into the pub, and Matt and Jodi chat and laugh and pointedly ignore the idea of breaking into and burgling an abandoned manor house.

Jodi is happy that the seed of the idea is planted, and confident that it will bloom.

Later, after they've eaten at the local Mexican restaurant, she and BB go home and crack open a bottle of wine. He drinks three glasses to her one, and she's still just merry when he's edging towards inebriated. He's a loveable, affable drunk, laughing and soft and more open about his own feelings and failings. They cuddle up on the sofa and watch an old movie. They start kissing, and the movie is forgotten. Jodi jumps off, pushing away his grasping hands and leaving the room; a minute later she's back, naked and spreadeagled above him, lowering herself teasingly down, telling him this is how she'll Mission Impossible into Morgan Manor's basement to grab the loot and that she won't leave a trace.

By morning, fuzzy headed, BB has agreed with the idea, and he's on the phone to Matt saying they should meet up to discuss "the adventure". Jodi has insisted on this. No texts, no electronic mention of what they're going to do. That's half of how they'll get away with it.

The other half is all down to her.

While BB is showering she sits in the garden with a coffee and thinks of her dead father, and how she's spent so many years waiting to make the bastard who killed him pay.

MATT

Matt woke at 3 a.m. and couldn't get back to sleep. Jangling nerves kept him awake and made him sweat. He threw off the bed covers and got cold; pulled them over himself again. Stared at the ceiling. Took deep breaths and closed his eyes, but opened them again to the imagined sound of a prison door slamming.

We're beyond suspicion, Jodi had said. *A local electrician, a PE teacher and a second-rate graphic designer working in a print shop.*

You're not second rate, BB had said. *You're really good.* Jodi hadn't answered, but she'd smiled. BB'd had lots of girlfriends, but Matt knew he really meant it when he said Jodi was The One. He saw it in the unguarded way he looked at her when she didn't know he was.

"Beyond suspicion," Matt said to himself, and close to four in the morning he got up and made coffee. He did so beneath the light of the kitchen extractor fan. He rented a small two-bed house he could barely afford, and neighbours were used to him leaving early for work, but even he was rarely up at this hour. He didn't want to raise any flags. "Beyond suspicion," he said again as he drank his coffee. He'd thought about those words a lot, and they sounded like the title of an average TV series in which all the characters were anything *but* beyond suspicion. But deep down he knew Jodi was right. They all had respectable jobs, and Matt knew half the people in town because of his electrical firm. Jodi had only lived there for a couple of years, true, but she was well liked, if low-key. She helped with litter picking and walked her elderly neighbour's dog.

Matt knew that BB still carried a bit of gambling debt, but he'd worked hard at paying it off. He'd even given him some money a year or so back, even though Matt's own situation wasn't quite as rosy as some people might believe. His company was doing OK, though still recovering from the hit he'd sustained during the Covid pandemic. But his divorce a few years ago had driven him to the edge of bankruptcy, and he'd been so upset during that period that he'd perhaps let Gemma take too much. If so, it hadn't been intentional on her part, but it wasn't likely she'd come to an epiphany and return anything to him. He rarely spoke to her anymore, but he knew she'd set up her own landscape design company up north. He thought there was a guy. That was OK, he hoped she was happy. BB often told Matt he was too fucking nice, and on this occasion that also translated as too fucking skint.

So beyond suspicion, maybe. But none of that would matter if they were careful.

He left home just after six. Driving out of town he had a brainwave and pulled into a quiet lane, parking up in a field gateway.

Dawn suggested itself across the eastern hills, and outside his battered van he took a moment to breathe in the cool morning air. He'd run each of the last four days to work away some of his nervousness, and his legs ached and felt stiff. It was a good feeling. Born and bred in Mariton, he still loved living there. Some might say his horizons were too close, and BB had left and come back a couple of times before he hit thirty. But this place was home. Matt sometimes suspected that staying was stubbornness, because it was Gemma who'd upped and left. In his mind he portrayed that as running away. That made him feel better, and he grabbed on to the best bit of advice his father had given him before passing away: *Be content with whatever you've got and you'll always be happy.*

In front of the van he scooped some damp soil from beneath the gateway and smeared it across his numberplate. It wasn't part of the plan they'd come up with together, but it seemed like a sensible precaution. Walking around to the rear to do the same, he froze and stared at the side of the vehicle. He emitted a short, snorty laugh, then carried on giggling. He hadn't laughed like this on his own in… forever. There was a hysteria to it.

On the van's side it said, *Matt Shorey, Elec/Tricks.*

Everyone in town knew his van. *That's why no one will see it,* Jodi had said, *because everyone's so* used *to seeing it.*

He wiped his hands on his jeans, sat back inside and took a few deep, slow breaths. Then he started off away from town and towards Morgan Manor, driving slow and safe, and wondering how the holy fuck BB had ever managed to persuade him this was a good idea.

It was Jodi. Her idea, her seed planted, the sway she held over BB. Matt adored her, and it was rare he'd ever felt so close to someone after such a short time. There was a vulnerability to her and also a quiet strength, and he thought perhaps their friendship was easy and pressure-free, and safe, because there could be nothing more. She and BB were tight, solid and in love even after such a relatively short time, and this made Matt feel so much more comfortable in her presence. He'd never been as confident around women as BB, and let doubts winnow away at him all the time, but his relationship with Jodi almost felt like that between siblings. She'd once said that together they were BB's solid foundation, and that he'd tumble without them.

There was that, and also the allure of a handful of cash if they found anything worth stealing in the manor. Jodi said she was good at deep searching on the net, following rumours, but that still troubled Matt. You had to know where to start looking for rumours, and he didn't think for a moment Jodi had googled "hidden treasure in Morgan Manor".

He'd settled his nerves, and allowed himself to be drawn in, for two reasons. One, it was an adventure with his two best friends, and something his life needed right now was adventure. Something unusual, and daring, and apart from the norm. And two, if they were caught breaking into the old, abandoned house, the most he'd end up with was a caution. In reality, that slamming prison door was a product of his overactive anxieties. The worst way he'd broken laws before were a couple of speeding tickets, being arrested for a drunken fight when he was seventeen and the occasional cash-in-hand payments he took for local work for people he knew well. He was hardly Mariton's organised crime kingpin. And all three of them were, as Jodi had said, beyond suspicion.

She's still a bit of a mystery, though, he thought as he hit the minor road that wound eventually around the foot of hill upon which loomed Morgan Manor. Easy-going, quiet, yet incredibly sharp, Jodi shared very little about her past. Scars on her chin and left forearm were from a bicycle crash when she was a kid, she claimed. They looked like more than that to Matt. BB seemed to accept when she said that she was boring and there wasn't much to tell, but Matt saw deeper. At least, he wished he could see deeper. BB had chosen his words carefully when he'd said, *It's like she's haunted*. For Matt, those four words summed up Jodi perfectly. Maybe what they were doing today was one way of her exposing and confronting her ghosts.

He arrived at the gates right on time. BB and Jodi were there in their running gear and backpacks, and by the time he left the road and approached the gates in a low recessed wall, they had them open ready for him to drive through. They squeezed into the front passenger seat almost before he'd stopped.

"Good morning!" BB said.

"You smell," Matt said.

"Charming," Jodi said.

"Not you. Him. You smell of roses and sweet dreams."

"I think... maybe... you're being sexist?"

Matt laughed, feeling his brief burst of hysteria still underlying everything. Being with his friends helped calm it a little. BB, brash and excited about doing something so crazy. Jodi, calm and quietly in control.

"So, you two boys ready for an adventure?" she asked.

"Oh yes!" BB said.

Matt headed up the long driveway that curved around the

gentle hill towards the house, and as they drew closer he could see more of it through the trees and undergrowth surrounding it. None of their planning had brought them close, other than Jodi who'd come out here on a night run just to see if there were any windows lit. She'd reported a quiet, silent place. Almost spooky.

"So what now?" Matt asked as he stopped the van and killed the engine. Morgan Manor's scarred painted façade was yellowed by early morning sunlight. The gravelled driveway was speckled with vibrant weeds and clumps of shrubs that had sprouted through the unused route. Most of the windows were either shuttered or, where there were no shutters, boarded over. The steps leading up to the wide front door were scattered with clumps of rotten wood from where a portion of the elaborate, wide porch had collapsed. If ever a building looked unlived in and alone it was this one.

Jodi opened the door and jumped from the van. Her feet crunched on gravel, and Matt scanned the building and surroundings looking for movement, signs of life, danger. There was nothing.

Jodi walked towards the old house. "Now, we knock."

JODI

Jodi knocked on the door. It gave a dull clump, not the echoing sound she'd been expecting. She felt foolish doing it, because the place was so obviously unoccupied. They stood in silence for a moment, a held breath.

"Nobody home," she said.

BB had already shrugged off his pack, and now he pulled out the claw hammer he'd been carrying, its head wrapped in a sock to prevent it banging against the other tools in there. Jodi carried her own tools, but hoped she wouldn't need them.

"Around the back, then," BB said. He led the way, and Matt glanced at his van before he and Jodi followed.

"It's fine," she said. "No one can see it from the road."

"Right." He sounded unsure, and now they were here and actually doing what they'd been talking about for two weeks, she knew he was nervous as hell.

She was nervous, too. She wouldn't let on; couldn't afford to. This could all come to nothing, but it might turn out to be the moment she'd spent years waiting for. The beginning of her future. Her dad's final moments called to her and played out in her mind, again and again, in all their flaming bloody violence. Her mother whispered a plea from years before, asking her to look after her father. But Jodi couldn't let herself be distracted. She shut her parents out. Guilt had made her adept at doing that.

They circled around the side of the house, gravel crunching beneath their feet. There was a side entrance down a short flight of worn stone steps, but a heavy metal door had been bolted across the opening. BB had brought tools, but Jodi hoped they'd find an easier way inside. At the rear of the house a brick wall curved outwards and disappeared into a mass of overgrown rose and clematis, too deep and wide to penetrate. It looked like an old walled garden. BB cradled his hands and Jodi stepped in and boosted herself up, one hand on his shoulder, the other feeling cautiously across the wall's head. No glass, no barbed wire, and beyond she saw an overgrown garden, large greenhouse and a wide glazed conservatory at the house's rear. Most of the glass was smashed, and that which remained was whitewashed, but it looked like a way in.

"OK, up and over," Jodi said. She hauled herself over the wall and waited while BB and Matt followed. They dropped beside her and the three of them stood staring at the rear façade of the old house. It had been grand once, and this large garden must have provided plenty of fresh fruit and vegetables. Plants had gone wild now, and a spread of knotweed had subsumed much of it.

They approached the conservatory. It was larger than Jodi's old flat, and she peered through one of the smashed windows into the shadowy interior. She had to pop her torch from her pocket and shine it inside to make out any detail. It was a mess. Smashed glass littered the floor, along with a couple of old scrappy sleeping bags, crushed cans and the remains of a small fire contained by blackened and cracked bricks. A stained mattress slouched in one corner, rusted springs protruding. Some old wooden furniture remained, rotted down or smashed up. The place smelled musty but not rank, so whoever had been using it was long gone. Maybe it had been a bolthole for kids to drink and screw, or perhaps a shelter for a homeless person or people.

At the rear of the conservatory where it met the manor's wall were three double-width doorways, each of them with metal sheeting bolted into the frames.

"Shit," Jodi said.

"This is a job for BB and his claw," Matt said.

BB shook his head. "I think this is a job for Mister Crowbar." He handed Matt the hammer and took a crowbar from his backpack.

The conservatory's outer door hung on rusted hinges, squealing as they pushed it open. It scraped across smashed glass and grit on the tiled floor, and Jodi stopped pushing as soon as the gap was wide enough for them to squeeze through. Something scrabbled in the mess, scampering away. She froze.

"I hate mice," Matt said.

"That was no mouse," BB said, voice low and laden with menace. "That was a rat, and a big one. Swallow a man whole."

"Dickhead."

BB picked his way to the nearest metal-sheeted door and started prying with the crowbar. The bolts were old and rusted, but they ground free of the wooden frame with ease. As he worked down the frame and pulled the door free of the wall, Jodi stood beside him and shone her torch inside.

"Oh, my God!" she gasped.

BB flinched back with the crowbar raised, and Jodi couldn't keep a straight face. She bent over laughing, and heard Matt sniggering behind them both.

"Oh, yeah. Very good."

"Get crowbarring," she said, still chuckling.

"Hysterical. So funny." The last bolt on one side came free with a *screeeee*, and Matt and BB grabbed the edge of the metal sheeting and pulled.

Jodi got a better look inside. A wide hallway with hardwood parquet flooring, timber wall panelling, a slumped water-stained ceiling and a swathe of spiderwebs right out of a horror film. Great. She hated spiders.

"Might be dangerous," she said. "Matt should go first."

"Of course he should." Matt pulled out his own torch and picked up an old chair leg from the mess in the conservatory, using it to sweep aside webs as he slipped through the gap and inside. Jodi and BB followed, and they were in. They stood in a wide hall leading towards the front of the house, with several doorways opening up on one side. Most doors hung open, and Matt aimed his torch at the jambs and heads, and behind them at the opening leading out into the conservatory.

"No sign of any alarms," he said.

Jodi took a deep breath. Musty, damp, the aroma of age and neglect. She wondered what this place had been like in its heyday and who had lived there, and there was sadness to the decay. She'd looked into the house's history as part of her researching the hoard of valuables supposedly hidden away here, and had discovered that the building's twentieth century had been traumatic. Owned by a local industrialist and landowner, three members of the family had gone away to war and never come home. That had set a rot in the place and those who lived there, which ended in the late seventies with a murder and suicide, inevitable stories of curses and hauntings, and claims of ownership so entangled in legalities and probate that eventually the place had faded away into history. Old black-and-white pre-war photos showed a grand building, imposing and homely at the same time, with wooden shutters, climbing plants softening harsh lines, and arched window and door surrounds presenting a characterful façade. It could have been beautiful again if someone had the money and inclination to make it so, but now it was probably too far gone to ever be restored to its former glory, and too damaged by events that had tainted it forever.

She wondered if there was anyone left alive who'd once walked these halls and rooms as a member or relative of the household, and whether their memories were good ones.

"Spooky as all fuckery," BB said. "How did we never come into this place when we were kids?"

"We almost did," Matt said. "It would've been a good dare, right?"

"All the stories said it was haunted," BB said. "Remember when Darney said he was coming here, then he wasn't in school for two weeks and rumour went round he'd broken in and was never seen again?"

"Yeah. He had chicken pox."

BB froze, head tilted. "I hear rattling chains."

Jodi rolled her eyes and started down the hallway. She flicked her torch back and forth, wishing that at least some of the front windows were uncovered to let in a sliver of natural light.

"Matt, you think any of the lights work?"

"Probably. But do you really think anyone's paying an electric bill?" She heard a *click-click* as he flipped an old-style switch up and down. Nothing happened.

"Adds to the atmosphere," BB said. "So where are we going, Lara Croft?"

"Study first. If not there, basement." She set off along the hall, remembering the layout plans she'd found of Morgan Manor and trying to adapt those grainy old scans online to actually being here. Information about the alleged collection of valuables was vague – and talk of what she sought within the hoard was brief and even vaguer – but she'd found mention of it being contained in both places in the house. The study seemed very unlikely, because the building had been empty for decades and there had doubtless been intruders scouring the place for valuables in that time. The basement, less unlikely. Wherever, she didn't expect an easy discovery. She was prepared to not find it at all. But she had to try.

"Great," Matt said. "Basement."

"You like basements," BB said.

"I most certainly do not. Especially the basements of abandoned and dangerous buildings with dubious histories."

"Ruth Bloom."

"Huh?"

"She gave you a blowjob in Darney's basement at his eighteenth birthday party."

"That wasn't a basement, it was a bedroom."

"A bedroom beneath ground level with no windows."

"A basement has rats and spiders and no lights and loads of old shit that's been chucked down there over the years. That was a bedroom."

"Because it had blowjobs?"

"Fuck you."

"You still liked it, from what I remember."

"In retrospect it wasn't the worst party of my life."

"Right. Ruth Bloom."

"But it wasn't a basement like this is going to be a basement."

"One less blowjob?"

"Rats and spiders and shit."

"You two," Jodi said through a smile. Sometimes when they got bantering like this it was almost as if she wasn't there, and she nudged aside the occasional sense of being excluded. They'd known each other forever, and there was so much history there that she didn't know and never would. She loved BB, and loved Matt as a friend, and she was so grateful for both. She couldn't tell them how grateful because that was complex and involved aspects of her own history that neither of them could ever know. So she hoped that love was enough.

"So, hey, Jodi," BB said, "how about Matt checks the study and you and I, you know, maybe check out the basement."

"No blowjobs," she said.

"Not even if we find the loot?"

"Maybe then." They'd reached the wide reception hallway. "Study's over there, but check this out."

"Woah," Matt muttered, and they all swept their torches

around the big space. They'd emerged from beneath a wide first-floor landing, and a staircase rose to meet it from the middle of the large vestibule. The ceiling here was double height, and the tall front doors were closed, bolted and sealed with metal straps and padlocks. It was heavy-duty security for an abandoned house, and made her more confident that there might be something here worth stealing.

"Where's the suit of armour?" Matt asked.

"Walking slowly around darkened corridors, axe at the ready," BB said.

Jodi aimed her torch past the foot of the staircase at a closed door.

Maybe it's in there.

"So, er, you mentioned a curse?" Matt asked.

"Anyone who steals the loot turns into a slug," BB said.

"Hauntings, curses, any old house like this that doesn't have them isn't worth looking at," Jodi said. She hoped that would be enough for him. She had mentioned the curse in passing, and had no wish to elaborate.

They crossed the hall and she tried the study door. It squealed open to reveal a small room lined with bookshelves. The shelves were mostly empty, but a few books were piled here and there as if left behind in a hurry. There was no other furniture. Heavy internal shutters were closed across windows in two walls, and disturbed dust swirled within torch beams. One wall was marred with blown plaster and a swathe of damp, and the bare floorboards beneath were rotting away.

"Where are the crown jewels?" Matt asked.

"Hey," BB said. He was standing close to one of the bookcase-lined walls, one hand resting on a small stack of mouldy books. "Ready?" He shifted a book. It dropped and fell apart, fanning loose pages across the floorboards.

Jodi glanced from BB to Matt and back again, eyebrow raised.

"Damn it," BB said, scanning the shelves for movement. "No secret room."

She aimed the torch around the floor and swept it back and forth along shelves, looking for anything that seemed out of place. The hoard would never have been left so exposed. If there was some sort of hidden compartment it might take them hours to find it.

"Let's try the basement," she said.

"Matt, start your Ruth Bloom-engine," BB said.

"If we don't find it there, we can come back and check the shelves."

BB's eyes went wide in honest excitement. "You mean there might be a secret room?"

"Cabinet, maybe," she said. "Cubbyhole."

"Cubbyhole?" Matt said. "The treasure I'm looking for will need something bigger than a fucking cubbyhole."

They followed her from the room and along the side of the wide staircase. Further back was the kitchen and utility rooms, but she paused and started running her hands over the tongued-and-grooved dark timber cladding on the staircase's side. A dado rail ran along the wall about a metre above the floor, and it seemed to be split in two places. She felt further. For a moment she thought there was nothing there at all, then she felt the horizontal seam in the timber boards, painted over several times yet still just noticeable through her fingertips. Between the vertical jointed boards there were also two small bolts, top and bottom, similarly covered in a layer of paint.

"Here," she said. She smiled back at Matt and BB. "Secret door."

"That's what I'm talking about!" BB said, and he went at it with his crowbar. The joints were thick with old paint and the door itself was screwed into the timber surround, but with a couple of minutes' effort the old wood started splintering around the screw heads.

Jodi glanced around as he worked and caught Matt's gaze. He smiled, she smiled back. Matt and BB felt at ease, larking around as usual, viewing this as little more than a foolish adventure. Matt was probably nervous beneath his smile, but BB was hyped and wired as a kid. She felt a tingle of guilt when she considered what she might be dragging them into, even by association.

"Got it," BB said. A few hard tugs and the door groaned free. A smell wafted out from the dark opening before them. "Well that's an interesting smell. I think you should go first, Matt."

"Naturally," Matt said, and as he stepped forwards Jodi put her arm out and stopped him.

"I brought us here, I go first," she said, more serious than she'd intended. So serious that neither of them offered a quip in response.

She shone her torch into the doorway and down the narrow stone staircase. The darkness of the basement rooms swallowed the light, and she took another deep breath before starting down. The steps were damp and slippery, and there was no handrail. She didn't want to steady herself against the stone wall. There were webs there, and holes between stones, and she tried not to imagine the size of the spiders making this place their home.

She breathed a sigh of relief when she reached the basement floor, then caught her breath as their combined torchlight revealed the extent of the room and its contents.

"Please tell me every box down here contains something priceless," Matt said.

"If that's the case we'll be able to afford Belgium," BB said.

"Why would you want to buy Belgium?"

"Beer."

"Just buy a brewery and have some change left over."

"This what you were expecting, Jodi?" BB asked.

"I wasn't sure," she said. "Different mentions, different specifics." The truth was there was only one place where she'd heard about the location of this hoard and what it might contain, and that was one of the obscure Facebook groups she had joined. She hadn't stumbled across mention of it on the net, like she'd told BB and Matt. She hadn't searched and researched what might have been owned by the household and left behind, or stashed here after the house was first abandoned. She'd read three sentences: *Rumour control – a long-missed Webster remnant is in Morgan Manor. In a pile of old family heirlooms. Downstairs study or maybe the basement.*

That was enough for her, but too much to tell BB.

"So let's get looking," Matt said. "You think we start at the back?"

Jodi felt a flush of despair. The basement was big, ten metres square at least, and scattered with piles of cardboard and wooden boxes of all shapes and sizes, three or four deep in places. Darker patches in the far corners might have been openings into other, deeper areas. It would take hours, maybe even days to search every box, and only she knew what she was really looking for. BB or Matt would cast it aside if they found it. The relic didn't hold any value in any traditional sense. Art was worth only what someone would pay for it, and the relic was not art. Far from it. If there was an opposite to art, that's what it was.

"Let's just spread out and get looking," she said.

"Even though you don't know exactly what we're looking for," BB said.

"Anything of value." Jodi shrugged and smiled. "Hey, it's just an adventure."

"Indiana Jones and the Spooky Spider non-Blowjob Basement."

"That the one with all the tarantulas and spikes and old corpses trapped in booby traps?" Matt asked, shining his torch up at the ceiling. The moving splash of light revealed rough wooden beams, spreads of dusty webs with the wrapped, knotted remains of old meals, and little else. Everywhere they looked spoke of time and dankness and a place long-forgotten.

They spread around the basement and started looking through boxes. BB prised a few wooden crates open and rummaged around inside, and found stacks of old china and ceramics that might well be worth money at auction. But it wasn't the sort of treasure they'd come looking for, and they could never transport it out of the house without attracting suspicion.

As she searched, Jodi kept glancing at BB and Matt, hoping that if they found what she wanted they'd say something, or she'd hear it clatter down when they cast it aside. The boxes contained all manner of household stuff that might have been stored down here after the murder and suicide, when the place was finally left empty in the late seventies. There were kitchen goods, including gadgets whose use none of them could make out. Several boxes contained old vinyl albums, and Matt got excited at some old Beatles LPs that he said might be worth some money. A stack of wooden crates contained tools of every shape, size and design. There was dismantled furniture, faded photo albums, tinned food decades out of date, many boxes of unopened carpet tiles, and plenty of other stuff that was nothing like what they were looking for.

Matt and BB started making a small pile at the bottom of the staircase, and Jodi recognised they were moving from a search for some sort of treasure to just searching. For them that was good enough. This had always been speculative, and they were enjoying the adventure of it all.

It was Matt who surprised them all.

"Holy fuck I think I've just struck… gold," he said, holding up a long, thin object in one hand.

Jodi's heart thumped and she shone the torch his way.

"What the hell is it?" BB asked from across the basement.

"Candlestick," Matt said. "In a box with loads of other stuff just like it. More candlesticks, metal plates and a wooden box with a padlock on the outside."

"That says 'contains riches' to me," BB said. He started moving across the basement, weaving around piled boxes. As he approached, Jodi could see he was carrying something in his right hand. He went to throw it to one side but she stopped him.

"BB, wait!"

They froze, looking at Jodi.

"What have you got?"

He held it up. "Old carving, or something."

"Let me see."

As BB came closer and Matt continued unpacking the box of possible treasures he'd found, Jodi felt an intense chill through her core. *Someone walked over my grave*, she thought, and though she had never been superstitious – stuff she knew and didn't know was fact, not rumour; cold hard truths, not unfounded stories – the thing BB carried drew her attention. She could focus on nothing else in the room.

"See? Just an old lump of wood." BB held it up. Matt dropped a metal plate and the resulting clang made them all jump. Something scurried from the box Jodi had been investigating and crawled up her arm, and she yelped and shook the spider away into the shadows.

"Oh, shit," Matt said, staring down at the wooden box he'd forced open. "Bingo. Bingo. And triple bingo." BB turned to see what he'd found, and Jodi stepped closer and took the wooden object from his hand. It was maybe ten inches long, wide and heavily knotted at one end, and its surface was rough and indented. At first she thought it was the random pattern of tree bark, but closer inspection told her these things were carvings.

She shivered, the hairs on her arms stood on end, and she smelled fresh, green wood. Growing, not dead like this thing.

She hefted it in both hands, and it felt so right. And so, so wrong.

HIDING FROM GHOSTS

JUNE 2000

WILDFLOWER

HIGH UP WHERE NO ONE WILL EVER SEE

JODI

Jodi is eleven years old – eleven going on twenty, her dad sometimes says – and it's only these past few weeks that her mum's allowed her out on her own. Not far, only through the back gate and out into the field and small woodland beyond, but that's enough for Jodi. It's far enough for her to try and escape reality, but even though she's just a kid she's already starting to learn that you can't escape your own fears. You can try to outrun them, but they have a way of sticking to you, like a shadow or the smell of cooking. Your fears are a part of you. The best you can do is try to find something to help you forget them for a while.

So Jodi is having adventures. She's climbed a couple of trees and carved her name in their trunks, high up where no one will ever see, and not so deep into the bark that she might damage the trees. She loves nature and the wild. She thinks that's part of the reason her mum is happy letting her out on her own. She's gone into the woods a little way and explored the old brick culvert in there, a tunnel that seems to go from here to nowhere. It's big enough for her to crouch and crawl inside, but it gets narrower the further she goes. When she is so far in that daylight hardly reaches she backs out again, scagging her T-shirt on a bit of broken brick, scratching her hands, feeling an instant of disquiet when she thinks the darkness deep down – deeper than she's been, in places she hasn't yet seen – is following her out. Flowing, as if the shadows have existed down there for ages on their own and her being there made them aware that they could edge outside. Maybe she'll go deeper next time. She runs from the tunnel back out into the field and across to the stream, and she spends a frantic, muddy hour building a dam and forming a pool in which she paddles up to her knees. When she is bored with that she kicks at the dam and forces it apart, and watches as water floods down the streambed and washes away some of the dried banking, imagining it is a fantasy land and whole villages are swept away by her giant's actions. She wanders back to the woods and goes to the old oak at its edge, thinks about climbing it, but instead she sits for a while inside part of the hollow trunk. She is hiding from ghosts, and then secreting herself away from marauding Vikings. For a while she watches aliens wandering back and forth in front of the oak tree, knowing they can't see her if she doesn't move.

Around mid-afternoon, hungry and thirsty, she runs back home, and even though she's been rushing around all day and kept busy and distracted herself with tree climbing and getting grazed knees and hands and scratched arms, and she is so muddy that she feels it drying and hardening on her like a second skin, her worries are waiting for her there. She sits beside them on the bench beneath the apple tree, and they put a hand on her leg and squeeze, just to let her know that you can't outrun bad things. She knows that anyway. Jodi is not a stupid girl.

"Hey, Wildflower, you're covered in mud and speckled with blood, so I assume you had fun?"

"It was great fun, Mum." Jodi smiles at her mother, whose name is Rose, and she smiles back. That makes Jodi start to cry. She sobs as the day catches up with her. Her mother hugs her and lets her cry, and that only makes Jodi more afraid. Her mum always tries to soothe her. This feels different. It's as if her mother has been anticipating these tears, and now the time has arrived.

"What's wrong, Mum?" she asks.

"Oh, Jodi." She hears tears in her mother's voice, but she can't pull back to look. She doesn't want to see her own mother crying.

"I saw Dad with medicine, and he was counting tablets and stuff."

Her mum is quiet for a while, hugging her beneath the apple tree and letting her tears slow. Jodi loves that bench, it's her favourite in the garden. She adores the way the smell of it changes throughout the year. Now it's fresh and clean, and in the autumn when apples started to ripen and fall there will be a warm, sweet tang on the air and the buzz of drunken wasps.

By then, she'll be sitting on her own.

"You know why I call you 'Wildflower'?" It isn't the answer to Jodi's question, but she doesn't mind. She thinks perhaps it's her mother's way of beginning to answer, and even though she's asked, Jodi isn't really sure she even wants to know.

"Cos it's a nice name?"

"It is. But it's not a real name, is it? It's a nickname. And it's because you're not like me. My name's Rose, and like my name I'm pruned and shaped, and teased into being something... something almost artificial. Some of that pruning I've done myself. But not you, my sweet girl. You're a wildflower. You're there because the world wants you there, and you're strong enough to always just be yourself."

"I don't get it," Jodi says. She's still hugged to her mother's side, but she twists and looks up into her face. Her mother is smiling but sad.

"You'll grow to understand," she says. "As you get older, you'll realise what that means. Keep your own mind. Be strong."

"Like Dad?"

"Your father's not as strong as you."

"Sure he is. He's *really* strong! Yesterday I was helping him build the garage and I saw him pick up two bags of cement!"

"I don't mean strong like that. I mean in his head. In his heart. He's... fragile."

"Does that mean, like, broken?"

"Not quite." Her mother looks even more sad. "Keep him safe and close if you can, Wildflower. Be there for him. Your dad thinks he's strong, but that means he won't bend with the times."

That is how Jodi's mother tells her she is dying. As an adult, guilt over her failure to do what her mother asked of her becomes a faultline that threatens to break Jodi in two.

BIG AS A BLUEBERRY

SEPTEMBER 2024

LEM

WORTHLESS BUT, YOU KNOW, MEMORIES

BB

BB never believed that they'd find anything of worth in that old house on top of the hill. It had been empty for so long that surely anything valuable would have been stripped away, taken by the owners or stolen by prospectors like themselves long before now? Jodi's certainty that there was something there had kept him intrigued, but for him this was just a lark. An adventure. This was him and Matt completing the childhood plans they'd made to raid and explore the place, and even if they found nothing, that was treasure enough for him.

Staring down at the box Matt had just forced open, BB began to wish they really had come here years ago.

"Is that costume jewellery?" he asked.

"Mate." Matt picked up a ring and held it up before BB's torch. The gold was pale and tarnished, but the rock glimmered, swallowing light and seemingly reflecting it even brighter. "This stone's as big as a blueberry."

"But it's fake, right?" BB asked this of Jodi, not Matt. She was watching them, eyes wide, grasping the old stick he'd found as if that was the real precious.

"Dunno."

BB took the ring from Matt and held it up, shining his torch onto it, into it. It was dazzling. When Jodi held out her hand he dropped it into her palm.

"Shouldn't you be on one knee?" Matt asked, and the two men laughed. It was vaguely uncomfortable, but BB shrugged it off. They'd never discussed anything so final and binding. He glanced sidelong at Jodi but she was looking at the stick thing in her other hand again. The possible-diamond ring lay forgotten in her palm.

"If this is all real…" Matt said, laying the wooden container on top of a pile of boxes. He pulled out a chain weighted with a locket, some earrings, several bracelets, a handful of brooches, placing them all on the box's open lid.

"Think there's more?" BB asked. "Where'd you find it?"

Matt nodded to his right where a heavy cardboard box lay open against the wall. Old books were stacked around it. "Buried in there, under a load of books."

"Buried. Right. Hidden – so there might be more. Jodi?"

"Probably more," she said, and he could see that she made an effort to tear her gaze away from the wooden thing. Her smile was false, forced.

"What is that thing?" he asked, and as he reached for the object she took a small step back, held it down against her thigh.

It was an involuntary movement, and her smile grew wider, more uncertain.

"Just like something my dad used to collect," she said. "Surprised me to see one here, that's all. Worthless but, you know, memories."

Memories. She'd mentioned her father a few times, but even so BB knew hardly anything about him. He'd been killed in a car crash when she was a teenager, and he guessed that was why she was never very keen to discuss him, and he'd never been pushy. *In her own time*, he'd thought, but as time went by and little more was said he'd let it go. In her own time might mean never, and that was fine. Now, this was a strange place to start talking about her dead dad.

"So what's it doing here?" BB asked.

"Lots of these old places had weird carvings like this." It was a lie, BB was sure. But that didn't matter. There was gold and diamonds here, probably other stuff buried deeper. He'd have time later to ask Jodi why she was being weird.

"Well let's keep it together with everything else and we'll carry it all out." He didn't reach for the carving, but he nodded down at the jewellery-strewn box.

Jodi tucked the carved wooden length into the deep thigh pocket of her running leggings and moved to another pile of boxes. Its end protruded from the pocket, clinging close to her leg. *Discussion closed*, BB thought, but when he looked at the valuables they'd found he let it slip from his mind. Jodi was private and secretive and sometimes pretty weird about her past, and that had never bothered him. He loved her for what she was now, not what she'd been, seen and done before they knew each other.

He could ask her later.

"Let's get digging," he said to Matt, and his mate's wide open expression made him laugh.

"What?" Matt asked.

"Your face!"

"I just never expected... You know."

"So it's an adventure *and* a payoff," BB said. "Bonus, right?"

"If we can find anyone to buy all this, yeah," Matt said.

"Let's worry about that later," BB said. He kneeled down by where Matt had found the wooden jewellery box, put the torch in his mouth and started rooting around some more. He brought out more books and piled them on the floor, glancing at the titles and covers as he did so. They were in pretty good condition, and he wondered at who'd put them down here, out of sight and mind for so long. His mother had brought him up to love books, and he always had a couple on the go. He liked libraries in a house because, as his mother had said, it made a place feel warm and gave it character. He wondered about who had read these books, what they'd been like, and how the books had ended up boxed away in the dark for so long. There was nothing modern here. Maybe they were a forgotten memory of the murder or suicide victims.

Then who owned the jewellery? He paused at that thought, listening to Jodi and Matt rooting around elsewhere in the cellar. An odd feeling came over him, a coolness, a chill. He'd held the ring, and maybe the last finger it had been on was a dead one. He snorted softly, but couldn't shake the idea. *This place feels weird*, he thought, but he wasn't sure whether it had felt weird before his thoughts of jewellery on murderous or murdered hands, or after.

"We should go soon," Jodi said.

"We've only been down here half an hour!" Matt said.

"And we've found plenty. And we can always come back. But time's ticking, it's almost eight and the roads will be getting busier. We don't want your van being seen leaving here."

"Right," Matt said. "Yeah. That would be uncool."

"Stick to the plan, man!" BB said, and he felt a rush of relief that they were leaving. The darkness and mustiness were getting to him. That, and maybe the idea that they were stealing a dead person's jewellery.

Matt gathered the valuables back into the wooden box and closed the lid, and as he snapped the catch shut something rang out.

"What's that?" BB looked around, flicking his torch up to the basement ceiling, wondering if one of them had set an old chime moving.

Matt brought out his phone and opened the screen. In its sudden glow BB saw his face drop.

"What?" Jodi asked.

"I set a movement alarm in the van connected to the dashcam," he said. "There's a truck." He held his phone out to show them both the view of Morgan Manor's gravel driveway in front of the house.

The truck was just rolling to a stop ten metres in front of Matt's van. It sat there unmoving, doors closed, tinted windows revealing nothing. It was a big Ford, two rows of seats in the cab, wide open bed in the back, a roll bar. It was the sort of vehicle often bought by rich people with no real need of a truck other than to drive their kids to school, but BB could see that this one was functional. Its body was bumped in several places, dirt splashed up the sides, and a short stepladder was tied against the cab roof.

"So who the hell is that?" Matt asked.

"Someone come to clean the windows?" BB said.

Jodi said nothing, but she stared intently at the screen.

"Why aren't they getting out?" Matt asked. "What are they doing?"

"Jodi?" BB asked, because he could sense her tension, hear it in her shallow breathing. She seemed not to hear. "Jodi!" He nudged her.

"Bad luck," she said. "That's all. We'll just have to—"

"Door's opening," Matt said. It was difficult to make out detail on the small screen, but BB saw the driver's door swing open and a tall man step out. He was dressed in dark clothing and wore a beanie over an unruly mass of wild grey hair. His face was heavily bearded.

He aimed a phone at Matt's van.

"Oh, that's just fucking—"

"We need to go," Jodi said.

"But he's clocked my van! Maybe we should go up there and—"

"We need to get away from here," Jodi said. "Matt, get that box. BB, hold this." She handed him her backpack and started tugging at the zip to open it.

"What's happening, Jodi?" BB asked, because the truth hit home all at once. They were here because of her, she'd found something that wasn't treasure to anyone else but her, she'd been on edge the whole time, and now she was scared.

No, more than that. She was *terrified*.

She pulled something from her pack, and BB almost laughed with the ridiculousness of what was happening.

"I'm sorry," she said, flustered and jittery. "I'm sorry, both of you – I fucked up and got it all wrong, but we have to go now!"

"You're holding a gun," Matt said.

"*Now!*"

"Why?" BB asked. "Who *is* that?"

"His name's Lem Baxter. He's the bastard who murdered my father."

SUNSET

JULY 2007

WRONG WAY, BOY

TRAPPED INSIDE

LEM

Lem's grandfather looks as stern as ever, the old sailor's weather-worn skin wrinkled and tough as untreated leather. His narrowed eyes and downturned mouth betray more than his familiar sourness, though. They also speak of pain. The old man has dished enough with his hands to know it – slaps for his wife and three children, punches to the faces of men just as drunk and cruel as him – and there's a subtle but definite shiver to the loose flesh of his neck and the firm set of his shoulders. Lem gets the idea that his grandfather has been suffering this pain for a long time, an agony to which he can never become accustomed. He's wearing the trousers, shirt and thick woollen tie he was cremated in, and the tie's knot has been tugged to the left and down to expose his throat, as if it's choking him and he is struggling for breath. He stares not at Lem, but through him towards some distant, inaccessible place.

Lem's mother is there as well, her gaze averted and aimed down at the uncertain ground. Her long dark hair is held up in a bun, but it's shifted to the left as if flattened against something not visible, or pressed that way by a constant breeze. Her head is similarly deformed by the falling wall that killed her. Like Lem's harsh grandfather she is also shaking, a flicker that draws her in and out of Lem's focus. He tries to ask if she is really there but he can't speak, and she wouldn't hear him anyway. Agony washes across her features in tidal shadows that will not abate. Her mouth tenses, rips her face into a wretched grimace, and then instantly resets to twist into that image of pain again and again.

Standing a few steps past his mother is Lem's Aunt May, a loving woman given to spells of depression that saw her wandering from home and being found sitting on bridge parapets or staring at the deep, endless sea, contemplating an abyss she finally met at someone else's hand. She stands with both hands pressed to the sides of her head, face tilted upwards as if looking to the stars, but there are no stars visible and her eyes are squeezed shut. Lem can't hear her scream but he sees it in every knotted muscle in her face and arms, every tensed ligament in her neck.

He looks for his father, but doesn't see him this time.

Past these people he once knew, and still loves in differing ways, a path leads towards a blazing white sunset splashed across a landscape he does not recognise. The scorched rolls and folds in the land, the charred skeletons of trees, the form of things is ambiguous shadow and shapeless light. *This world is a whisper given form*, he thinks, and though Lem is a hard man who entertains only one real fear, the idea chills him to his core.

The sunset feels like the edge and end of this world, and it's where he is heading. He hears music coming from there, and it's the freeform jazz his father and mother used to listen to when they were on camping holidays, Lem off exploring and playing in the heather, his parents sitting in deckchairs beside their camper van and awning, drinking wine from plastic cups and smoking and enjoying the summer and the unreliable consistency of the music. Lem knows each note before it comes, as if it's him playing it. He has never played a musical instrument, but he thinks that through this sunset and on the other side he might. The warm glow pulls him on, drawing him along the path past his relatives who shiver in agonies he doesn't yet understand. It lures him with a promise of something better beyond.

It's the usual bullshit ideas of an afterlife he has never believed in, but he can almost hear it through there, smell it, taste it on the air. The peace. The tranquillity. The freedom from every bad thing he has done in his life, and everything yet to be done. He's been here and sensed that place before, and he has always been denied it. And he *craves* it, more than he's wanted anything. He's tired of this wretched life that should never have been his in the first place.

His forwards movement ceases and he frowns as he feels hands gripping his upper arms and chest. He's level with his mother now, and he turns to look at her, wondering why she is still here on this side.

I know, I know why, and I can't try to fool myself otherwise.

"Not yet," his mother says, though her mouth does not form the words. He melts at the memory of her voice, and perhaps he even cries. "We're stuck here, Lemuel, and you can't leave us behind."

I'm not leaving them, they left me and I know why they're trapped here like this in so much pain—

"Wrong way, boy," he hears his grandfather say. The voice does not come from the man behind him and to his left. It originates all around him, as if the world is speaking.

"You haven't finished," his Aunt May whispers into his ear from everywhere.

The sunset coaxes him on, and he wants to break into a run towards the comfort that lies within its embrace. He's a tired man and weary, and the years have left their scars, weighing him down with so much restless and relentless time.

"I said wrong *way*!"

The hands grasp harder, pulling him back. Lem wants to break away and run, but he was always a boy who listened to his grandfather. The old man was not someone to disobey.

I know why they're pulling me back, he thinks, and something breaks in this world that isn't real. Something bleeds through. It's a colour and texture, and a sense of something foul and corrupt. Not like the light he so wants to meet. If this place is a whisper given form, that other place starting to intrude is a scream.

"Lem!" He knows the voice but cannot place it. It's more distant and vague than his dead relatives' voices, yet there's something more tangible about it. He feels a breath against his face. Smells garlic. Tastes blood on his tongue, coppery like an electric shock. "Lem!"

It's not my time, he thinks, and his grandfather and mother and aunt hear those words, because for just a moment their agonies seem to cease and they watch him pull away and recede from them. They watch with the hope that he might one day end their pain.

To do so, he must confront his own.

"I never signed up for this, Lem," Wayne says. "Not for this."

Lem tries to respond but can't. Reality has crashed in around him, and it is overwhelming. He's lying on his back, and if Wayne wasn't bent over him he would be staring up at the clear blue sky. It's tainted with a haze of pollution, a breath of toxicity, nothing like the purity of that place he'd been dragged from. He tries closing his eyes as if to rediscover a dream, but Wayne slaps him across the face. The pain doesn't bother him – Lem feeds off pain, takes edge from it, it sharpens his nerves and wits – but the shock startles him more awake than before, more there. And he doesn't like it.

He glares up at Wayne. His long hair is tied up in a ponytail, and Lem reaches up to grab it. But he is holding something in his hand.

I've still got it.

"Come on!" Wayne says. "You with us? You back with us?"

"Us?" Lem asks.

Wayne glances aside, and Lem senses someone standing just out of sight. There's no threat from them, but their stillness and silence is troubling.

"Us?" Lem asks again.

"Come on," Wayne says. "You know Jodi's here. Can you stand? I thought you'd gone. I thought you had a fucking heart attack or something, and that—"

"Maybe I did," Lem says, and Wayne doesn't respond to that. He leans down and grabs Lem beneath the arms, heaves him up into a sitting position, and Lem leans against him and looks around. It's like waking up from a deep slumber and reassembling yourself, gathering those bits of you that matter from dreams and nightmares and deeper, stranger travels, and forming them together into the same you that fell asleep. Lem sometimes wishes he could wake up and make himself someone or something else, but it hasn't happened yet. That time might come if he manages to finish what he has begun.

He sees the figure standing to his right, staring at him in terror, and remembers that this is Wayne's daughter. A young woman, but still just a kid, really. What the fuck he was thinking bringing her along, Lem doesn't know. But then as Wayne says, he didn't sign up for this. None of it. He didn't know what was going to happen.

Looking the other way, Lem sees the body of the man he killed. The old fuck is curled up against the base of a stone wall, ruined head tucked down towards his legs facing away from them. Lem can just make out the misshapen skull, and the exclamation marks of blood on the wall. The guy's right hand still clasps the taser he used to fry Lem.

"What did you do?" Lem asks.

"Me? You did that. What the actual fuck? We could have just run and—"

"He saw us."

"So?"

Lem looks at the object in his hand. "So I came for this, and he shouldn't have got in the way."

"Holy shit, Lem," Wayne says. He sounds wretched and tired, and Lem looks back at the young woman standing a few steps away from them. She is shivering even though it's warm in the morning sun. Her auburn hair is tied in a ponytail shorter than her father's, but her denim jacket is the same. He wonders if she worships her dad. Probably. He smiles, but the traumatised teen looks right through him at the body lying against the wall, and she reminds him of how his grandfather was looking through and past him, perhaps back towards this place. He knows the old man was not shocked or disapproving. He's done the same, and worse.

"Come on," Lem says. "Help me up."

"I don't know if I should," Wayne says. "I don't know if maybe I should just call the police, tell them what happened—"

"Tell them you broke into this house and killed him?" Lem nods at the body. A wasp circles the bloody head, thinks better of it, and moves on.

"I didn't kill him," Wayne says, and he looks at his petrified daughter as he speaks. "Jodi. You saw. It'll be alright. You saw."

Lem reaches with his free hand and clasps Wayne's jacket collar. He still feels weak and his heart flutters and the memory of somewhere far away drifts across his vision, teasing him with an imagined paradise that should be his. Perhaps it still will be, one day. When all this is done.

He's far stronger than Wayne in any way that matters. He pulls his supposed friend down and close, smells garlic on his breath. They ate curry the previous evening and drank a few beers each, talking over the plan again and again. It didn't involve the house owner showing up and firing a fucking taser into Lem's ear. He was supposed to be in France on business.

"We're leaving," Lem says. "Just as we planned – the same route, the same timing, the same place this evening. Just as we planned."

"This wasn't in the plan." Lem is impressed with how long Wayne holds his gaze. Not many people can. Maybe he sees a reflection of what Lem has just seen, and it offers its own allure.

"Get us out of here," Lem says. "Help me to the van. You're driving."

Wayne glances at his daughter Jodi one more time, then helps Lem stand. They hobble across the overgrown lawn towards the driveway, and the old van parked there. It's as nondescript as you can get. Jodi follows, keeping her distance.

Lem feels woozy, and by the time they reach the van he has to lean against its side. He frowns and closes his eyes, resting his forehead against warm metal, and recent events that seemed so sharp became murky, drifting through his memories and reforming in different shapes and shades. The only sound is his own troubled breathing, the buzz of insects in the summer sun and chirruping birds. Gravel crunches as someone moves from foot to foot.

He holds the object tight in his left hand. It is the most solid thing in his life.

"Help me," he hears Wayne say, and he isn't sure if he's talking to him or his daughter.

Lem's heart flutters, his vision swims, and then he is in the passenger seat and someone's clipping the seatbelt across his waist and chest. The van starts moving. Sunlight dazzles the windscreen and strokes warm fingers across his face. From the narrow rear seats he feels the girl's eyes on the back of his head.

"You should get to a hospital," Wayne says. Lem doesn't reply. They both know they can't do that.

Lem looks down at the object nursed in his lap, now gripped

with both hands. *I got it*, he thinks, and despite everything he feels a sense of satisfaction. Somewhere far away his dead family smiles. That is why he's doing this. It's the reason he left that old fool dead against the wall, and why he grips the thing in his hands like his life depends on it.

"You didn't have to kill him," Wayne says. "He was half your weight, twice your age. You didn't have to beat his head in like that. If you hadn't gone at him he wouldn't have fired the taser. We could have…" He continues talking but his words fade, their meaning blurring and then smudging into white noise. Lem's head nods as if asleep and he looks at the thing in his lap again. Two feet long, the length of oak is as thick as his forearm. Its surface is uneven, the shape of the tree branch retained even though it has been worked and carved with an array of designs. He tilts it, and at either end the cut wood contains the pale moonlight-yellow of something else trapped inside. Something not wood, and not tree. Some of the carved designs he recognises, and one of them is smeared with blood from where he smashed it into the old man's face. It is a rook with spread wings, and Lem smiles, because he wears a similar design high on his chest. Even though he is used to them by now, such coincidences never fail to please him.

"I'm done with all this, Lem. That's me finished. You didn't have to kill him."

Lem looks up. They're moving along narrow country lanes, and he waits until Wayne slows to negotiate a tight bend.

"I never do," Lem says, and he slams the relic with all his strength across the bridge of Wayne's nose.

As he pulls back and strikes a second time he locks eyes with Jodi in the rearview mirror, and she begins to scream.

JODI

Jodi sees the madness in Lem's eyes, and the threat, and she knows that Lem won't stop until they are both dead. She barely has time to throw herself across the back seat as the van veers from the road and down a small bank, and slams into a stone wall. She isn't wearing a seatbelt – her dad's whispered instruction, after he'd strapped Lem into the van – and the impact throws her into the rear of the front seats, winding her, pain knifing across her shoulder and hip and left foot. The van's motor is screaming and she smells burning, fuel, smoke. Someone is uttering a wet shout and she can't tell who. Maybe it's her. She tastes blood and spits, only realising that she's lying on her back when the blood spatters down into her eyes. Something pops and crackles and she has a sudden clear image of breakfast in a camper van when she was four or five, her parents eating bacon sandwiches, her eating her favourite Rice Krispies and listening as they snapped and crackled and popped in the bowl. She was always convinced that she could tell the three sounds apart. The van's engine is screeching now, and there's an intense vibration hammering through the vehicle and blurring her vision, a juddering that becomes heavier and more insistent as wheels grab and grind at ground that refuses to move beneath them.

Dad, she says, but maybe she only thinks it because her mouth does not move.

The stench of smoke is rich and acrid, stinging her nostrils and making her eyes water, and she knows she has to get out. She rolls on to her side, reaches for a seatbelt, and pulls herself up just as there's a deep, throaty *whoomph!* A wave of heat shoves her in the back, forcing her up and over the rear seats and into the van's rear storage compartment, despite the pain and blood and the fears for her father. One of the back doors is hanging on smashed hinges and she pushes herself towards it.

Fire picks at her. She smells it singeing her hair, feels it crackling at the seats and plucking at her denim jacket as if to snatch her back. She has to turn around and look, has to help her dad, but the heat is a solid wall that's forcing her up the van's slightly sloping floor towards the open back door, and when she does turn to look she can't see anything inside the front of the van except fire. She squints and raises her hands to her face, peering between fingers. Even that is too much. She kicks and pushes with her feet and tumbles out, falling backwards onto damp grass and wet mud. Banging her head gives her voice at last.

"Dad?"

He's dead, someone says. It might be her or might be her mother, telling her an adult truth and berating her for not keeping him straight and safe. *He was dead before the crash, Lem smashed his face in with that thing and you saw the blood, you heard the crunch of breaking—*

"Dad!"

She scoots back up the shallow bank to the road and keeps kicking, pushing herself across the muddy lane and scraping her forearm and hands on sharp cruel gravel, because the van is ablaze. Its front is buried against the wall and swallowed by fire, hungry fingers swirling in the air like dancing demons reaching for the trees and bushes beyond the smashed stonework. Smoking shrivelled leaves fly high above the heat, trying to escape the flames just like her.

"Dad," she says, this time through tears. They do nothing to soothe her burning eyes. They scorch her soul. "Oh no, Dad, please don't be dead." More tears, and then the pain of her injuries start to winnow past the shock. Something stabs in her left shoulder, her hip rages, and her left foot feels numb and swollen inside her trainer. Her chin drips blood. The fire roars and screams. Glass cracks, metal snaps and buckles, a tyre explodes. The stench is a sick stew of acrid plastic, burning fuel and other smells she doesn't want to identify or sense ever, ever again.

She stands swaying in the road, and for a second or two she considers circling around to see her father one last time. *But what if he's aflame, melting, changing*, she thinks, and that idea is awful. But instinct steers her every movement now. She takes a few staggering steps along the road towards the front of the van, the heat pulsing against her and drying her eyes, stretching her skin.

For a moment she sees through and past the flames. She blinks, wetting her eyes. *Did I really see that?* She holds her hands up, as if to part the roaring conflagration, and she sees him again.

Her father. Impaled on a tree on the other side of the wall. A broken bloody mess, motionless, hanging there, while voracious flames dance across the ground around him, creep and crawl up his legs, his back.

He's like a witch tied to a wooden stake, the cleansing fires rising to consume.

In that all-encompassing heat, the cool hand of grief clasps around Jodi's heart.

As she looks, the passenger door is kicked open and Lem falls out. He hits the ground hard. He's on fire, roaring as if to challenge the thunder of flames, adding his voice to the conflagration. He rolls across the grass and onto the road, splashing and writhing into a wet pothole, scattering burning brands that might be clothing or skin. Jodi is more terrified of him than the fire, and when he kneels and goes to stand, she runs away on her sprained ankle. Behind her the sound of angry flames and Lem's pained, furious roar urges her on. She promised her dying mother that she would look after her father, help him bend with the times, but she hasn't done that. He's been too stiff and straight and now he is broken, and she is alone. She has failed her dad, and her dead mum, too.

As she reaches a low wooden fence, beyond which is a forested area, she pauses and glances back along the road at the blazing van. It's engulfed now, and she cannot see the thing she hoped to see. Lem is not lying dead and burning beside it. He's standing in the road, away from the blaze, head down and arms held out from his sides. He's no longer on fire, but his clothes are scorched and blackened and still smoking. So is his head.

Jodi falls over the fence and dashes into the overgrown woods, leaving behind the safety of a road through life and taking to the wild. Her father prepared her for this, giving lessons that no teen girl should ever need to learn. She hated every moment, knowing that it was the opposite of what her mother wished for them both. But she was young and confused. That was the excuse she gave herself when he told her those things, and it was what she grabbed on to as time went by and she looked back on those terrible, painful times. She was only a kid, and at least by staying with him she was protecting her dad as best she could. Influencing him where possible, trying to look after him. Not everything could be her fault.

When she considers it safe she stops and stomps on her BlackBerry, scattering the parts and crunching the sim beneath a rock. She feels a tug as she does so, a hollowness, as if her soul is being untethered from reality and normality. She's preparing to disappear just like her father taught her. *He's the most dangerous man I've ever met,* he said, *and he's got me mixed up in dark things, unnatural things. Things that shouldn't be. I'm going to do my best to break my ties with him. But if something happens before I can do that, you'll have to run, Jodi. Run and hide. I'll show you how.*

What might happen? she asked. He didn't answer, but she saw the look in his eyes. A desperate fear that he had lost any control of the situation. That was answer enough.

She has to ensure that Lem will never find her.

Later, sitting deeper in the woodland, letting bitter tears of burning loss come at last, she vows that one day she will find him.

HAIR DYE

JODI ALONE

PLANS CHANGE

BEING WATCHED

Jodi is alone.

It's been three months since the crash, the fire and her dad's murder. She did not return home that day. Instead, she went to a place where her father had taken her only a couple of weeks before to stash a small bag ready for such an occasion. It contained a thousand pounds in cash, spare clothing, scissors and hair dye, and a debit card to a new bank account. Her name on the card was still Jodi, but her second name had changed. Jodi didn't like that. She was still her father's daughter.

She spent the rest of that dreadful day getting as far away from the scene of the accident as she could, after tending to her wounds – the scratches and cuts, and the singed hairs across her forearms – and ensuring they could not be seen. She used only public transport.

Every night for the next three months, she fails to dream.

The nightmares are there, she knows. They're a weight within her, a dark, growing pressure in her heart and soul, but they do not manifest. She's glad about that, but also afraid. She worries that if and when they do come, and the dam of her grief bursts, she might lose herself too much.

Get lost but stay in control, her dad said. *Keep a tight hold on who you are, but don't let anyone else see. You'll be your only best friend. Control is the thing. Everything that happens to and around you has to be your choice.*

She has a new phone but uses it sparingly. She stays in a different place every night, and the cash and money in the new account allow for that frequent movement. Cheap hotel rooms blur into one. Buses and trains trundle her back and forth across the country.

People approach her, sometimes to help, but she always smiles and moves on. *Don't be noticed*, her dad said. *Don't cause a scene. Be forgettable.*

The dam of dreams breaks at last, but it doesn't give way to nightmares. She spends so much time moving, hiding, trying to be someone who Lem cannot find however hard and long he might choose to search, that her grief takes care of itself. To begin with she cries herself to sleep most nights, but the tears soon dry up. They give way to a deeper mourning that settles around her bones, making her feel heavier and more loaded down.

Most nights after that she dreams of her mother not dying, her father still being alive, and how her life would be so much fuller if any of that were true.

When she wakes, Jodi is alone.

It's almost two years later when she has the first real nightmare, and the next day she starts looking for Lem.

The nightmare affects her whole day. She can't remember much about it – mostly she's pleased for that, but she also wonders whether remembering might help her box it up and shove it aside – but her day is haunted with the scent of burning flesh, the sound of crunching bones and the feeling that she is being watched.

Even locked inside her small bed-and-breakfast room, she is being watched.

She's been staying here for almost three weeks. The old lady who owns the house is polite but not intrusive, passing the time of day when Jodi enters and leaves but otherwise leaving her alone. Jodi doesn't think she'll stay much longer. She's working in a local bakery, going in at four in the morning and finishing by midday, and one of the guys there has taken an interest in her. Yesterday they had sex at his place following an after-work drink in a pub close to the bakery. It wasn't very good.

She thinks his tattoos might have brought on the nightmares.

Jodi knows the times and destinations of trains from the small local station, and soon she'll pack and leave, even though she'd paid up for three more nights. But first she has to attack the subject of her dark dreams. She's thought about this on and off over the past couple of years, but she's always resisted searching for Lem. The idea of taking revenge upon him for her father's death is always there, but she fills her time with being quiet, keeping her head down, staying safe.

Her irrational fear is that if she looks for him, he might stare right back.

So she spends the afternoon in her room on an old second-hand laptop she's bought, riding her landlady's internet as she starts to carefully, covertly dig around. After four hours of looking, she discovers that Lem Baxter does not exist. There's no trace of him online at all. No birth certificate, driving licence or news items. No social media, old photos or mentions that might refer to the Lem she seeks, however indirectly.

It's as if he is a ghost.

What she does find is something far more intriguing.

Using the words "Baxter relic curse", she scrolls down three pages of unconnected results until she finds a scan of an obscure newspaper article from 1975. It describes the mysterious and bloody death of a man called Andrew Baxter, who was stabbed many times in an alleged criminal feud, badly injured in a car crash when he escaped, and then finally killed when a truck full of beer barrels ran him down. The story concludes with a short interview from an anonymous source who claims to be a distant relative of Baxter, who says, "He was always obsessed with some crazy idea that an old witch called Mary Webster put a curse on our family. He thought that finding some relics belonging to the witch might lift the curse, and that got Andrew involved in some bad stuff. It looks like the curse finally came home to roost."

Jodi tries to look deeper, but there is no more. That is the only article she can find about Andrew Baxter's death, and there is no mention of any child who might have been Lem.

But it gives her a way to start looking.

Jodi keeps her eyes open for more information about the Mary Webster relics.

She still moves around regularly, but the length of time she stays in one place sometimes grows to several weeks, even three or four months. It depends on where she is, how safe she feels and who she meets. She makes friends, who make her feel welcome and included. Sometimes she has a boyfriend. But she's always careful to maintain a distance. She knows that people regard her as cold, and she can't help that, because it's the way she's grown up. She breaks some hearts.

Along the way she picks up a variety of skills, some of which she carries from one place to another. She's always been interested in art from a young age, and she finds that she's naturally gifted at graphic design. There's always places she can sell this talent – print shops, advertising agencies, design companies – and sometimes she considers setting up her own business online. She can move around and still work, and she's confident that she could establish a decent, consistent business.

But Jodi is wary of establishing any online presence. The idea catches fire and then fades away just as quickly. Mostly, she can't get too excited about such things. She still lives with a bag packed ready by the door.

There's no evidence that Lem had ever come looking for her, and she views that as a good thing. It means he can't find her. But she keeps looking for him, and several times she finds mention of the Webster relics online. They're in obscure Facebook groups – she always uses a pseudonym – Discord channels, reports on local community news websites or other places buried in the deeper, darker web.

She becomes something of a detective. It's an interest, it fills her lonely evenings when she's not running or swimming or reading, and she still has that vague idea of revenge. Over time, and the more she looks, it becomes a need.

The nightmares are only occasional, but rich as ever.

Twice, she perceives the presence of the relics in reports of murders. Both times a chill goes down her spine when she imagines Lem, probably scarred by the crash and fire, battering those victims to death with another relic.

The fact that he's still looking for them is a strange comfort to her. It means that she has a way to find him.

Soon after her twenty-second birthday, which she spends alone hiking in the local hills, Jodi chances across mention of a Webster relic on a message board buried deep in a shady corner of the web.

She had a particularly harsh nightmare the day after her birthday. She thinks it was because she thought of her parents a lot that day, especially her dad, wishing he'd been there to celebrate with her. The bad dreams brought her awake screaming, sweating and convinced that her hair was on fire.

Finding whispers of a relic gives her an idea that has been brewing for a while. Lem is obviously still focussed on those weird things, whatever they are, and she wonders whether she can find one and get it before him. After that, her thoughts are vague. Lure him in and get him arrested, perhaps. Tease him with it by planting mentions across the web. Or maybe just destroy it so that it is lost to him forever.

The man claiming ownership is called David Roth. Jodi establishes that he's a dealer for high-end thieves, a fence, and over the next two days she gathers as much information about him as she can. It becomes an obsession. It's been a long time since something has excited her so much.

She moves to a city close to where Roth lives and rents a room. One day before she plans on contacting him, she finds a local news report saying that Roth has been murdered. Delving deeper, she discovers that he'd been killed in his own home, cut up, torn to pieces and spread around the house. His son William discovered him.

Jodi flees from that place, cutting back and forth across the country, and for a couple of days it feels like it did when she was eighteen.

She had been so close to Lem, and so close to such terrible violence.

It's a few days before she can breathe easy. It will be a lot longer than that before she dares go looking again for mention of the relics. She finds a new place to live for a while, a new job, and she shuts out anyone who might become a friend.

Jodi is alone.

Over a decade later Jodi finds herself in a small, nice town called Mariton. She lands a job designing corporate and private artwork and adverts at a printing shop, and she settles in well.

After the first two weeks there she thinks, *I'll stay for six months. No more.*

And then Jodi finds love, and her life changes forever.

REVENGE

SEPTEMBER 2024

HER BOGEYMAN

BLEEDING A BIT

JODI

I've put the man I love and my best friend in terrible danger, Jodi thought, and at the same moment she feared they wouldn't remain her lover and friend for very long. Not with the way they were looking at her. She had much to explain but so little time, so she turned her back on BB and Matt and hurried to the base of the staircase.

She was convinced that Lem hadn't heard about this Webster relic. She was certain that he wasn't even a member of that obscure Facebook group. She'd intended posting news of it after finding it, under a pseudonym and somewhere she thought he *would* see, and that was supposed to be the beginning and the end of her revenge.

"What's he doing?" she whispered, afraid her voice would carry up the stairs, around the empty house, through closed and shuttered windows and across open air to Lem. A ridiculous notion, but he was her bogeyman. She still dreamed of him sometimes. She refused to call them nightmares, because she wouldn't give him that, an admission that he terrified her. He wasn't worth that much. But her dreams were dark and red and blazing, and sometimes she felt the pain of anguish and rage, even though in dreams you weren't supposed to feel anything at all.

"They've just walked out of view, heading for the manor," Matt said.

"'They'?"

"Someone's with him. Skinny guy, young."

"Jodi, what the fuck's happening here?" BB was right behind her.

"I owe you both an explanation," she said. She tapped the wooden relic in her leg pocket. "He wants this. That's all I have time to tell you now, but later, when we're away, everything."

"So he's dangerous," Matt said, and Jodi glanced back at him. Her expression must have been enough to communicate that, yes, Lem was dangerous, because Matt hurried to them at the foot of the staircase, wooden box cradled in his hands.

"Which way will they come in?" BB asked.

"I don't know," she said. "But we can't be trapped down here."

"This is fucked up," Matt said, voice breaking.

"Matt," Jodi said. "We'll be fine." But he was looking at her gun. He was afraid of her, and she could hardly blame him. Everything he knew about her, all the nights out and laughs, whatever BB had said when he and Matt were out doing something on their own, it was all a lie. No words were needed to communicate that. It was all in the gun in her hand.

She clasped the weapon tight and started up the stairs. She hadn't fired it in over four years, since long before she'd come to

Mariton and met BB and started to hope that she might be able to settle down to a normal life at last. Keeping her head down, yes. Staying low and quiet.

She did the same now as she stalked upwards, and the gun in her hand felt so alien. *It's an extension of you*, the woman who'd sold it to her had said. She'd had a hard history scored into her scarred arms and cold eyes. It didn't feel like an extension of Jodi now, and the idea of pointing it at someone, let alone pulling the trigger, made her feel sick.

Even Lem. She hated his guts, but she was not a murderer, and would never stoop that low. None of this had ever been about that. She sought a different revenge.

Three steps from the doorway at the top of the stairs she turned off her torch. BB and Matt did the same. She listened, mouth open, and heard nothing. Another step, another, and leaning forwards she could see along the corridor beside the wide staircase and towards the large reception hallway. There was no sign of movement, no sound.

Where the hell are they?

She imagined Lem standing two metres away, pressed back against the side of the staircase, waiting for someone to stick their head out from the basement doorway. She imagined so well that she heard him there – just a scrape of a boot on decades-old dust – and caught her breath, leaning back into BB.

"What?" he whispered in her ear, and she shook her head.

Spooked, she thought. She mounted the last step and peered around the doorframe, gun held down beside her leg, finger resting across the trigger guard, barrel tapping the wooden object in her pocket. There was no one there.

Someone spoke, distant and senseless. Jodi was sure it came from beyond the other side of the staircase, back the way the three of them had entered the manor half an hour before.

Someone else issued a harsh *shhh*.

She glanced back at BB and nodded along the dark corridor, away from the hallway and towards the kitchen and utility rooms that lay in that direction. She had no idea how long they had, whether Lem and his goon would come directly to the basement, or what she'd do if they did.

BB shoved her but she shook her head, lifted the gun and aimed it along the corridor towards the front hallway, saying without speaking, *I'm the one with the gun*. He didn't argue. He stepped out of the basement door and ushered Matt along towards the kitchen rooms, before putting his hand on Jodi's shoulder and squeezing softly as he backed that way himself. She went with him.

A bang, a muffled curse. She tensed, then heard someone chuckling. It might have been Lem. It had been fifteen years since she'd last seen him, but she remembered his laughter, hollow and empty, only full and honest when it was cruel. His companion must have hurt himself, she thought, because this chuckle sounded real. He was also careless, and that was good. He'd seen an electrician's van and probably assumed someone was working on the manor.

Lem's overconfidence would help them.

BB guided her back, and then they were through an open doorway and into the remains of a big kitchen. There was a ceiling lightwell here that had been partly boarded over, but some of the boards had come loose allowing morning sunlight inside. It showed a large square room, walls lined with the remnants of free-standing furniture that were swollen and slumped and rotting down to the floor. In the middle of the room was a preparation table, scattered with broken glass and decades of dust. It smelled stale and old and undisturbed, and dust swirled and danced in light-beams as if startled at their intrusion. A mummified rat lay on the table, big as a small cat.

"No door," Matt whispered. He looked really rattled now, and Jodi hated herself a little more every moment that passed. But she also felt the weight of the relic in her pocket, as heavy as the past fifteen years.

"That way," she said, pointing at a door in the room's far corner. "Utility rooms, there'll be a door outside."

"If it's not bricked up or locked or—" Matt began, but BB was with him then, whispering something in his ear and guiding him around the kitchen central island towards the door in the corner. Jodi went after them. Her heart fluttered and her senses were alight, fight or flight sharpening reality. She was taking flight, even though a little part of her wanted to fight. She'd always struggled against that part, denying its allure. After everything Lem had done she refused to be as bad as him.

The door in the corner was partly open, and Matt pushed it wider. Its hinges creaked and BB grabbed his arm, and they all froze with breath held. Jodi glanced back at the kitchen entrance. No movement, no sound. She hoped Lem was checking the study first, and if so that would give the three of them the chance to slip out unnoticed.

If they could open a door or window. If the metal shuttering wasn't too strong. If they didn't have to backtrack and try to exit the way they'd come in.

"Looks good," Matt whispered, and Jodi looked past him and

BB along the narrow corridor beyond the door. On the right were three windows, all of them boarded over, and on the left closed doors leading into utility and storage areas. But the door at the end of the corridor was external, and the bottom corner of it was rotten enough to let in a splash of sunlight. One good push and it would crumble, and she was sure that would be enough room for them to crawl out. Then away, and then she would explain some of what was happening, and continue with her plan to hurt Lem as much as she could.

Matt went first. The floorboards creaked as he hurried along to the far door, clouds of dust rising behind him. BB followed. Jodi looked back over her shoulder towards the far end of the kitchen. She didn't see him fall.

A crack, a crumple, and then a thud and BB cried out, one short sharp shout that he immediately managed to cut off.

She slipped into the corridor and pulled the door behind her, almost closed but not quite. BB had fallen through rotten floorboards. They should have known they might be fragile. The door was crumbled around its base, the walls were stained and bubbled with years of damp, and they should have been more careful.

She moved along towards him, waving Matt back towards the external door.

"Keep to the edges!" Matt said, and she did as he said, testing each step.

"BB?"

"I'm OK," he said, and he giggled. For a moment she thought he really was fine, and that the giggles were because of his own jackass stupidity. But then she detected an unsettled edge to his laughter, and from behind she could see how he was straining to hold himself in a certain position, or away from another. He'd gone through almost to his waist, and his hands were braced on the cracked rotten boards on either side. His shoulders were tensed beneath his T-shirt, triceps knotted, and his arms shook as he held up his weight. "I do think I pissed myself, though."

"BB, I'm coming on your right side, just hang on and—" She stopped talking the moment she looked up and saw Matt's face. Ashen, shocked, he looked back and forth from BB to Jodi. "Matt, what?"

"I think I'm bleeding a bit," BB said. "Gotta... best get me out. Or maybe... No. I haven't pissed myself. It's blood."

Jodi froze, thinking quickly. As soon as Lem and his helper made it down into the basement he'd know that someone had been here before him. He'd seen the van, so he would be ready for someone else being in the house.

Confronting him face to face, ever again, had never been a part of her plan, but now she had no choice. And what she heard next sealed the deal.

"We'll look around, find out who's here before we go down there." That was definitely Lem, his voice deep and growly from many years of cigarettes and booze, and it gave Jodi a chill. For over a decade that voice had haunted the darker places in her dreams, its presence forming shadows she always turned from and tried to escape.

"I'll give us time," she said, and BB glanced around at her, face pained. "Matt will get you out." Then she was gone, heading through the kitchen towards the far corridor, gun held out before her, full of determination.

And terrified.

BB

BB's arms quivered as he held himself as high and steady as he could. The pain was coming in now, and what had started as a cool numbness in his left leg and hip burned and screamed. It was wet down there too, and he felt blood running down his leg, pooling in his trail shoe.

Matt kneeled before him, but not too close. He probed out with one hand, like a man checking thin ice, and the floorboards flexed beneath him.

"Wonder how deep it is?" Matt said. "If you try to climb out you might hurt yourself more, or it might just crumble."

"Mate, there's a lot of blood," BB said, and he saw his friend register the urgency in his voice.

"Wimp," Matt said, examining where BB was trapped through the floor. He lay down and stretched out one hand, feeling down beside BB's hip.

"Buy me dinner first," BB said.

"Last time I saw you this pale was after Slater's stag night in Torquay, we'd been drinking all day and hit that strip club, you bought a bottle of tequila with…"

"Sunday," BB said.

"Yeah, right, Sunday. Bet that really was her name, too. Next thing I knew you were asleep propped up in a shop doorway outside, so I staggered you back to the hotel, and the colour of you next morning at breakfast…" He felt around, then froze and his face fell.

"What is it?" BB asked.

Matt drew his hand out carefully and held it up. It was soaked with blood, running down his wrist into his sleeve, dripping onto the floor.

"Lots," BB said. He remembered Sunday, and how she'd agreed to come back to his hotel and then vanished when his eighty-pound bottle of tequila was gone, and he couldn't remember anything else about that evening and not much about the next day. It was a grey haze, much like what he felt now. Woozy. Light.

"OK, mate, let's get you out of there and—"

"Artery," BB said.

"Maybe just a big cut."

"Either way…" BB looked at his friend's red hand.

Matt crawled closer and the floor creaked beneath him, one board cracking and flicking up a haze of dust. He caught BB's eye, smiled, but it was brief.

BB blinked slowly and the pain in his hip and leg spread and grew, consuming his whole leg. The fun had gone out of the day. He wondered what fun Sunday might have been. He looked around for Jodi but she wasn't there. He blinked, and it was so slow that he wondered if he'd slept for a while.

Matt had moved, now braced against the wall beside him and with his hands beneath BB's armpits. BB felt pressure and he pushed with his hands, but instead of rising he felt himself falling, as if his head was suddenly lower than his feet.

"She didn't come with me," he said.

"Who?"

"Sunday."

"Push, BB. You're too fucking big and ugly for me to haul you out on your own."

"Where's Jodi?"

"Push!"

"Where's Jodi?"

Matt didn't answer, and BB tried to turn around to see, but the corridor was dark now and he could hardly see anything at all. He heard water dripping in the basement beneath him and wondered if he'd fallen right through an old pipe, then remembered that he was bleeding.

Bleeding a lot.

"Tourniquet," he said.

"Got to get you out first." Matt hauled and whatever had speared BB and stuck him there turned, twisted, ground against bone. He opened his mouth and screamed, and buried in that scream was the loud *crack* of a gunshot.

JODI

Jodi walked from the kitchen with the gun held out before her, and Lem and his sidekick were standing at the basement door, Lem shining a torch down into the darkness. The sidekick was young and skinny and short, with a shaven head and tentacle tattoos curving up from his neckline and across his left cheek. Jodi thought the tattoo artist might have been a seven-year-old kid. A piercing in his nose had gone septic, his left nostril red and swollen shut. She might have felt sorry for him, but his eyes glimmered with a promise of violence, and she thought he'd delight in it.

Lem saw movement and twitched the torch into her eyes, dazzling her. She crouched and aimed at his stomach. She was six metres away and could not miss.

"Want me to take that gun from her and—?"

"Shut up, Rash," Lem said.

"Don't tell her my name, man, what if—"

"Shut. Up."

Rash shut up.

Jodi twitched her aim to the sidekick's crotch and back to Lem, right and left again. She smiled, trying to exude calm and control. The last thing she wanted in the world was to shoot anyone. Even after what Lem had done to her dad, the idea of putting a bullet in him was not what drove her. She was a good person, as her dad had been. She'd not lower herself to Lem's level. She was brighter than that, better. There were more intelligent ways to make him pay.

At least, she'd thought so. He was never meant to be here, but now he was and his presence was huge, not just physically but in her perception, that burning raging figure that had haunted her dreams for the past decade. She'd always believed that seeing him in the flesh would lessen the monstrous threat, but that hadn't happened. She was terrified, but doing her best to hide it.

I'm the one with the gun, she thought.

"Who the fuck is she?" Rash asked.

"The one with the gun," Lem said. "I know you?"

"You're kidding, right?" Jodi asked. She squeezed her lips together, berating herself. *No weakness! Don't give an inch. He's fucking with you!* For now, she was braced with her left leg in front, kneeling on her right knee, so that the relic in her right leg pocket was not visible. She so wanted to taunt him with it, but not yet. This was all about BB. If Lem saw what she had he wouldn't stop, he'd walk into bullets to get it. She'd then be guilty of murder as well as breaking and entering and burglary.

Lem tilted his head to one side. She could still only see the skin around his eyes. The beanie was pulled down and his beard was expansive, tangled and speckled with grey. He moved the torch up to her face again and Jodi tensed, but he was only taking a look. He aimed it down again and in the poor light she saw his cheeks bulge as he smiled.

"You've changed your hair. Me too." He pulled the beanie from his head. It was as if doing so opened up his face because she saw his eyes then, just as dark and cold as she remembered, almost bottomless in the poor light. He turned slightly to his left, then right, to give her a full view. The hair on his scalp was patchy, islands of wiry fuzz in spreads of ugly scarred skin, and his left ear was a melted mess. His left cheek was hollow and flat. Most of his beard was fully grown in, but there was a gap along his left jawline and neck where it only grew in silver clumps. She could see strange spiderweb designs on some of the scarring, and she thought perhaps they were creases in the skin or cauterised veins. Or perhaps he had chosen to mark these wounds with tattoos.

He had other tattoos on other scars. She'd seen some on the day they'd first met, then others late one night when he and her father were drunk, and Lem had recounted some of these illustrated stories of his life – the curling snake on his left arm, healed injuries adding their own dark pink waves; the five fat black spiders crawling down a wound from beneath right armpit to hip. He'd spoken of his cause then, too, and his insane quest to gather these strange, scattered relics to lift an ancient witch's curse on his family. He'd told them so much, drunk, and never for an instant had Jodi believed that he hadn't meant to tell them. Lem was not a person who did things by accident. His wounds and tattoos, and that strange fantastical story, had stuck with her.

On someone else these burns might have looked pitiful and sad. On Lem they only made him more monstrous.

"Looks like you got away better than me," Lem said.

So now he knows who I am, Jodi thought, but she didn't react. She had to maintain control.

"Into the basement, both of you."

"I don't like spiders," Rash said, and Jodi held in a laugh. Lem's expression didn't change.

"Through the doorway," Jodi said. "Down the stairs. You've got a torch, and your friend will protect you from creepy crawlies."

"I quite like it up here," Lem said, glancing around at the damp featureless corridor.

"Looking down the barrel of a gun?" Jodi asked. "Held by someone whose father you killed?"

Lem frowned for a moment, then he was expressionless once more. Whatever he felt or thought was kept inside, because he had no reason to express it to the world. She remembered that about him. His face when he'd battered the old man to death at the farm was the same as when the three of them had shared breakfast at a roadside café earlier that same morning. Cold. Dead.

Rash moved first. Jodi had been expecting it, he was younger and probably keen to impress the older thug he'd hooked up with. He darted at her, faster than she'd expected, a flowing shadow with grit grating beneath his boots. She switched her aim to him, standing and taking a step forwards to meet him. He froze. She kept the increased pressure on the trigger. Aimed at centre of mass, she'd end up blasting a hole in his chest. *I don't want to kill anyone*, she thought, but she said, "I can end this with two shots."

Rash was wired, up on his toes, eyes wide. Jodi still wasn't sure if she'd shoot him first, if it came to that. Lem was her bogeyman.

"OK, fuckface," Lem said, and for a moment Jodi thought he

was referring to her, venting a thread of anger in readiness to take her on.

"But—" Rash said, and then Jodi realised Lem had been talking to him.

"Down the steps," Lem said. "You go first. In case there are spiders. So did you find it?"

Jodi realised this last was directed at her. She felt the weight in her right leg pocket, braced behind her, and turned away from Lem.

"Not yet," she said. "But I will."

"Lock me down there and you think you'll still find it?"

"It's not down there."

"*Hmph.*" Lem looked into the doorway. "Seems I'm getting false information."

"We found jewellery," Jodi said. "Diamonds. Gold. Nothing else."

"Doesn't matter if you found it or not. I'd find you, and take it from you." Something changed in Lem then, and in the poor light and under pressure Jodi wasn't *certain* that she saw his expression falter as he let down his guard, his focus turning within, just for a moment. "It's the last one," he said. She sensed the weight of that statement in his cold black heart.

Rash tensed again, rocking on his toes, and as his eyes went wide Jodi heard a short, loud scream from behind her, and her finger twitched against the trigger. The gunshot was shockingly loud but she retained focus, knowing that the second following the shot was when she'd be at her most vulnerable. Torchlight flickered around the corridor, adding to that chaotic moment. Heart racing, she tried to breathe deeply, taking in the scent of smoke and dust shaken down from the ceiling, and she aimed at Lem and shouted, "Stand still!"

He was standing still. So was Rash, leaning against the wall beside him with one hand pressed to his shoulder.

"She shot me, Lem, she—"

"Shut up, fuckface," Lem said, and Rash instantly fell silent. Jodi glanced back and forth between them. Rash took his hand away and studied the groove the bullet had ploughed across the top of his shoulder. His T-shirt was torn but his skin was barely broken, blood seeping rather than pouring.

"Not such a good shot," Lem said.

"Yeah, I know. I meant to miss." She shrugged. "I guess you're paying him enough to buy a new T-shirt?"

Lem waited, still and silent, and Rash started down the basement stairs.

"Poor bastard," Jodi said. "Being stuck down there with you."

"You know we won't be down there for long."

"Long enough."

"Long enough for you to get back to Matt Shorey's place, eh?" Jodi gestured with the gun.

"Since that day you ran, I've killed… well, I've lost count how many people. While you've been hiding yourself away, terrified that I'd find you and finish the job."

"You don't scare me."

"Right. Well, you didn't expect me to be here, plainly. So…"

She gestured with the gun again.

"So you wanted to get the relic before me," Lem said.

"I still will."

He looked her up and down, and she knew that if he saw

the thing tucked into her trouser pocket he'd come at her, and she'd have about half a second to decide whether she could live with murder in her heart. She adjusted her stance, turning her leg further away. She hoped it looked like she was bracing herself better to shoot.

"He was screaming," Lem said. "After you ran away and left me on fire in the middle of the road, your dad started screaming. He went through the windscreen because he didn't have his seatbelt fastened. He told you not to fasten yours too, I'll bet. He knew me a little too well by then, and I reckon he guessed I'd want to do away with him and you after you'd seen me murdering the old guy. So we hit the wall, he flew through the smashed windscreen. Impaled on a tree branch. Nasty. Lots of blood, guts, all sorts. Shit himself. The fire got to him, too. Something else we have in common." Lem touched his scarred face and fake-shivered, and Jodi almost pulled the trigger then, all her fear and rage putting four pounds of pressure on a five-pound trigger. But she thought of her father's face, and her mother's voice saying, *Be brave, Wildflower*, and she eased back.

"But I saved him," Lem said.

Jodi froze, trying not to let her reaction show. *But I saved him.* No, her dad was dead. If he wasn't he'd have come looking for her. Unless…

Unless he thought she was dead, too, and they'd both gone to ground.

"Bullshit."

Lem only shrugged.

"What happened? Where is he?"

Lem shrugged again. Smiled. He was fucking with her.

"You've got three seconds to start down that staircase or I'll kill you."

He did as she said, and as she edged forwards she saw him silhouetted by his torch as he descended the staircase. In the harsh light, Rash stared up past Lem at her. She thought there was a flicker of fear in his eyes, and she wasn't surprised, even though he was obviously used to violence and wretchedness. Anyone would be afraid of being locked in the dark with that beast.

Jodi waited until Lem was at the foot of the staircase, then slammed the door shut and threw the bolts at the top and bottom.

I could open the door again and shoot them both. Keep shooting down there till the gun's empty. Two corpses in a basement never visited. They might be there for months, even years. And I could stop hiding.

She'd lied, she *was* afraid of Lem, but that didn't change who she was. And now his words about her father had planted doubt, even though he lied. He *had* to be lying.

But I saved him.

She stepped back and stared at the door, and realised just how ineffective the small bolts would be with Lem battering against the door from the other side. But she still had the gun, and she hoped they'd stay down there long enough for her, Matt and BB to get away. *Lem knows Matt's name from his van!* she thought, but that was a problem for later. Right now they had to go minute by minute.

She dashed to the kitchen and carried an old chair back to the basement door, wedging it firm beneath the dado rail. Once Lem and Rash decided to break out, it might give them a couple more minutes. If that. She'd have to make every minute count.

She turned and ran through the kitchen and into the corridor beyond. BB sat propped against the far door, and Matt was trying to tie something around his leg. BB stared along the corridor but she could tell by his eyes that he didn't see her. She had never seen so much blood.

"Oh, Jesus," she said.

"It's bad," Matt said. He looked at her, down at the gun, but asked nothing about the gunfire. All he cared about was his friend.

"We have to go," Jodi said. "We don't have long. Hold on, BB." He didn't reply. He gave no indication he'd even heard. "Matt?"

"I've tied it off but…" She knew the "but". There was so much blood, and the ragged wound in BB's leg was still gushing, despite Matt's belt cinched tight around his thigh.

Edging around the broken area of flooring, trying not to look at her boyfriend's blood spattered all over the pale wood, she stepped over BB's legs and past Matt to the rear door.

"What happened?" Matt asked.

"Nothing good."

"Did you—?"

"No." She tried the door, already knowing it would be locked. She turned back to Matt. He nodded, and picked up his rucksack and moved past her to the door. He was pale, eyes wide.

"Get it open quickly," she said.

"Look after him." In those three words Jodi heard so much fear. There was accusation, too. Or if she didn't hear it, she put it there herself.

She kneeled beside her bleeding boyfriend. This was all her fault.

MATT

Matt was an electrician by trade, but he'd always been handy. Friends came to him for help. He was known for it. He'd built stuff in BB's place, plumbed in a new bathroom, and it was almost accepted that he was there when BB needed anything done. He was always rewarded with a beer and a takeaway, and it was a comfortable part of their relationship. Once, BB had called when he'd locked himself out of the house, and Matt had turned up with a locksmith's kit designed by a burglar while he was still in prison. *He doesn't need to burgle anymore,* Matt had said, and he was inside within five minutes.

He wished he had that kit now.

The door was screwed into the frame, and he could have sorted that in a couple of minutes with his electric screwdriver. The lock was more troublesome. It was an old mortice lock and it was rusted solid. He went at it with BB's crowbar, and the frame started to crumble.

How the hell had it all gone so wrong, so quickly? They were running from someone he hadn't even seen, Jodi had a gun, and this simple friends' adventure had become something so much more dangerous. And BB had hurt himself on a fucking floorboard!

He glanced back. Jodi was down beside BB, tightening the tourniquet.

"Jodi."

She looked up at him, eyes wide. "Hurry," she said.

From back through the kitchen Matt heard a heavy, dull thud. Jodi glanced behind her along the corridor. Her gun was on the floor beside her. Her fucking *gun*!

"What the hell have you done to us?"

"Get us out of here, Matt," she said, and his name sounded odd in her mouth, as if it were the first time she'd used it. He didn't know her anymore.

Matt worked at the lock with the crowbar, scraping away splintered and crumbling wood and exposing the rusted metal. There was more banging from deeper inside the large house, and Matt was afraid. Jodi said the man there was the one who'd killed her father. She'd fired her gun. He had no idea what was going on, who she was, or what they were doing here, and his friend was bleeding to death.

Matt had never been a violent man but he felt like breaking something, so he channelled his rage and fear through the crowbar and into the lock. It cracked, metal grinding against metal, and then the bolt sprung free of the receiver in the frame.

"Got it."

"Pull it open."

Matt tugged, and as the door opened inwards it dragged a mass of undergrowth with it. Ivy had grown across the doorway and rooted itself in the old wood, and the door soon froze in place. He hacked at it with the crowbar.

More banging from back through the kitchen, and then the cracking of wood.

"Up," Jodi said, lifting BB with her shoulder beneath his left arm. "Matt, here." She plucked something from her pocket with her other hand and lobbed it. A folding knife. It looked like something gardeners might use. Jodi was not into gardening.

He opened the blade and used it to start slicing through the ivy. He could see through it to outside, so it wasn't that thick, but he didn't know how long it would take to hack away.

"Maybe we should go—"

"Just keep going!" she said. She had her gun in her other hand now, and that weird carving sticking out of her pocket.

This is all about that, Matt thought, *and she mentioned a curse, a fucking* curse, *and she lied to us about more than I can fathom right now.* A chill went through him, raising the hairs on the back of his neck, shrivelling his balls. He'd held that odd chunk of wood. First time he'd touch it, he hadn't known quite what the sensation meant. It was like something ice-cold feeling blazing hot.

He caught BB's eye. His friend offered a weak smile and Matt looked down at his leg, not bleeding so much now that the tourniquet was tight, but blooded dark from thigh down. His trainer squelched with blood now that he was standing up.

Matt sliced and hacked at the ivy, maintaining pressure on the door, and soon it swung open far enough for him to squeeze outside. He pushed through then turned and shouldered the door, bracing his feet and shoving hard. Birds sang, oblivious to what was going on inside Morgan Manor. The day moved on. Something rustled away through the overgrown garden, chirruping.

"Come on!" Matt said, reaching in for BB and realising he'd left his rucksack with the box of jewellery propped against the wall inside. He hated himself for thinking about it. "Jodi—"

She shoved the rucksack along before them with her foot, and Matt plucked it up and slung it behind him. BB was there then, leaning through the door and slumping down when Jodi let him go. Matt took his weight and staggered back, hugging his friend to him and leading him out through the part-open doorway.

Jodi followed, glancing back inside at the sound of something breaking, cracking. She tugged at the door but thick ivy strands were trapped beneath it, jamming it open.

Matt was already trying to guide BB through the overgrown garden and towards the front of the house, but plants grabbed at them, BB was barely helping, and with every second that passed his weight bore down more and more on Matt's shoulder. His head lolled.

"BB! Mate!"

"Huh…"

Jodi joined them, swinging BB's free arm over her shoulders. "Come on." The gun swung from her other hand. "You still got that knife?"

"In my pocket."

They carried BB between them, dragging him along what had once been a path, using his weight to help them forge ahead and haul his trailing feet through grabbing plants. Soon they emerged into the fresh sunlight that splashed across the front of the house. The truck was parked in the centre of the wide half-moon driveway; Matt's van tucked further away beneath tree cover.

What if they came out the way they went in, from the other side of the building? They'd be closer to the van. What if they've got guns, too?

"Straight to the van," Jodi said. "Unlock."

Matt dug into his pocket and clicked the remote locking button. The van's lights flashed and it let out a *beep* that was pretty much the loudest sound he'd ever heard. He looked back over his shoulder the way they'd come; no sign of anyone.

"Put him in the back," Jodi said.

"But—"

"No time."

They reached the van and leaned BB against it, and he slumped with his chin on his chest, breath fast and light. Jodi held him upright as Matt opened the van doors, then they negotiated him around and inside, Matt shoving boxes and tools aside, sitting him on the bed and easing him down onto his back.

"Knife," she said, hand held out. He caught her eyes, his best friend, and didn't know her at all. He hated her then, and a raw anger rose within him. But she was in charge. Whatever was happening here, whatever was going to happen, she was going with the flow, while it was threatening to drown him. Matt put the knife in her hand.

"Get him in, shut the doors, start the engine and pick me up."

"Pick you up where?"

Without answering Jodi ran back towards the truck, knife in one hand, gun in the other. Matt tried to shove BB further into the van but his friend was dead weight—

Don't think that, don't you dare even think it!

—and BB let out a long groan, and blood pulsed from the wound in his right thigh. Matt saw it properly for the first time through his torn running tights, a pouting, meaty wound black with thick blood.

"Sorry, mate," he said, and he grabbed BB's feet and bent his knees. He cried out again. Matt paused and exhaled, leaning in to comfort BB.

"Stay right the fuck there!" Jodi shouted.

Matt jumped up and looked around the van's open rear door, and there were two men standing close to where he and Jodi had just dragged BB from around the side of the manor house. One of them was tall, bearded and his face and head looked messed up. The other was scrawny.

The tall guy looked at him and smiled.

Jodi was standing close to their truck, pointing her gun at them. Matt had no idea whether she was a good shot – just one of the three million things he suddenly realised he didn't know about her – but the men did as she said.

She kneeled and poked at one of the truck's tyres with her knife. It took a few hard stabs, then he head a long angry hiss as the tyre deflated.

"Hi, Matt Shorey, electrical engineer," the tall man said. Matt didn't like his voice. It was flat and unafraid, as if today's events were nothing to him.

And what are they to Jodi?

"Get in, Matt," Jodi said as she hurried back towards his van.

"I expect you have a website," the guy said. "Home address? One man band, so I'm guessing so. Business probably not so good? Wife and kids at home?"

"Matt," Jodi said, and he did what she told him. He started the van and glanced in the mirror to check on BB in the back. He was little more than a shadow.

"You OK, mate?"

A groan. Matt wasn't even sure it was in response.

The skinny guy strode past the tall, scarred man and started walking towards Jodi. She took three steps towards him, gun pointing his way.

"I've already shot you once," she said. Matt had both windows down, and her voice was clear and sharp above the idling engine. The skinny guy hesitated, then turned to grin at Matt. Matt didn't like judging on appearances, but he looked like an utter fucking psychopath.

Jodi walked sideways to the front of the van and paused. Matt realised her problem. She'd have to edge out of view of the two men for a moment to jump into the passenger door, and the skinny guy was now maybe a four- or five-second dash from the driver's side.

"Let them go, fuckface," the big man said. "She's got what I want, I see it in her pocket. And I see what it's got her. All that blood. Tangled up in shit she shouldn't be touching. Funny, really. Most people don't believe, but she will now. Bad luck for sure, eh, Jodi? And I didn't even get to lay a hand on him."

"You'll never have it," Jodi said, and something about her voice and what she said next told Matt this was significant. This was a moment Jodi had been waiting for, and relished. "You'll always be looking. Your family will always be hurting. And that's why I'm leaving you alive."

The man's face changed, and Matt's stomach dropped. He felt an instant of dizziness and queasiness, because he'd never seen such a hollow expression in a human face. If it hadn't been for the dawn colours playing across distant hills, he might have believed those eyes were black holes.

Jodi stepped beside the van and opened the door, and as she did so the skinny guy took a few fast steps. Matt half-raised the window and locked his door, then he heard a *crack!* and the man grunted and turned a quarter circle, hand grabbing his upper arm.

"That time I meant to hit you," Jodi said. She was standing on the passenger door sill, hanging on to the surround and pointing her gun left-handed across the bonnet. The skinny guy clasped his arm as blood dribbled through his fingers, face creased in pain. Beyond him, closer to the house, the older man stared with dead eyes.

"I'll find you," he said. He spoke softly, but still Matt heard.

"Go, Matt."

"I'll find you all. You know I will, Jodi."

Matt hit the gas. It was up to Jodi to hold on tight. He wanted the fuck out of there. As they skidded from the gravelled parking area onto the driveway curving down and around the hillside he watched in the mirrors, expecting to see the two men darting to the truck, punctured tyre or not. The younger man did, but the older man watched them go.

Matt almost believed he was staring into his eyes.

BB

BB guessed he was dreaming, but the dream kept coming back to one moment, and when it hit that moment he suffered the pain all over again – he was stuck in a hole and something was stabbing into his left leg.

One time the hole was in the park in Mariton, close to where he and Jodi had once made clumsy love on their way home from a drunken night in the Hen pub with Matt and a couple of other friends. He couldn't move however much he tried, and though he shouted, Jodi could not hear him. She was beneath the trees, leaning back against a trunk with her jeans down around her ankles. No one else was with her, but she acted as if he was there. He wanted to move and tell her to stop, wait for him, but he was stuck fast. Each time he opened his mouth to shout the pain lanced in and stole his voice away.

They had been in a house, the smell of damp and neglect rich and warm in his nostrils. They'd gone there for an adventure. He and Jodi, the love of his life. And Matt, his best friend, so different from him and yet with so much in common, history and secrets and catchphrases and knowing nods. The house was larger on the inside than without, and the more they walked the longer the corridors, the more numerous the closed doors. *It's here somewhere,* Jodi said, even though she was already carrying the wooden carving she'd gone there to find. Jewellery and gold and gems lay scattered in the dust, but it was a lump of wood that had drawn her. He'd always known she was odd. *What's your story?* he'd sometimes thought, though he never asked in such blunt terms. You'll *never fully know*, she might have replied if he had.

Another time the hole was halfway up the path to his little house at the edge of Mariton. It had been his parents' home, and he'd only recently started sharing it with Jodi. It was an arrangement new to them both but which they were enjoying. Now, though, she stood at the open front door calling his name. She looked concerned but didn't come outside because it was raining, even though she often loved to run in the rain. BB waved both arms but she didn't see. He called her name, but if he couldn't hear his own voice, how would she? The pain consumed him, and the rain carried the tang of blood.

He held out his hands but the water collecting in his palms was clear. He brought it to his mouth. Blood.

They'd left the house being followed by people, two men he'd never met, hazy in his dream because he wasn't sure he'd actually seen them. Jodi had been afraid. He hadn't liked that, he wanted to protect her, even though she'd tell him to get his alpha-self fucked if he even suggested she needed looking after. She was fit and strong, and she'd shown him a few of her martial arts moves. *She could kick your arse*, he'd told Matt once, but what he'd really meant was, *She could kick my arse.* They'd horsed around a few times. Mostly it had ended with him in some sort of painful judo-lock. Occasionally she'd let him win.

And he was stuck in another hole, this one clasping him in a soft but firm grip, keeping him close, refusing to let him go, and whichever way he looked or listened the pain came in. It was more distant and numbed, but somehow he understood it was worse than ever before. More serious. His senses were dulled. It was misty all around, vague, as if he were viewing this dream through smeared sunglasses. He heard a rhythmic *thunk, thunk*, and felt movement against his back and hips and legs, but the sensation belonged to someone else. The pain became an absence, burning and desperate.

Perhaps someone was calling his name.

It's like she's haunted, he thought, and there was Morgan Manor with dark basements, endless corridors, that carved chunk of wood clasped in her hand. His thoughts became confused. Senses withdrew. He'd thought it was his heart going *thunk, thunk,* but now no, no, it was something else, somewhere more distant.

BB struggled to hold on to himself and the world. A great distance grew all around him, and at least it took away the pain. The hole he was trapped in grew larger, infinite, and as he fell without moving his final thought was, *There was supposed to be a lovely light.*

JODI

"Where do we go?" Matt asked from the driver's seat. "Hospital, right? Jodi? Will they follow us there? Why did that guy kill your father? What the fuck have you got us into?"

The words flowed over and around her but Jodi couldn't distinguish one question from another, nor formulate a logical response. Words failed her. Pain pulsed behind her eyes. She was sweating and freezing cold, hugging herself against BB, trying to share warmth because she knew that his would be leaving him now. If she kept him warm for as long as possible maybe she could hold on to memories, rather than allowing in the new unbearable reality.

"Jodi!" Matt shouted.

"Just drive," she said. "Not home. Take turnings."

"I'm going to the hospital."

She looked up, past scattered boxes of electrical equipment and tool racks on the van's sides, towards the front seats. She caught

Matt's eye in the rearview mirror. His gaze stung her so she looked away. How will I ever look him in the eye again? She looked down to BB beneath her, rocking gently with the movement of the van. His eyes were half open. Or half closed.

"I'm so sorry," she whispered to BB, the person she loved, the clown and hero and decent man.

"What?" Matt asked. "Hospital?"

No hospital, Jodi tried to say, but she couldn't get the words out. Neither could she say, He's dead. She could only lean over his body and wrap him in her arms and listen as Matt's voice grew louder, more pleading, and more wretched as realisation dawned.

"He's gone," she said at last. "Just drive. Out into the lanes, away from Mariton. Get us lost, Matt. We need to get lost."

A VERY
GOOD MAN

NOVEMBER 1976

EMPTY
WORDS

THE WOOD
FOR THE TREES

LEM

Lem is not even a teenager, and they've just buried his father.

"He was a good man, Lemuel, a very good man." Even as she says those words Lem's mother's voice fades into an embarrassed whisper, because she knows how far from the truth they are. They're words you're expected to say about someone at their funeral. It's just Lem and his mother left now. There were twenty people at the graveside, and only a few of them had returned to the house for the wake. The front door closed an hour ago behind a man whose name Lem didn't know. He ruffled Lem's hair – even though he was almost thirteen and way past that sort of treatment by an adult – and kissed his mother on the cheek, then went out into the rain. The wake left behind the stink of cigarette smoke and alcohol, a living room and kitchen scattered with plates of half-eaten ham sandwiches and cheese-and-pineapple sticks, and the sense that things aren't quite over. Lem doesn't know where that feeling comes from. Maybe it's because he has yet to start mourning his dead father.

Over forty stab wounds, he heard one of the men at the wake saying to another. They were standing close together in the backyard, smoking, drinking his dead father's Scotch, and they didn't know Lem was in the outside toilet listening to everything they said. *Popped his right lung. Punctured his liver. Hard bastard, he's survived bad stuff before, but...*

His mother hasn't moved from her chair since the last man left. She's smoked half a dozen cigarettes and sipped from a small glass of sherry that seems to replenish itself without her moving. Hair is coming loose from her hair bun. She's always liked wearing her hair like that, *old fashioned and original*, she says. Lem hasn't moved either. He's still sitting at the small dining table at the back of the living room, aware of the big worn armchair that was his father's. Its emptiness is the most powerful presence in the room.

Then he crashed the car he was driving, managed to get out, slipped on all the blood running down his legs. Half the smashed windscreen buried in his face. Battery acid splashed all over him. He should've been dead three times over by then. They say he stumbled into the road, cos the smashed glass had blinded him, and it's a dray full of beer that did for him. Dragged him three hundred feet along the road. Yeah, Andrew was a hard bastard.

Lem is waiting. His mother told him she has something to tell him. Every time she speaks and then falls silent again he wonders if that was it, but so far there's been nothing he hasn't heard a hundred times before. Hollow platitudes float on skeins of cigarette smoke. Silences hold more weight than empty words. There's an open can of beer on the table that he's been eyeing.

She sighs. Stubs out a cigarette. "I promised your father I'd tell you a story," she says, "but it's just a load of old bullshit. Something that … affected him. Drove him to do some of the things…" She looks up at him then, red-eyed and reduced.

"It's OK, Mum. You don't have to."

"I promised," she whispers, and her eyes flicker towards the empty armchair. "The same story was told to him when your grandfather died. Lemuel, you're such a good boy, always have been, and you'll grow into a good man, eh? Just like your father. A good man." She nods a dozen times as if to convince herself of those words.

Lem remembers seeing his dad beating someone outside a pub once when they were on holiday in Cornwall. He must have been eight years old, maybe nine. It's far from his only memory of the man's brutality, but for some reason it sticks in his mind more than others. Maybe because it was at the end of a good day. They'd been crabbing together in the harbour, the reek of the sea settling in their clothes, and then his mum had bought them all Cornish pasties and they'd sat on a bench eating them, laughing as seagulls swooped in and stalked their food with red-tipped beaks – *dipped in the blood of dead sailors*, his dad had said, and he'd laughed and ruffled Lem's hair and told him he was joking – and then afterwards they'd had an ice cream before going back to their rented cottage and getting ready for dinner at the pub. So it had been a nice day, one when he even saw his mum and dad holding hands as they walked around the fishing village thronged with tourists. And it had ended with his dad stomping on a man's head in an alley around the side of the pub, and kicking him in the face until it was red, all red, nothing else. He'd known Lem was watching.

Never let anyone look down on you, his dad said afterwards, trying to justify this extreme revenge for some imagined slight. They were sitting on the sofa in their cottage while Lem's mother bathed his father's knuckles, sliced open on another man's teeth. Lem had his head on his dad's chest, cuddled in, smelling sweat and beer and cigarette smoke and the sad ghost of their good day. His dad's heart, *beat… beat… beat…*, slowly and in complete control.

Now his dad is dead and buried, and Lem's mum is calling him a good boy and telling him he's the man of the house, and she has a story to tell. And Lem doesn't want to hear it. She'd promised his dad, and that could only mean it was something bad. He knows that, even though he's barely a teenager. Deep down he knows that *everything* about his dad was bad, and he's terrified that what she's going to say will stamp that same badness onto his own soul.

"It sounds stupid, really," she says, and she actually laughs. Lem hasn't seen that in a few days, maybe weeks. It lifts his heart and he smiles. Then his smile slips away when she says, "But he never thought of it as stupid. And I've seen things… known things… that make me think there's something to it after all." She turns to Lem, and her next words sound rehearsed and recited from memory, spoken with a tear in her eye. It's something she wished she'd never have to say, and he never wanted to hear. "Your father spent his life trying to lift a curse that was cast on his family. And now that he's gone…" She looks away and sniffs, wiping at her eyes.

"Don't say it, Mum."

"Now that he's dead, Lemuel, that task falls on you. This is something I've had ready to say for years, and I've dreaded doing it with every breath. But here we are. And you need to hear."

She tells him the story.

*W*itches and trees, trees and witches. The stories of the two often converge and blend, and this one more than most. This tale is a true merging of witch and tree. There are places where you can read more – obscure magazines and one or two old books – but the details change depending on who is doing the telling, and how they discover the tale. Your father always knew that. That's why he kept things to himself, focussed, concentrating on what he knew and disregarding everything else. You'll have to do that as well, Lem. You'll have to focus. Set aside lies and hone in on the truth, even if that truth is different for you than it ever was for your father.

You'll need to see the wood for the trees.

So yes, the tree and the witch. That's where the story starts, and not as long ago as you might imagine. When you think of witches I expect you think of the dark ages, and women and men tied to stakes and burned alive. That did happen, to some bad people but mostly good ones. This story is much closer to us than that, in time and place. So close that Andrew often said he could reach through and touch it. When I asked what he could reach through, he'd look at me strangely, and his answers weren't always the same. Sometimes he'd say, I can reach through the lies to the truth. Other times it was the other side of a dream. Once, he said he could stretch past death to whatever lies beyond.

I guess that's where he is now. And now, he'll know the real truth of things.

The story goes that a witch came after his family, a little over two hundred years ago up in Derbyshire. His great-great-great-grandfather beat a child for stealing some grain from his farm, and the child died. He or she belonged to a young couple from the local village, and that young woman's mother was allegedly a witch.

She lived on her own, apart from the rest of the village, but she was liked well enough, and helped villagers with various ailments and problems. She used herbs and roots to make medicines. Her name was Mary Webster, and she knew which mushrooms to eat and which to leave alone, and how sometimes the weather and sun and moon touched the moods of those villagers she existed to help. There were no black cats or pointed hats or broomsticks for Mary Webster, no silliness like that, but...

Well, maybe some silliness. Maybe some darker stuff we're not so used to believing as true.

The thing is, Webster didn't come after your father's ancestor as a witch, but as a grieving grandmother. She visited him to offer a chance at atonement. But he was not a good man, and he shoved the woman away from him. Told her to leave or he'd kill her like he'd killed her grandchild. Crying, grieving, hurting deep inside, she'd offered him a hand to hold, an opportunity to express regret, and he threatened her with a closed fist.

Mary Webster returned three days later. They say she went to condemn him for his crime and lay some sort of punishment upon him, but she never had the chance. The brutal man ran her through with a pitchfork the moment she set foot on his land. He impaled her, then dragged her across his yard and into the woodland behind his home. He pinned her up on an old oak tree, cut off her hands and tore out her tongue so that she could make no shapes, perform no spells – I guess even he believed some stories about what she was, and how she'd come there to lay a curse on him – and then he left her to hang there and die.

But that night he died in screaming pain, his insides boiling and his eyeballs bursting and... the stories are horrible.

Next day, his wife and three young sons went to try and save the woman, but they found something amazing. Mary Webster was dead, but also something more. That old oak tree had grown around her, absorbed her, trapping her within its embrace.

Grieving their dead husband and father even as they tried to understand his crime, they cut down the tree, and chopped it up, and over the next seven days the dead man's three sons spread those parts across the countryside. They dropped bits of the tree containing the remains of Mary Webster into holes and caves, and the basements of old buildings and abandoned churches. Some accounts say the tree's parts only stopped bleeding when they threw the last relic into a church crypt.

So that was the end of the witch, and ever since that day illnesses, deaths and bad luck have haunted your father and his family. Whether or not Mary Webster truly went there that day to curse the family, her slaying made that curse manifest.

It's touched us too, Lem, but we've also had your father. A strong man. A hard man. He's spent his life searching for those wooden objects containing the remains of the dead woman, Mary Webster, to try and bring her back together again. Because he believes that making her whole, making her safe, will assuage her rage and lift her curse. He found five relics and hid them away. And I can tell you where.

So there it is. Nine days out of ten I think the story is a load of old bullshit. He told me once, not too long ago, that he isn't even sure the curse wants itself lifted, and that old dead witch doesn't wish herself made whole again. Now Andrew is dead, killed when he was looking for another relic. And his was a hard death.

Today is one of those days when I believe.

"Well, I *don't* believe," Lem says. His mother glares at him but he doesn't look away. In the end, she does. "You can't make excuses for Dad," he continues. "It's not fair to tell lies about why he was like he was."

"Lies, truths, they're all mixed up, Lem."

"Mixed up like trees and witches?"

She lights another cigarette, takes another sip of sherry.

"I love you, Mum. I love Dad, too. But I don't want to live my life like him. I don't want to be a bad man."

"He wasn't born bad, Lemuel. He was made that way by the curse he spent his life trying to lift. I saw him die and come back twice, and I think there were other times, and don't you think—"

Lem stands at last, in the middle of the room filled with the detritus of a wake, the last echoes of a life. "Die and come back? Relics of a dead witch? A curse? It's like one of those Hammer films Dad lets me watch on a Friday night. I'm sad he's gone..." Lem is crying now, but behind the tears he knows what he has to say. Knows he *has* to say it, because now might be the only time. This feels like a point in his life that will fork depending on the decisions he makes *right now*. He senses a weight, and it's not just the absence in his father's chair or the sound of that gruff voice stored in the walls and floors of this home. "I'm sad he's gone, but I won't let the stupid stuff he believed in make me like him, Mum."

She stares at him for a while, and he thinks he sees something like pride in her eyes. But cigarette smoke and tears blur his view – her smoke, his tears – and he can never be sure.

Four months later his mother is dead, crushed beneath a falling wall in a freak accident, and Lem's life is never the same.

HOLLOWED

SEPTEMBER 2024

GOSHAWK

'THUNDERSTRUCK'

MATT

Matt did what Jodi said and drove, took turnings, and within fifteen minutes of leaving Morgan Manor's main gates he knew that they would be safe for a little while. He'd headed along the main road away from Mariton, taken a left after the Blythan Arms, driven down the single-lane track, turned right before Halford's Farm, then wound up into the wooded hills known locally as the Rolling. He'd gone running in the Rolling with Jodi a few times, and she'd always eased back so that he could keep pace. They'd only done a few miles, eight at the most, and he'd got to know some of the fire tracks and forestry roads, discovering a few places he'd never been even though he'd lived in Mariton his whole life.

They were parked on one such track now, and he kept the engine running. He couldn't bear the silence.

"They won't find us here," Matt said, staring through the windscreen. His breathing was fast and shallow, as if he'd been running rather than driving. He was sweating. It was almost nine in the morning. He was ready to turn around and look into the back of the van, because it had all gone quiet back there. He'd look and Jodi and BB would be sitting with hands over their mouths, trying not to laugh because it had all been a big joke on him. The heist, the shooting, the blood, that tall vicious bastard and the skinny guy with a bullet in his arm. All a gag, and he was the victim.

He saw BB and Jodi running away from the van laughing, doors hanging open. He imagined the rear empty, doors still closed, no sign of any blood or the loot-filled rucksack or Jodi and BB at all, because he must have had a nightmare and been sleep-driving, and it was lucky he'd not crashed. Or he'd turn around and find that the silence was because Jodi was also dead, lying with wrists slit by her own knife because she could never live with what she had done.

At last he turned in his seat and was faced with the nightmare he already knew was real. BB was lying motionless, and Jodi leaned over him, arms around his shoulders and head resting on his chest. She was sobbing quietly, shuddering as she took in a breath.

"Jodi. They won't find us here. But we need to get BB to a hospital."

"He's dead," she said, barely a breath, and it was as if the words came from everywhere. She didn't move as she spoke.

"He might not be," Matt said, but it was a stupid thing to say. If BB wasn't dead, then why had he listened to Jodi and driven out into the sticks instead of to the hospital in Mariton? *Because I haven't got a clue what I'm doing*, he thought, and he heard BB laughing at him and calling him a stupid prick.

Jodi looked up and he had never seen that face. She was hollowed by shock.

"He's dead, Matt," she said.

He looked at BB's body, lifting himself so that he could see into the van's rear. He stared for a while.

"Turn the engine off," Jodi said.

"Why?"

"Just turn it off. I need to think."

"No, you don't," he said, but he turned the engine off anyway. The sudden silence and stillness was shocking, and he opened his door to let some of the outside in. It should never have been that silent, that still, while BB was with them. He was alive and vital, always joking and laughing, always on the move because he didn't know how to be motionless. "Neither of us needs to think. We need to go to a hospital with…" He looked down at BB, seeing him properly for the first time since leaving the manor. "He died while I was driving and…" *And I wasn't even there to say goodbye, he didn't hear me, he didn't hear my voice when he was dying.*

Jodi looked at him and shook her head. She was seeing much further, concentrating, frowning. "I need to think."

"No!" Matt shouted, and Jodi jumped. "*No!*" he shouted again, louder, watching his oldest, best friend for any sign of movement. There was none. He remained still and not there, and Matt couldn't understand how that could be. Not so quickly. How could he have gone from being the man he was to this motionless, empty body? Where was he now? How could everything that made the friend he'd loved just… stop?

"Matt—"

"You *don't* need to think! Your thinking got us into that place, to take that thing." He nodded at the wooden carving still sticking out from the leg pocket of her blood-soaked leggings. "It got BB into that hole and got him *killed*! So you don't have to think *anything*. We're going to the hospital with my dead friend, and if we get into trouble for breaking into an old house so be it, Jodi, I couldn't give a fuck. Not a single fuck."

"That's not the trouble I'm worried about," she said, and he knew what she meant. He saw it in her face, and he'd known it from the moment they drove away and he saw that look of outright, blazing fury on the man's face. The man who Jodi said had killed her father. There was so much he didn't know, and every scrap of what he didn't know made Jodi more of a stranger to him.

"But BB," he said. "We can't just… What do we…"

It was as if someone reached in and took out Jodi's bones. She slumped down against the van's back doors, shoulders falling, upturned hands landing on the floor liked clawed, dead spiders, and her face crumpled and twisted as tears flowed. She cried silently to begin with, with no breath to give, then she shuddered hard as she dragged in some air and wailed. Matt had never heard a sound like it. He turned and dropped back into his seat, then slipped from the van and moved around to the front, leaning back against the bonnet and looking out into the woods as Jodi cried behind him. He didn't know how to comfort her. He wasn't sure he was in a position to comfort himself. He started to shake, and a buzzard drifted through the trees to his right, barely flapping its wings as it tilted left and right to avoid the branches. BB loved birds of prey and could identify them from a distance – buzzard or red kite, sparrow hawk or kestrel. He'd always wanted to train a goshawk. They were one of the hardest birds to train, he'd said, and he thought that was cool. He would never own a goshawk now.

Matt pressed his hands to his face, but he still saw a world without BB in it. He heard birdsong welcoming in the day, smelled the damp pine morning, saw the buzzard alighting in a tree, and BB remained not there.

"We can't just leave him somewhere," he whispered, and the birds sang back in agreement. BB had a brother in Birmingham, and his mother was still alive in her seaside place in Cornwall. They would have to be told. His brother ran a fishing tackle shop. His mother came to visit sometimes, and she wore colourful clothing and loved a gin and tonic. "We can't just leave him."

From inside the van he heard the familiar opening tones of AC/DC's 'Thunderstruck' as his phone rang.

LEM

Lem drove with one hand and held the phone to his ear with the other. He didn't speak, only listened. The guy said nothing when he answered, and Lem heard only the sound of early morning birdsong.

"Is that Muriel?" he asked, injecting a lightness to his voice. Matt hung up. Lem dropped the phone into the door pocket.

"Who's Muriel?" Rash asked.

Lem glanced sidelong at him and didn't even offer a response. Fucking idiot. He had no doubt that Rash wasn't his real name, not even part of it, and that he'd taken it on because he thought it sounded hard, or cool, or intimidating. All Lem thought of when he spoke the name was speckled red spots on a scrotum.

It had taken twenty minutes to change the truck's wheel. Jodi and the others were long gone by then. Lem knew he had to act fast, stay in control of the situation. At least Rash was mostly quiet. He was too busy dying from the graze to his arm.

"Can't believe she shot me," Rash said.

"Can't believe you stood in the way of the bullet."

Rash looked at him, about to say something, but thought better of it.

"Got that address yet?" Lem asked.

"Only just got reception, it's looking. There." He pointed along the road at a sign that read MARITON: VILLAGE OF FLOWERS. The sign was carved into a chunk of timber set into a huge rock that had been placed beside the road, its base sitting in a spread of wildflowers.

"Lovely," Lem said. His mother had loved flowers, and Lem always thought of her when he saw displays like this. She'd have said, *It's like a rainbow came apart and got rooted here.* She was quite poetic when it came to things she loved, and he knew she'd died with so much left to say. The wall had crushed all those poems from her head.

"Got it," Rash said. "OK, past a church on the left, then second right. You think they'll be there?"

"Nope."

"Then why are we going?"

"So that they know we've been."

Lem pulled into a small lay-by beside the church. He picked up the phone and stared across at Rash.

"What?" Rash asked.

"We walk from here."

As usual Rash nodded as if he knew what was happening, but he didn't. Not at all. He was useful for his smattering of local knowledge, and use of his truck had proved worthwhile for the past couple of days, but there was very little between his ears. Even his squid tattoo had too many tentacles.

"I'm feeling a bit faint," he said.

Lem glanced at the blood-soaked sleeve of his jacket. "We'll get it fixed up soon," he said. "Put this on." He shrugged his own jacket off and dropped it in Rash's lap. It was several sizes too big, but it would cover up the blood and stop any awkward questions. Lem didn't like the idea of getting someone else's blood on his clothes, but it would be far from the first time.

That buzz of excitement came in again and he bore down on it, smothering it beneath his familiar steadiness. He couldn't afford distractions.

But he'd *seen* it. Stuck in her pocket, she'd tried hiding it from him to begin with, but you couldn't hide a relic from Lem. They were too much a part of him, and his life, to be hidden away when they'd so recently been exposed. It wasn't that he could smell them or taste them on the air, exactly. It was more as if he felt them, a gentle touch of his ancestors' expectant fingertips stroking his neck and shoulders, like excited children gathering around a party performer. She had it, and at the end when she and her helper were driving away, she'd teased him with it.

She could have put a bullet in his chest a dozen times, but she'd refrained. Lem wasn't sure it would have killed him anyway. Not for good. But the fact that she'd held back told him plenty about her intentions. Taking the relic was meant to taunt and hurt him, and that was why he would take it back from her. He had no doubt about that. It was simply the way things were.

He'd already smelled blood that morning, and for once he hadn't been the one to draw it.

Lem pulled on his beanie to cover the burn scars on his head and upper face, then they left the truck where it was. He pocketed the keys. Rash had stared at him the first few times he'd done this, but Lem's casual ownership of his vehicle had never been questioned. Rash might be thick as shit, but he already knew Lem well enough to accept things as they were. His survival instinct made it so.

"You're navigating, but don't make it look obvious," Lem said. He followed Rash past the church, then they took some turnings and ended up walking towards the end of a cul-de-sac. Lem nodded as they passed a couple of pensioners chatting outside a small grocery store, and he tried a smile. They both glanced away. He knew he had that effect on people, and that the burn scars presented a visage that mirrored his soul. So be it. He'd been ugly inside and out long before Jodi abandoned him to die on the road beside the blazing van.

"This is it," Rash said, looking down at his feet.

"Which one."

Rash nodded his head without looking up. Lem put a hand on his shoulder, just a hand's width from the gunshot wound, and squeezed enough to elicit a whimper.

"Ouch! Lem!"

"You couldn't look more suspicious and shady," Lem said. "If this is you trying to act casual then please, please try and act like a remorseless baby killer. Now, which house is Matt Shorey's?" He let go of Rash's shoulder, and the skinny man took a deep breath and raised his head. He pointed across the street at a small semi-detached house with a hawthorn tree in the front garden and a splash of yellow roses climbing a trellis around the front door.

"Don't point," Lem said.

"What? Then what do I do?"

Lem crossed the road and strode up the short driveway as if he belonged, and he heard Rash scurrying after him. He glanced left and right as he went, but saw no one watching them. The small front gardens up and down the street had hedges and trees along their borders. That was good. It meant these people liked keeping themselves to themselves.

Lem headed down the side of the house and through a gate into the back garden, pressing himself against the back wall and checking to see if anyone overlooked the small patio area. There was no one. Rash followed him and pulled the gate gently closed.

"What now?" Rash asked.

"Now we make sure they know they can't come back here," Lem said. He took out his phone and held it ready to take photos. He held it up and snapped a picture of Rash first, before his companion had a chance to turn away.

"Fuck's sake!" he said. "Nothing to identify me, Lem!"

"Don't worry. Won't matter."

"But if—"

"Don't worry," Lem said again, and Rash fell silent. Lem was used to being in control. It was something in his voice. Sometimes between blinks he saw that long winding path heading towards the light, and the blurred shadows of his wretched family members standing there in pain, and he wondered whether his true voice came from that ambiguous place beyond life and before death.

There was patio furniture, a table beneath an open parasol, a fire pit packed away against the side of a garden storage building, plant pots scattered around the patio and the edge of the lawn, all planted with heathers and other perennials. A shovel was propped against the garden store.

"I'll get the patio doors open," Rash said. Lem nodded.

It took three minutes for him to pop the lock, and Lem held his breath as Rash slid the door open. No alarm sounded. No dog barked. Rash glanced back over his shoulder and Lem nodded.

"I'll find a towel or something for my arm," Rash said, and Lem followed him into a neat kitchen with a snug to one side. While Rash opened drawers searching for something to bind his wound, Lem took in the surroundings. There was plenty of stuff he could have used, but he sought something special, and distinctive. He'd know it when he saw it.

Rash slipped his coat off and handed it to Lem, then he ran a hand towel under the tap and leaned against the sink. He winced as he pulled off his shirt. There was a small, tattered hole in his arm, a couple of inches below his armpit and slicing through the top edge of his bicep. Lem twirled his finger and Rash turned around.

"Gone through," Lem said.

"I'll clean it, then can you bandage it up for me?" Rash asked.

Lem nodded as he turned away and went through into the living room. One alcove was lined with books. A huge TV hung on the chimney breast. There was a drinks cabinet in one corner, with several bottles on top along with a couple of decanters.

Maybe those, Lem thought.

He strolled around the living room, then took a step back and looked out through folding doors into the hallway. Beneath the stairs was a cupboard door that stood ajar. A few shoes spilled out, and inside was a glint of metal. Lem opened the door with his boot. Golf clubs. He grunted, turned away, then glanced back again when he registered the other thing he'd seen. He smiled inside, knowing that it would barely touch his face. He remembered his father. He always did at times like this, though it was usually the dead man of scars with windscreen glass embedded in his face. He tried to imagine a smile on his old man's face. As with Lem it was mostly unseen.

Using his handkerchief to hold it, he took the object and headed back through the living room to the large kitchen. Rash was still at the sink, wincing as he cleaned the bullet wound.

"Did you find any bandages?" he asked, then he looked down at what Lem was carrying. "What's that?"

Lem propped his phone against the bread bin, facing out, and scrolled to WhatsApp. He adjusted its position so that he could see Rash standing at the sink.

Rash chuckled uncertainly, wanting Lem to think he knew what was going on.

"Track pump," Lem said. "Good one, too."

"So we're gonna send that Matt Shorey dude a video?"

"Yeah, sure. Let him know where we are."

"Waiting for him, like," Rash said.

Lem grunted and touched the video call button. The ringing tone began. "Smile for our friends." Rash dropped the bloody towel and stuck up his middle fingers.

"Come and see us, fuckers, and we'll see who shoots straight next time. Right, Lem?"

"He hasn't answered yet, fuckface." Lem blinked, and silhouetted on that winding path his father watched, smiling on the inside. The ringing stopped and he heard a crackle of connection.

"Right, here we go," Lem said. He swung wide and hard, gripping the handle and tube on the track pump so that the heavy metal base connected squarely with Rash's temple.

"*Gurk*," Rash said, stumbling sideways against the sink. He stood swaying for a moment, then the deep dent in the side of his head started leaking blood and other slick fluids. Lem had seen this before. He knew Rash was already done, but he didn't just want to kill him. He wanted to spread him around.

"*Gurk*?" Rash said, and as he reached for the bloody towel he'd dropped on the draining board, Lem swung again. Three more times. He picked up the phone and aimed it at Rash as he slumped down onto the kitchen floor.

One of the many things Lem had inherited from his father was a strong, cold heart that barely beat faster whether he was fighting, fucking or killing. Now with his heartbeat not quite edging above sixty, Lem dropped the track pump and picked up a carving knife, still using the handkerchief. Matt Shorey, Electrical Engineer, must have enjoyed his cooking. The knife was keen.

JODI

Jodi knew who had made the call by the look on Matt's face. She didn't want to see, but had to. She didn't want to move on to whatever came next, but she *had* to, because this was all her doing. Every minute of this day, every damned bloody moment was because of her and what she'd planned and done.

She had to clamber over BB's body so that she could lean on the back of the driver's seat and see. She did so carefully, trying not to touch him, as if he'd become so much more delicate now that he was dead. Matt was standing in the open van doorway. His hand holding the phone was shaking. Jodi closed her own hand over his, and together they watched a man being murdered in Matt's kitchen.

"This is now," Jodi said.

Matt pulled away and turned the phone facedown, staring at her. Shock stole his expression, but she saw her own guilt reflected in his eyes. He dropped the phone onto the driver's seat but they still heard. A wet *thunk*. A grunt. The *shtick* of a sharp blade parting clothing and flesh. One of his expensive kitchen knives, she guessed, plastered with his fingerprints.

Jodi grabbed up the phone and went to thumb it off, and in that moment she glimpsed what Lem was doing in Matt's house less than ten miles from where they were. Rash was dead now, she had little doubt of that, but Lem was slicing him slowly, carefully, so that he could still aim a phone with his other hand. She disconnected and dropped the phone as if it were hot or infected.

"So that we can't go home," Jodi said. She closed her eyes, swallowed down the sick. Her stomach felt heavy and hot. She opened her eyes again and looked at Matt. "He got your number from the van, address from your website."

Matt didn't seem to hear. He leaned against the doorframe and stared past Jodi, through the passenger door window and into the woods beyond.

"Matt!"

He glanced at her.

"We can't go home."

"Police," he said. "He's murdered someone, on camera, in my house, and—"

"That was live. We didn't screenshot, didn't record, didn't see his face. That guy's body is in your house, and if we go to the police we'll have to explain that as well as…"

"As well as BB," Matt said, looking past her into the van's darker interior.

"Yeah."

"So what do we do?"

"We need to—"

"What the *fuck* do we do? Now that you've got us into this shit that's got BB killed and some thug murdered in my kitchen by another thug, just what the actual fucking fuck do we…"

Jodi reached out and grabbed Matt's hand and he didn't pull away. She squeezed and he squeezed back.

"We have to stay ahead of Lem and figure that out."

Matt thought about it, not meeting her eye. He stared at the silent phone facedown on the driver's seat, and she knew he was seeing the blood, the red, the mess of a dead person in his house. *At least he doesn't have a family*, she thought, then she realised that his family was her and BB and that she had broken it beyond repair.

"We have to meet him," Matt said.

"No."

"Somewhere public, open and safe, like the King's Arms. He won't do anything stupid with so many people around. Then we give him that thing you've got in your pocket."

"I can't do that." She let go of his hand and leaned back.

"Why not?"

"Because it's what he wants."

"Good! It's *good* that's what he wants, because you have it, so give it to him and he can fuck off, or we can use it to lure him in and get him arrested!"

"I took it because I knew he wanted it. The details don't matter, and there's stuff you don't know about me, but I've spent years thinking he killed my father—"

"The details don't matter?"

"Matt, please. For me, finding this thing before him was some sort of revenge. But he said that my dad didn't die after all. I don't know how that can be, and most of me doesn't believe it. But if I give this to Lem he won't just disappear from our lives. He's fucking *brutal*, Matt. He's killed people, I don't know how many, and he'll take one of us to blood the relic."

"What do you mean?

Jodi sighed. "It's stupid. He believes in a curse around these things and his family, and it's driven him mad, made him like he is. But he's utterly focussed in collecting all the relics, and my father and I were with him when he found another one. And he believes when he finds a relic, he has to blood it. He did that by killing my dad, or so I thought."

"We've just seen…" Matt couldn't finish. He didn't have to.

"Lem probably had that planned for Rash all along."

"So throw it away. Bury it. Hide it."

"And then what?"

They were both silent for a few seconds.

"He'll come after us," Matt said.

"Right. He'll look until he finds us, then he'll torture us for its location. We've got to grab any advantage having that thing in our hands gives us."

Matt laughed, a short sharp snort without humour. "A curse."

Jodi pressed her hand against the relic in her leggings pocket. She hated the feel of it and everything it represented.

"You had no right," Matt said.

"I know. I'll do whatever I can to make things better."

"You can bring BB back to life?" He glared at her.

Jodi looked away.

"Jodi?"

She started to shake. She couldn't control it. Shock, grief and anger scorched her body and mind, taking over and setting her muscles cramping and quivering, but no tears came this time. Her eyes stayed wide and dry, and wretchedness flowed from her in hot waves. She leaned on the seatback, and the more she wished reality would take her away from the awfulness of what she had done and caused, the clearer everything became. If it weren't for her stupid need for petty revenge after so long, BB would still be alive. She had lost the man she loved, and Matt had lost his best friend. Dizziness washed over her and she puked, turning her head to the side just enough so that the vomit spilled across the door sill and outside rather than onto the van's seat. Her stomach clenched again, knotting painfully. She felt weak, almost fluid, as if she would melt into a puddle and never reform into the woman she had once been.

"... still..." she heard. Matt's voice, but distant. "Jodi..."

She felt him holding her, and then he was leaning over the seat and hugging her so tight that it hurt. And it felt good.

"I'm sorry..." she said, but it wasn't enough and it never would be. She was glad when Matt did not reply. Instead he held her a while longer as her shaking gradually settled, and the heat of her grief and guilt seemed to chill in the cool morning air.

"So what do we do?" Matt asked at last.

Jodi hauled herself over the front seats and Matt moved back to let her out. She breathed in the fresh morning air, not realising just how much she'd been smelling BB. His blood, his death. She wished Matt would embrace her again so that she could hug him back, but that moment was past.

"We need to leave BB where he'll be found," she said. "Then go somewhere safe, and figure out the best way out of this."

"Driven by what?" Matt asked.

"What do you mean?"

"I mean, is this all about your father now? You really think he's still alive?"

Jodi had to think about that for a moment, but not long. And when she spoke she really believed what she said. "No, I don't believe that. This is about our safety, first and foremost."

"Promise?"

"Promise." She remembered her father that last time she saw him, helping an injured Lem into the van. She remembered the sound of Lem caving in his face with the relic he'd stolen that day, again and again. She remembered the crash.

Jodi knew that she was a great liar. Perhaps so good that she could even lie to herself.

LONGSHIP

APRIL 2007

A GOOD THIEF

HORNED HARE

JODI

Jodi has turned eighteen, and she has just bought her dad a pint for the first time. They are sitting outside the Longship on the banks of the River Wye. It's a cool spring day, but the sun's out and it's warm enough for them to sit out on a bench in the garden, closer to the river than the pub.

"Same again?" Jodi asks.

Her dad drains his pint and smacks his lips. "Same again! And a bag of peanuts. Dry roasted."

Jodi grabs their glasses and walks across the garden towards the pub. The grass still hasn't received its first cut, and the place has that untended look that might turn some people away, but she likes it. Flowers are blooming, shrubs in scattered planters coming to life, and daffodil bulbs sprout as if the world is waking from a long slumber.

Jodi is officially an adult now, but in her mind she's been there for a long while. The weight of what her mother asked has always been heavy on her shoulders, but her dad's doing OK. He's got a job and they share a nice flat, and he's staying out of trouble. Even though he never says anything, she knows that he's doing his best to make her proud.

Today's one of those days when she feels unaccountably upbeat. They come from time to time, and often it's just a brief moment of delight and contentment that thrills through her and makes her smile. She's always welcomed them because whatever might be troubling her in life – school, boyfriend stuff, or the deeper, more profound sadness about her mother and everything that's been missing – these moments always cut through to the more satisfied, relaxed heart of her, the part that she grabs hold of and thinks of as her "core calm". It's the place she always wants to be, and where she dwells as much of the time as possible.

She kicks through the last of the long grass and enters the shadow of the pub, and inside she exchanges pleasantries with the barman and he's smiling, and she wonders if he's having a core calm moment as well. Pints in hand – cider for her, real ale for her dad – she goes back outside, and someone is sitting in her place.

Her feeling of peace evaporates immediately. She stubs her toe on a brick path verge buried in the grass and spills some drink, cursing as it speckles down her jeans. The sun is still out but it feels cooler than before. Her dad is watching her, and the other man sitting beside him is staring out over the river, smoke rising about his head. Her dad smiles but it seems forced. Either that, or Jodi's mood change paints it that way.

She walks across and puts her dad's drink before him. Then she heads around the table and sits opposite her dad, and that's when she catches her first glimpse of the stranger. He has his elbows on the table, hands steepled in front of his face, cigarette smoking between two fingers, and he raises one forefinger in greeting. His mouth twitches in what might be a smile, but she suspects it doesn't touch his eyes. He doesn't take off his sunglasses, and it's another three weeks until she sees those lifeless eyes. By then it's too late.

"Who's our new friend?" Jodi asks. The man has intruded and spoiled their time together, and she can tell her dad doesn't know him.

"Name's Lem. I'm told your dad's a good thief," the man says. His voice is cold and dry, and reminds her of a dream she once had. It was a nightmare she experienced several times after her mother died, in which an unseen man spoke to her from inside her mother's coffin. The younger Jodi always woke terrified that she would finally see this man.

"He's retired," Jodi says.

"Like I said," her dad echoes.

The man shrugs.

"You've got blood under your fingernails," Jodi says. If it really is blood, from something bad, most people would claim it's oil or dried chocolate or something else.

The man raises his finger again, not in greeting this time, and inclines his head to look down. "Cut my hand at work," he says. "Sorry." He puts his finger in his mouth and his cheeks suck in.

Jodi glances at her dad and he shrugs slightly. She shakes her head and nods towards the car park. Her dad picks up his pint and takes a long swig, and Jodi does the same.

"Honestly, I'm sorry to trouble your day," Lem says. "And it's such a lovely one." He looks up at the sky and Jodi takes the opportunity to size him up, while he probably isn't looking at her. She still can't really tell behind the sunglasses. He's very tall, over six feet, and broad, and he has a mass of flowing black hair and a big beard. A proper beard, her mum would have said, one that grows in well and is thick and looks heavy. It's slightly unkempt, but not enough to make it scruffy.

"No trouble at all," her dad says. "Get you a beer?"

Lem glances back down at Jodi, as if he's deciding whether he wants her here or not.

"I'm fine, thanks," he says. "Driving. You?"

"I'm leaving my car here," Jodi says.

"Special occasion?"

"My daughter's eighteenth," her dad says. "You police?"

Jodi raises her eyebrows, and Lem laughs out loud, just once. It's more like a cough. He takes a final drag on his cigarette and leans down to stub it out beneath his boot. Jodi will see him do that again and again over the coming weeks, and it becomes a habit she never really understands. It speaks of concern for other people, and the environment, and Lem has neither.

"Far from," Lem says. "Far from."

"He's retired," Jodi says again, and she sees the first flicker of annoyance from her dad. Lem doesn't see it – he really can't, because he's looking at her – but she's sure he picks up on it.

"Does an old thief ever retire, or just get nicked?" he asks.

Jodi nods down at his bare forearms. "Nice tatts."

"I've got plenty." He traces the tattoo on his left arm. "Got this snake to cover the scar from a farming accident in Devon. Tractor rolled, and I was thrown from the window. Driver wasn't so lucky."

Jodi looks closer and sees that the python curling around his wrist and across his forearm is following a deep, ugly canyon of scars. He lifts the hem of his T-shirt to reveal the left side of his stomach and chest, lean and muscled. A strangely horned hare is tattooed beneath his armpit, its mouth an ugly pink scar. "Fell off my bike and handlebar snapped, tore me open down the side."

"What about that one?" Jodi asks, pointing at his neck. He drops his T-shirt and pulls the neckline down to reveal the edge of a wing, feathers extended.

"Just looked nice," he says. "You got any?"

"I'm only just eighteen," Jodi says. She does have one, a small daisy on her thigh that even her dad doesn't know about. She doesn't want to admit to it. For some reason she believes that Lem is lying about his, and that the injuries they cover are no accidents. "Dad's got a couple, though."

"Jesus," her dad says, rolling his eyes and scratching his forearm.

"USS Indianapolis?" Lem says, and her dad bursts out laughing. She doesn't understand, and the fact that Lem hardly smiles disturbs her. Everything about him does, and suddenly she wants away.

"I'll get more drinks," Lem says, and before either of them can object he's up and away to the pub.

They should have left then. But something keeps them there, and when Lem returns he has a pint for himself, and says he'll leave his car there as well. He does not mention his former career for the rest of that afternoon, and when Jodi goes onto soft drinks he and her dad keep drinking. When the two of them walk home and Lem jumps into his car – five pints down, still wearing his sunglasses, and steady and calm as if the alcohol has barely touched him – he and her dad have swapped phone numbers and arranged to meet up again at some point.

And that is when their business is done, and their fate written. That afternoon should have been one long core calm moment for Jodi, but it becomes a turning point in her life that she will always wish had never been taken.

KOJAK

SEPTEMBER 2024

A WICKER COFFIN

YOUNG MASTER KING

MATT

"When we were kids we used to call him Kojak," Matt said, and the memory of him and BB running past Kojak's place and shouting that name brought the ghost of a smile that did not fit his face.

"Because he's bald," Jodi said.

"Right. He lived in a different caravan then, just along the river from the one he's got now. You can still see the old one, or what's left of it."

"BB's never mentioned him," Jodi said, and Matt took a brief stab of delight in that. *Good*, he thought, *it's good that he hasn't told you everything about me and him growing up*. It felt nice having something that was just him and BB, a precious memory, even though that memory consisted of teasing the mad old dude who lived down by the river. Even back then Kojak had seemed old, though Matt guessed he can't have been much older than fifty. He hadn't seen him in a couple of years, but he knew that BB had cycled past last year on one of his rare mountain bike forays, and he'd told Matt that Kojak was still there, sitting by the river on the dock he'd built illegally, fishing and smoking and living his best life. BB had always admired Kojak for that. He'd stopped and refilled his water bottles, had a chat, then gone on his way. Kojak wasn't the ogre they'd believed him to be as kids, and Matt was constantly amazed that the old man didn't hold any grudges against them.

"Wonder if kids still give him grief," he said, and it was something that had never crossed his mind. He really hoped they didn't. Kojak made money foraging the riverbanks for wild garlic, mushrooms and other plants that he sold at local weekly markets, and he was also a whizz at anything mechanical. People took boats to him for fixing, and there were still a few locals who risked the pitted track to his caravan to get their car serviced.

"So you think he'll... you know, find him?" Jodi asked.

"If we leave BB close by, Kojak will find him," Matt said. Even speaking those words aloud felt awful. Leaving his friend's body anywhere felt horrific. But...

"BB loved the outdoors," Matt said, more to himself than Jodi. "We were pissed once, talking about whether we wanted burying or burning. Soon after his dad died, I think this was. I said I wanted to be cremated, and BB came up with the idea of being buried out in the wild in a wicker coffin. He reckoned you could do that. Need a licence apparently, and I don't know how serious he was. Sounds crazy to me. A wicker coffin..." He trailed off.

"Matt," Jodi said, touching his arm.

He shrugged her off. "I'll drive."

Jodi fell silent and Matt drove, heading through country lanes towards the river. He had to slow a couple of times when cars came in the opposite direction, but he didn't recognise anyone. He was glad about that, but it did nothing to settle his jangling nerves. Whatever might happen with Lem, what they were about to do was a crime that would leave them with countless awkward questions to answer.

It was as far from normal behaviour as Matt had ever contemplated, but he understood why they had to do it. They were in terrible danger. Jodi had always struck him as calm and in control, and he had never seen her so afraid.

After a while she said, "I suppose he's out of the way. Off-grid."

Matt did not reply. Most of the reason he'd thought of Kojak was that he really didn't want to go anywhere near Mariton right now. He had visions of seeing Lem standing outside his house waiting for them to arrive. Or if they sneaked into the town along one of the smaller back roads, he'd be waiting for them wherever they went. Whatever they did with BB's body, wherever they left him, Lem would be there. Like a zombie smelling flesh, a vampire craving blood. He would track them down by the scent of death, seeking it for sustenance and being drawn in by their fear, dread and grief.

Matt knew people like Lem existed, but he'd been lucky enough to never cross their paths.

They reached the gateway to the rough track that led down through woodland towards the river. Jodi jumped out and opened the gate, and for a second Matt considered flooring the accelerator and powering off along the country lane. Out to the main road, back to Mariton, and he'd be outside the little hospital there within half an hour. He'd tell the truth about everything, because he didn't have the capacity to build lies, especially complex ones that could withstand scrutiny. With Jodi suddenly not in the car his awareness of his dead friend's body lying behind him grew more acute.

"So, what do you think, buddy?" he said. He watched Jodi opening the gate. BB didn't answer. "Straight outta here and back to how we *should* handle shit like this, eh? Authorities. Police. I'll take the smack on the wrist, then let them handle Lem and…"

And the dead man in his house. Killed with his own track pump, which was covered in his prints, and one of the expensive knives he'd bought online because he fancied himself as some sort of wannabe-chef. They'd believe him, surely? They'd know that he couldn't build a lie, and that everything he told them was true?

Jodi waved him forwards and the moment was then – turn through the gate or head off along the road. She tensed, and he knew that she knew what he was thinking. Her hand went to the carved thing in her leggings pocket, and it was that gesture which made him edge forwards and turn through the gate. *He'll want to blood it*, she'd said of the relic. Matt had already witnessed Lem's brutality, and the memory of that made him feel sick and would stay with him forever. A man that dangerous, that driven, would be ready for Matt to surface.

He drove through the gate and Jodi closed it behind them, then she jumped back in the van and they headed down the rough track and into the woods. She said nothing about his decision, but the silence between them was heavy.

Matt couldn't help thinking he'd just passed one of those important forks in life. He only hoped he'd gone the right way.

"So is he all 'get off my lawn!'?" Jodi asked.

"He's a friendly old guy. Lives like he wants, has done for decades. Off-grid, like you said. Got to respect that." He parked the van where the woods ended and opened the door. Jodi grabbed his arm before he had a chance to jump out.

"If he gets weird, we'll leave quickly," she said. "One track out of here, and if he calls the police—"

"He won't," Matt said.

She frowned.

"He doesn't like them. History."

"Right. You going to tell me what history?"

"I don't know it." *Just trust me*, he almost said, but instead he shook off her hand and said no more. He wanted to take control of this fucked-up situation, and much as he hated what he was about to ask Kojak to do, *he* needed to be the one to ask.

"So how do you know we can trust him?" she asked.

"Someone needs to find BB, Jodi. I can't just leave him out in the open, dump him, and just hope that someone comes along. Someone needs to find him today, not tomorrow, so that animals…"

"OK," Jodi said. "OK."

Matt got out of the van and heard Jodi opening the other door, and he started towards Kojak's caravan. He hadn't been down this way in years. It brought back a rush of memories of when he and BB used to play along the river as kids, building dams in small feeder streams, skimming stones, swimming on warmer days, and teasing old Kojak who lived out here on his own. It had never been spiteful teasing, and Matt only remembered the guy laughing at them and waving them on, as if to shoo them away like troublesome flies. He and BB had never hung around for long. They were not cruel kids, and there was more fun to be had elsewhere. Streams needed damming, stones needed skimming. Precious memories to make.

The caravan was in a surprisingly good state of repair, well cleaned and settled into a site which had obviously grown around it. There'd been several half-hearted attempts to evict Kojak over the years, but he'd always managed to hold on to his plot. Probably, Matt thought, because he hadn't *lost* the plot. People who knew him said he was eccentric but all there.

The caravan door opened and, as Kojak stepped out, Matt had the sudden realisation that even after all these years he didn't know the guy's real name.

"Hi," Matt said.

"Hey, Matt." Kojak swung the door wide and leaned on the doorframe, glancing past Matt at Jodi beside the van.

"You... remember me."

"Sure I do." He pointed, and for a second Matt thought he was gesturing at Jodi. "Always good to know the town electrician, and I've been meaning to give you a buzz."

"Oh, yeah?"

"Bastard solar panels are playing up. You'd know about them?"

"Sure, if it's not a mechanical problem. Even then I'd give it a go."

"Damn things – never wanted them, but since they've been in I've only had to use my jenny ten per cent of the time, even less when it's a good summer. Store plenty of power in a rack of batteries I've set up behind the van, can't see them cos of the hawthorn trees I planted back there in '02, maybe '03. So I've grown to love them, really, and I've had a mess around with them myself but..." He shrugged. "They're not cars. Who's she?"

"Jodi. My friend BB's partner."

Kojak raised his eyebrows and smiled. "So how is young Master King?"

Matt opened his mouth but didn't know how to reply. *This just isn't happening,* he thought. *I'm not really here asking the village outcast to lie about finding my best friend's body. I'm really not.*

The silence hung just one side of awkward until Kojak said, "Forgotten my name, haven't you?"

"I'm not sure I ever really knew," Matt said.

"So maybe Kojak will do."

Matt smiled with one side of his mouth. "I'd rather not."

Kojak shrugged as if he didn't care. "Hi, Jodi," he said. "I'm Gerald."

"Hey, Gerald."

"So where's BB?"

"He's in the van," Jodi said.

"Well tell him…" Kojak trailed off, and the soft smile on his face fell slowly to nothing. "What's wrong with him?"

"We need your help," Matt said, and any thoughts he'd had of laying a foundation, bleeding out the story, fell apart beneath the weight of what had happened as it crushed him down. It brought out the truth in a featureless flood, like blood across rotten timber. "BB died, Gerald. Someone is after us. A bad man. A murderer. And there are reasons we can't go to the police."

"He kill BB?"

"No," Matt said, and he tried to expand on what had happened but could not. His throat was hot, his eyes full, and he realised that if he tried to put the past two hours into words, none of it would make any sense.

"BB died in an accident," Jodi said. "The three of us broke into Morgan Manor because we'd heard there were valuables there, and a bad man called Lem Baxter arrived at the same time. While we were trying to sneak away from him, BB fell through some rotten floorboards and slashed his leg. Tore his artery."

"Huh." Kojak took a cigarette from a pack in his shirt pocket and put it into his mouth without lighting it. His hands were shaking, ever so slightly. "So you want to dump poor BB's body with me."

"We want you to find him," Matt said. "Somewhere along the riverbank. Call it in, look after him until they come and take him where he should go. He shouldn't be in the back of the van being dragged around, just lying there."

"You and he good mates, yeah?"

"Best friends from kids."

"I remember the two of you coming here. Harmless little sods. Out doing what kids should be doing, really. Apart from teasing old Kojak, that is."

"We didn't mean anything by it. And you can't have been that old."

"I'm eighty-five now." He lit his cigarette and dragged hard on it, burning a third of it in one go as if in defiance of his age. He coughed heavily, hand over his mouth. "Damn Covid, still fucking with my lungs. So you two don't want to hide here, then?"

"We'll go somewhere else," Jodi said.

"Sounds like you know where somewhere else is. Same as you know this bad man Lem Baxter."

Matt glanced back at Jodi but she didn't elaborate.

"So how do I know you didn't kill him and you're trying to frame me?" Kojak asked.

Matt went to speak but the pressure behind his face held in his words, and he wasn't sure what to say, or whether he could say anything.

"Yeah," Kojak said. "I guess I'd know if that was the case." He descended the three steps from the caravan door and approached, and Matt saw him as a blurred shape through watery eyes. He might have been twenty years younger living in his other caravan, and perhaps BB was standing behind him, ready to shout *Kojak!* and run away laughing, leaving Matt in his wake. He'd always been faster than Matt.

"That's a sad way to die," Kojak said.

"Just bad luck," Jodi said, and Matt saw Kojak's eyes go a little wider.

"No one dies of bad luck," he said.

Matt heard a bird calling high up, probably a buzzard. BB would have known. Something splashed in the lazy river to their right, a silvery shape catching the sun. The riverbanks were wild and overgrown with ferns as high as his shoulders and banks of brambles heavy with ripening blackberries. The river provided a gentle background whisper to the scene, and Matt could understand why Kojak found this place so calm and magical. What they were asking him to do might steal the magic away forever.

"Did you find your valuables?" he asked.

"Huh?"

"What you went to Morgan Manor for? I've heard stories, but assumed the place had been ransacked ages ago."

"Some jewellery," Jodi said.

"We can pay you," Matt said, and Kojak threw down and stomped his cigarette.

"I don't want stolen jewellery with blood on it," Kojak said. "So what makes you think that bad man won't come here?"

"He doesn't know where we are," Jodi said, "and we're going to take care of him."

"Get him arrested?"

"Yes," Matt said. Jodi said nothing.

"You want coffee?" Kojak asked. "I want coffee. Only had one cup so far this morning, and it usually takes three to get this old brain going, but once it is going it doesn't fucking stop." He turned and headed back up the steps into the caravan.

"So…" Matt said.

"I've seen all sorts of stuff in this river," Kojak said, leaning back against the doorframe. "Car floated by after one of the big floods a few years back, music still blasting from inside. I saw a coffin passing by about twelve years ago, they reckon it'd been washed in from a churchyard thirty miles upstream when the bank collapsed. Must'a been an expensive one, still whole. Twenty years ago, maybe twenty-five, roundabout when you boys started coming down this way, a big raft drifted by with a load of people fucking on it. I never did find out what that was all about. Maybe they were making one of those dirty movies. Never found a body, though. And it's not that I want to. But I believe your story – you more than her, Matt, because I don't know her. And poor Sam King. So yes, I'll help you. While I'm making coffee, you two can put him on the riverbank just upstream. No way I want to see that. There's a fallen tree there he can get tangled in." He paused, head to one side. "*Be* tangled in. You never spoke to me about this, I don't know anything. I didn't know you were here. I'll just find him, phone the authorities, and that's my whole story. Got it?"

Matt nodded. He tried to thank Kojak, but it came out as less than a whisper.

"Coffee," Kojak said. He disappeared back into his caravan, leaving Matt and Jodi standing there in the warming autumn day.

Matt turned and Jodi was staring at him, and he knew that these next few minutes would constitute another moment that would change their lives forever.

This morning was made of them.

JODI

Driving back up the track from the river, Jodi couldn't help feeling that she'd left part of herself behind that she would never be able to retrieve. It had died with BB, and now it rested on the riverbank with him, waiting to be found. Kojak hadn't said as much, but she knew that he'd leave BB for a while, so that at first glance it looked like he'd fallen in while out running, drifted, been washed down the river. It was far from perfect, but she had to focus on the short term now. Any time beyond Lem, and discovering the true fate of her father, would form a part of her future life.

My future life without BB, she thought. Her heart was barren. Her soul hung dead in this flesh and bone wrapping.

You're there because the world wants you there, and you're strong enough to always just be yourself, her mother had said that day when Jodi realised she was going to die. Jodi had tried to live up to that ever since.

She had to be strong.

"We have to hide that rucksack," Jodi said.

"Uh-huh."

"It could help us afterwards. When this is all over we'll both be damaged, suspected. I'll lose my job. Your firm, who knows?"

"Don't care."

"You should care, Matt. BB would. He'd want us to be OK."

Matt didn't reply. He slumped in the passenger seat, the rucksack full of jewellery and other stuff that might be worth money nestled between his feet. He hadn't wanted to drive after they'd placed BB by the river, most of him on the bank, his feet trailing in the water. They'd propped him against the fallen tree that Kojak had mentioned, branches and undergrowth ensuring that he'd be held tight. Jodi had untied the tourniquet that had failed to save his life, and had taken his phone from his pocket. He'd been heavy. They were sweating by the time they'd finished. BB's face was calm, eyes closed, and it even looked like he had a small smile on his lips. *It's no wicker coffin*, Jodi had said, but Matt hadn't acknowledged her comment. She'd felt the depth and weight of the men's friendship all around, in every birdcall and the sigh of the indifferent river passing by.

Now, she couldn't blame him for his silence. In fact she was glad. To work this out and see them both through to the other side Jodi needed to be in control, and sitting behind the wheel was a small but important part of making that so.

She drove them up the rough track from the riverside, heading through the woods towards the road at the top of the hill.

"This isn't ever going to be over," Matt muttered.

"Everything we do from now on is to make sure it is," Jodi

said. "As much as can be, anyway. I can't think past Lem, but that rucksack is our link to the future. So we need to hide it, and use it as our anchor."

"Very poetic."

"Thanks."

They approached the gate and Jodi slowed, hoping Matt would jump out to open it. He did, but before doing so he touched her hand on the wheel. That was all. He didn't say or do anything else. It meant the world.

Through the gate and out into the narrow lanes again, Jodi drove away from Mariton heading for a place where she thought they could hide the rucksack. She kept one eye on the rearview, worried that Lem would find them somehow, but the chance was so remote and unlikely that she had to shove it to one side. She couldn't spend the rest of her life looking over her shoulder.

And that was something she had to think about. Her intention had been to steal the relic as some small, personal revenge for what Lem had done to her father. That had blown up in her face, and at the same time suggested the possibility – vague and unlikely though it was – that her father might not have died in the crash and fire that followed.

Might actually still be alive.

After fleeing the crash and losing herself, terrified that the burning blazing melting Lem would pursue her and kill her as well, she had gone to ground. Then she had looked for her father. She'd found one mention of the crash in the local press, and the reports said the fire had been so intense that the police were searching for human remains. There was nothing from that day that had given her any hope that he was still alive. Sometimes, she woke up in a sweat and still heard the crunching impacts of Lem caving her dad's face in with that relic.

She had found nothing to dissuade her from the certainty she had carried forwards – that her father was dead.

Even the slight possibility that might not be the case made what she'd wanted to do so much more complex. She had always planned to steal away the relic and then hide it somewhere Lem would never, ever find it. She knew how he was driven by discovering them, and over the years she'd read more reports of random murders across the country that could possibly have been him finding more of those things, stealing and blooding them with the death of another poor innocent. To keep him forever searching, and always in pain, would afford her some small form of personal revenge.

Now, things had changed. If she could lure Lem in with the relic and glean details about where her father might still be, then the police could pick over whatever was left of his soul.

But Lem was cunning and brutal, and he had remained at large all these years. Ironic, considering his family supposedly lived beneath the shadow of a curse.

"So where are we going to dump this?" Matt asked, kicking the rucksack at his feet.

"I know someone who might buy some of it. But for now we need to just hide it and—"

"Really? What are you, some sort of master criminal?"

"Far from it."

"So?"

"Someone my dad used to know, long time ago. But that's for after. I was thinking the old sewage works. No one goes there."

"Because it stinks of shit."

"Perfect."

Matt said no more so Jodi assumed he agreed with the idea. She wished she could talk to him some more, move closer, but there was so much darkness between them now that she feared she might never get close again.

They drove in silence for a while, windows down, cool morning breeze blowing away none of that terrible morning. The van felt so empty now that they no longer carried BB's body. He had always been a man who filled uncomfortable silences.

The entrance to the road that led to the old sewage treatment plant was padlocked as Jodi had expected, so she drove further along the lane and parked in a wide lay-by often used by people coming for a walk along the valley.

"Shouldn't we get further off the road?" Matt asked. "Only, all it'll take is for him to drive by. My van's hardly inconspicuous. And what if he's already tipped the police off about that dead guy in my house?"

Jodi gripped the wheel. She hadn't been thinking straight. Matt's fears were real, and it was possible that Lem would have already ensured that someone found the butchered remains of Rash in Matt's house. They were wanted people now. The small town's lively Facebook page could be alight with the horror of it all. *And he was such a nice, quiet man...* It was known that the three of them hung out together, so BB's and her place wouldn't be safe either. Lem had cut them off from everything they knew and put them on the back foot, and now they had to think laterally to try and keep one step ahead.

She touched the thing in her pocket. It felt warm, as if leaching heat from her.

"Fuck it," she muttered.

"What, you hadn't thought of that? You saw what he did to that poor bastard, in my house, and you just thought that didn't matter?"

"We need to dump the van and get another vehicle."

"Don't tell me, you can hot-wire cars as well?"

"Maybe an old model."

"Seriously?"

She shook her head slightly. "Just gimme a second." *But we don't have many seconds left*, she thought, because every moment, every action was digging them a deeper hole that it would be harder to crawl out of. She closed her eyes, mentally travelling the local roads and lanes, searching for a place where they could pause and reassess just where the fuck they were, and what the fuck they were going to do. And with her eyes closed, BB came into her thoughts, grinning and passing some quip, and his presence cleared her mind and focussed her attention on where she really needed to look.

It wasn't the roads and lanes that presented the answer. It was the trails.

They took anything that might be useful from the van – *Weapons*, Jodi couldn't help thinking as they grabbed screwdrivers and other tools that would fit in her running pack – and left it as concealed as they could. It was tucked into the edge of a woodland, driven fifty metres down a fire road and then off into a deep ditch to one side. It was stuck fast now, and Jodi had felt a stab of concern when the van's front end dipped and its back end lifted. That was it, they were without transport. But they were definitely safer without it, and they were both fit and ready to run.

She knew just where they were and where they were heading.

"It's two or three miles," she said to Matt.

"No problem," Matt said. "Though I'm not really dressed for it." He wore work trousers and a T-shirt, both of which were stained with BB's dried blood.

"We'll take it easy," she said. It was almost ten in the morning, and dog walkers would be out in force in the woods and along the river where she planned on heading. They'd have to be careful, and remain unseen if at all possible. *I'd be much better on my own*, she thought, but quickly shoved that idea aside. Responsibility for what was happening, and had happened, lay heavily on her. Matt was a large part of that weight.

"That'll be found soon," Matt said, nodding at his van.

"Doesn't matter, we'll be away."

"So just where are we going?"

"There's an old dredging barge moored along the river, couple of miles south of Moon Bridge."

"That thing's still there?"

"Last time I went out that way. You been there?"

"I saw it a few years back when me and BB took a couple of canoes down the river." His look of naked loss made her turn away.

"Well, if it's still afloat we can rest, take stock, make plans. Hide the rucksack there, hopefully. Got your phone?"

Matt tapped his pocket.

"Can I have it?"

He frowned but handed it over. Jodi aimed it at his face and unlocked it, then swiped around until she found WhatsApp. The last call was an unknown number. She typed, *We're going to hide it from you forever, unless you tell me about my father*, sent the message, and locked the phone. She gave it back to Matt.

"Don't answer anything, let it buzz," she said. Matt only nodded. He didn't trust her, she could still see that in his eyes, and she couldn't blame him. If he thought she was playing games and risking their lives for her own personal gain, he was right. That had been the case all along, though she'd never intended it to be that way.

But they were out of options. They had to see this through to the finish with Lem – him arrested or dead in a ditch, and the truth about her father revealed – before they could take even one step beyond what had happened. Instead of continuing trying to persuade Matt of this, she turned from him and started running. Matt fell in behind her, wearing the rucksack filled with the bits and pieces from the manor, and soon they were jogging through the hilly woodland that led back down into the valley. They would hit the riverbank a dozen miles downstream of where they'd left BB, and she found herself wondering if his blood was part of that waterway now. Would he wash past her and Matt as they sat in the old dredging barge wondering what the fuck to do, swilled down towards the sea, consumed by the water and made part of it? It was a notion he'd laugh at.

The last time she'd been running several hours before, BB had been behind her, and all this was a bit of stupid fun, even for her. The relic and what it meant had been on her mind, but more than that was an adventure with the man she loved and their best friend. Now the heart of the matter rubbed against her right leg as she ran, a sickening presence, both heavy and gruesomely intimate. She thought about the crazy curse driving Lem, his unblinkered belief in what he was doing, and the sick tattoos across his body that told the violent story of his quest. He'd have had more since that last time she'd seen him with her father. She had no wish to see them. She'd hoped she would never set eyes on Lem again, but her rash foolishness had brought him crashing back into her life.

Maybe it was inevitable, she thought, but she hated that idea. She'd always brushed off the concept of fate.

Everything that had happened, and was about to happen, was on her.

ALMOST ALIVE

LEM AND THE RELICS

FIVE FAT SPIDERS

NØ OFFENCE TAKEN

Lem Baxter is eighteen years and three days old when he kills his first man. He uses the ragged chunk of wood he's come to the dusty and run-down antique shop to buy, and which the owner refused to sell to him. On the second strike he feels a change come over him. The object – he's already come to know it as a relic, because of what he knows of its history and the mythic status it holds for his family – was cumbersome, spiky and unwieldy when he first picked it up, but now it seems moulded to his hand, shaped perfectly to his grip, warm and close against his palm. It has become a part of him, and he smiles as he swings it to smash the man across the face one more time.

Shelves shake and shimmer, a glass bowl tumbles and smashes, a tall piece of corner furniture falls into a stout oaken chest, cracks and breaks apart, and Lem sees himself disappear as a big mirror shifts as if not wishing to bear witness. His senses are sharp and slow, his heart steady and unruffled. This is just another part of what it takes, and what he knew would come. He's learned things over the years since his father died and his mother was killed in that freak accident. He's come to accept. He understands that this is his calling, and as blood spatters his face and he smells the desperate sour breaths of the man who will die at his hand, he is more than ready to answer.

The man staggers to one side and blood sprays and drips across his white shirt. It splashes the large mirror like spots of rust. His cheek and left eye are slashed and torn, and as he raises one hand, Lem returns the swing and cracks three of the man's fingers. He cries out in pain, shouts for help, and Lem drives forwards and pushes him down into a spread of small side tables. They smash and scatter.

The relic feels different. Almost alive. He has a wooden crate of the five objects that his father found hidden away, but this is the first one Lem has discovered on his own, after a long period of research and searching, quizzing and questioning. Most of those he questioned gave up their knowledge willingly; a couple needed some gentle encouragement. Finding this relic has made real all the things his mother told him and which he has grown to believe, solidifying a story he once thought was make-believe.

As it is splashed with the man's blood, the relic whispers to him more of the truth.

"Please," the man says, holding up his hands to ward off more blows, fingers on his left hand mangled question marks. His face is a red mask, left eye pulped and wet. His mouth hangs open and barely seems to move as he pleads for his life. "Please... please."

Lem pauses in his attack, lowering the relic that is now a part of him. He glances at the front window, so loaded with old furniture and antiques that he can hardly see through to the pavement beyond. The door is locked, sign flipped to CLOSED when he entered.

The man sighs with relief, perhaps thinking that Lem has stopped his assault.

He has only just begun.

He lifts the chunk of wood and it sings with joy as he brings it down into the man's face. He strikes again and again, the impacts shifting from hard to wet, his victim's limbs thrashing, more furniture breaking as the shop owner struggles his last, and Lem's breathing barely increases. His senses are sharp, but still it takes him a few moments to realise something is wrong. The man is dead beneath him, settling and dripping as blood flows and muscles contract and twitch.

Lem's next gentle breath is a wheeze.

He kneels up and then keels over, turning so that he does not land on the blade protruding from beneath his left armpit. He thinks it's a letter opener, its brass handle the head of a dragon. As he shifts the relic across to his stricken hand and reaches for the blade, pain bites into him with ragged, merciless teeth. He groans and rolls onto his back, staring up at a ceiling that is networked with cracks and spider webs. *My father's curse has come to take me*, he thinks, and he tries to raise himself into a sitting position. The pain is too great, and he feels white-hot fire pulsing across his chest and setting his heart aflame.

He blinks, and between blinks he has shifted onto his side, and there are flies buzzing around the ruin of the dead shopkeeper's head. Lem has the relic cuddled close to his chest. His left arm is held up and away from his body, and his wound consumes him. Blinking again, the flies have vanished and the shop is consumed by a bright light that does not seem to originate outside.

There is someone else there with him. The presence fills the shop, and Lem catches a scent that he knows too well and which for some years has only haunted his dreams. It's sweat and beer and cigarettes, sweet and foul at the same time.

"Not yet, boy," his father says. He's sitting in a rocking chair deeper inside the shop, barely visible past scattered shelves and furniture, his face glimmering with a hundred beads of shattered glass. As he rocks, the runners crunch shards of broken mirror on the floor. The movement is in time with Lem's steady heart, and the sound provides a sombre musical beat to his father's words. "Your time's not now, you've plenty left to do."

"Dad," Lem says, and it's the first time he's said that word in years.

"Lying there, pissing your pants," his father says. "Toughen up. Don't let anyone ever look down on you. You know what happens when they do."

Lem's memory flashes back to his dad stomping on a man's face behind a pub, and in a pile of ruined antiques he sees the shopkeeper's face, and it looks the same.

"On your feet, boy! You've got shit to finish."

The rocking chair stops moving, and for a beat shorter than a breath Lem feels a sense of crippling loss. The light dulls, shadows grow out of dusty corners, and he blinks himself back to the shop's shadowy interior once again.

Or perhaps he only opens his eyes.

He's alone once more, and it takes him a few minutes to lift himself into a standing position. The blade is still stuck between his ribs, and he knows enough to leave it there until he can find some help. He also knows where to go. He's had to grow up fast without parents, and he is already used to the world his father used to inhabit, a land of dark streets and shady corners. It could be said he was a resident from the first day he was born.

The rocking chair is empty, of course, and the flies still buzz around the corpse. It is a whispered song of the dead that Lem will make his own.

First murder, first serious wound, first tattoo. The tattooist does not ask where the wound in his side comes from. Nor does she ask why Lem chose a peculiar, horned hare design. Lem has heard that she is not a woman prone to asking questions about things that do not concern her. She's the sort of person he will grow to recognise and value.

Later, he lifts his left arm in front of his mirror, wincing as the deep wound inside still tugs as if angry it did not steal him away. He holds the first relic next to his new tattoo and compares the carved horned hare with the ink. The tattoo is more refined, smoother and easier to make out. He isn't sure that's the way it should be, but he has plenty of time and many more relics with which to learn.

He sits in the dark that evening, a bottle of whiskey in one hand and the relic in the other. It's been blooded with the shopkeeper's blood, and he can feel its strange vitality drawing on his soul. *Witches and trees, trees and witches*, his mother said that day of his father's funeral when she first told him the story, and he realises that he can't keep this thing with him forever. He has the ones his father found before he died, and this new one, and now Lem must gather the rest. He has to find somewhere secret and safe to keep them all.

By the bottom of the bottle he's reliving an old happy memory, and he knows just the place.

※

When Lem is twenty-five he tracks down his third relic to an art gallery in Hay-on-Wye. That someone might mistake it for a piece of art amuses Lem, but it's also weirdly apt. The second one was an ugly fist-sized knot of wood, and he'd used it to cave in the owner's head in an old farmhouse in Pembrokeshire. He'd heard about it on TV, when the owner took it on a programme thinking it might have been worth something. It was, but only to Lem. He'd caught himself on barbed wire climbing a fence to try and avoid the farm dogs, and a couple of weeks later the jagged scars running down his right side were covered with five fat spiders. If he turned the relic just right, and the light fell on it at a certain angle, he saw a shrivelled spider looking at him askew, as if angry at what he'd done.

Don't be angry, he'd said as he hid the chunk of wood away with the first one he'd gathered, and those his father had found before him. *I'm bringing you back together again.*

This third relic has a grotesque beauty about it. Though Lem is young, even he knows that art doesn't necessarily have to be beautiful. But as soon as he walks into the gallery he's drawn to it on the wall, past the metal sculptures and stone carvings, past the oil paintings and watercolours and charcoal scratches of unknown landscapes. He stands in front of it and stares, and he understands why someone has chosen to put this thing on their wall.

It's been worked and carved, rough bark removed and the smooth wood beneath scored in sweeping swirls, spiralling lines. He shifts slightly left and right, admiring how the gallery's flat white light shines from its polished surface. He leans further so that he can see the cut end and the shifting colour-tones of its insides, and then the woman is standing beside him.

"Beautiful, isn't it?"

Lem catches his breath. He hadn't heard her. The relic had him hypnotised.

"Can I see it?"

"I... er, we can't move it from the display. These pieces aren't for handling."

"But they're for sale," Lem says. It's not a question. He turns to look at the woman, and she takes a nervous step back. He smiles, but it does nothing to settle her. He's seen this himself, in the mirror, how the weight of his life is already evident in his eyes. Old eyes in a young face, someone once said to him, and maybe that's what startles some people. He doesn't think so, though. He thinks it's what he has seen and what he knows. The truth of terrible things reflected from inside.

The woman blinks and smiles nervously. She's maybe as old as his mother would be now, well dressed, and Lem thinks, *She doesn't have people like me in here.*

"We're actually closing in a few minutes," she says. "If you'd like to come back in the morning I'm sure my husband can discuss it with you. I'm more familiar with the paintings and photographs, it's Ian who has an interest in the sculptures."

"Sculptures," Lem says, and his eyes are drawn back to the relic. He reaches out and plucks it from its wall fixing.

The woman gasps and takes another step back. "Really, you're not allowed to handle the artwork, it's a display, not a shelf in a shop."

Lem looks at her again, and behind the fear he sees the disgust. She doesn't like him. She sees him as beneath her. He's used to that, has been used to it his whole life, and his father told him to always stand up to people like this. He saw his father doing it many times, with fists and feet.

"It's for sale," Lem says again.

The woman is quiet for a moment, then says, "We're closing soon."

Lem glances at the door. It's a cold day, it's been raining, and the streets of the small Welsh town are no longer very busy. Dusk is settling. He looks at the thing in his hand, weighing it and feeling the perfect balance. The wood feels warm against his skin, like it has always been there.

More than that, it feels hungry.

"I'll come back in the morning," he says, and as he hears the woman sigh in relief he swings the heavy object in an arc, pivots on his right foot, and cracks it across her throat.

The woman grunts and stumbles to her left, reaching for a floor display cabinet and missing. She goes down. He doesn't know how badly hurt she is, and it doesn't matter. He stands beside the woman and looks outside, through the display windows that are once again speckled with rain. A car passes by, lights fractured in the downpour. The street lamps have come on.

Lem glances down at the woman. She's staring up at him with

wide eyes, one arm twisted beneath her, the other grasping her throat. He's not sure if she's breathing.

She tries to say something, but he can't make out her words. They'll make no difference. The object is melded to his hand now, as if those carved swirls and whorls were always meant to fit his palm, his fingers, his fingerprints. This relic was always part of his lifeline.

The woman speaks again before he kneels down and kills her. It sounds like, "Billy". As she dies she fights, and he earns two deep scratches across his forearm. He's glad. They are brands of his mission.

A few minutes later Lem leaves the gallery just as someone approaches the front door. He pulls up his hood and zips it up so that it covers his chin and mouth. The relic is tucked into his coat pocket, both ends heavy with the blood he held it in. No paleness of bone and carved wood now. Just the dark purple of remembered flesh.

The girl is probably in her teens but still short, still a kid. Her own coat is tight around her. A school bag hangs from one shoulder. *Ah, Billie*, Lem thinks.

She nods at Lem and steps back, and to begin with she doesn't realise that something is wrong. At her age Lem was already alert and sharp, already used to bad things. This kid didn't know bad things, not yet.

I could just follow her inside and kill her too, Lem thinks, and the idea inspires no strong emotion in him. Not bloodlust, nor sadness. He has already blooded the relic, so there is no need to kill any more.

Lem turns away and walks along the pavement, heading for an alley that twists past shops and cafés towards where he parked his car. He is halfway along the alley when he hears the first muffled scream.

※

He waits a while before getting the next tattoo, and does so a long way from that little South Wales town. The healed scratches on his forearm form part of the design, pale pink waves in a swirling, twisting pattern of black lines and splashes of pale blue. The tattooist is a young woman listening to some bland rock music, and she tells Lem about her favourite band and how she met the lead singer once, and how one day she wants to form a band of her own. He smiles and nods and enjoys the pain, feeling the needle prickling over the scratched scars of that third relic and painting them away. *You should be in a band*, she says as she wipes away smeared blood and ink, revealing the artful swathe of the design. *You've got the eyes for metal.*

※

Lem is forty-seven, and it's been almost four years since he has discovered any of the remaining relics. He thinks there are only a few left now – he's never been quite certain just how many there are – and at times like these his enthusiasm for the search wanes. That's when he spirals into dark places, but his father always shouts him back. He's there waiting for him, urging him to wake up and be what he was always meant to be. Over three decades dead, still the old man can shout loud enough to put the fear of the Devil into Lem.

He knows what's going to happen today. It gives him a tingle of something that might be excitement. His expression doesn't change, his heartbeat sits at around sixty, but he drums his fingers on the steering wheel as if they are already holding the relic he's come to find.

"You sure he'll be here?" the man in the passenger seat asks. He calls himself Yam, and is indignant about the spelling. His full name is William and he hates Will. Lem thinks he's a prick. He's also a junkie, and so is more likely to be a liability than a help. But he set up this meet for Lem, and he'll provide another service later, when the deal is done and they are alone.

Over the years, Lem has learned to be more careful about the bodies he leaves behind. There are patterns, not least in the fact that they're always bludgeoned to death. He's used fire and knives to sometimes hide the fact, and occasionally he's attempted to dispose of the corpses once they've served their purpose and blooded the relics. But that all takes time, and the more complicated his efforts, the more likely they'll lead to him making a mistake.

He's spent long enough with Yam to know that he won't be missed. Nobody cares about dead junkies. One less drain on the system.

"You told me he would," Lem says.

"Yeah, but that's only what he told me, and you've spoken to him since then, and I have no idea what you said, and you're a spooky motherfucker so who the fuck knows if he's gonna show or not?"

"Spooky motherfucker," Lem says.

"Yeah, well, I mean… those burns, man. Make your face

look…" Yam falls still and silent. Lem knows his sort, all bluff and bluster until the shit hits the fan. The silence stretches until Yam says, "Don't mean nothin' by it."

"No offence taken." Lem means it. It takes a lot to offend him.

He glances around, checking the mirrors for any movement. They're waiting in an old open-air car park that belonged to an industrial complex that was knocked down years ago to make way for new housing. The houses were never built, and now the site is overgrown with weeds, scattered with fast-food wrappers and used condoms, and at night there's an occasional torch flash from a junkie looking to score. Lem has been here three times to scope the place out, and he thinks this is as good a place as any for the trade. It should be easy, just a handing over of cash in exchange for the item. He offered five hundred, and David Roth bit his hand off. It was part of a haul stolen from an antique dealer in Lincoln four weeks before, and Roth obviously thought the stuff was still hot. That's the exact term he'd used. This was the first time Lem has dealt with an American, and it makes him think of the cop shows he sometimes fell asleep to on TV.

It will be hot, Lem thinks. He glances across at Yam and smiles. His burn-scarred face barely moves. Yam nods and smiles back, but it doesn't reach his eyes. He's nervous as hell, and Lem realises he should do what he can to settle the twitchy prick down.

"Go for a beer when this is done?" he asks.

"A beer? Sure," Yam says.

"Good pub nearby?"

"I guess the Star is pretty good."

Yam probably thinks it's the best place for him to score. Lem nods, because the Star is a few miles out into the country, and he can already think of three or four places where they can pull off and park with no one seeing them. This relic is short, thin and sharp, and he can already feel it warm and moulded to his hand as it punctures Yam's skin and slips into his gut.

Something flashes in the distance, and dusky light glimmers from a windscreen as it enters the car park through the exit gates. Theirs are the only two vehicles there. The other car pauses for a moment, then starts rolling towards them.

"Stay chill," Lem says. "This won't take long."

Yam doesn't reply. Lem glances across at him. His knee is bouncing, the movement vibrating through the car. Yam set up this exchange, and Lem was happy to let someone else do the dealing for once. He examined the background, made sure things were smooth, ensured that everything was set up to his liking. The brief call he'd made to the man approaching them now was necessary. He is always aware that he cannot afford to leave patterns between corpses, however many years apart they might be.

The relics form a pattern he cannot avoid, and that is a risk he has to take. It's also a risk that has never come home to roost. His family ensure he continues in his task, never more so than in those moments between blinks when he starts to believe he can't.

"Chill," Lem says again, and Yam grows still, breathing deeply.

"I'm good," Yam says. He's far from good, with old clothing that might never have seen the inside of a washing machine, bloodshot eyes and tracks of a bad habit along his arms. Lem never trusts anyone, so that makes taking on someone like Yam less of a threat. Lem will always have one eye on him.

The car stops a few paces from them. It's a brand-new Mazda, bright blue, recently washed and polished. The guy who steps from the car wears a matching blue suit. He's over six feet tall, solid. He looks like a lawyer, not a thief. Maybe he thinks he's some kind of crime lord. Lem notices that he's left his motor running, so he starts his car and does the same.

"What?" Yam asks.

Lem says nothing. He opens the door and gets out, and Yam follows.

"Evening," Lem says. He takes off his beanie and looks up at the clear summer sky, turning a deep blue as the sun hits the western hills.

"Evenin'," Roth says. His voice is loud. Maybe he's just shocked at Lem's scarred scalp and patchy beard.

"You've got the antique?"

The man glances from Lem to Yam and back again, then reaches into the Mazda's back seat. He brings out the relic wrapped in brown paper, glancing around to see if anyone else is watching.

Lem laughs, like gravel in a tin. "We're alone, it's OK." He takes a roll of notes from his pocket. His eyes are on the wrapped relic in the man's hands, it draws his attention, and he hears the whispers of his ancestors in the scrape of grit beneath his shoes as he takes a couple of steps forwards. Maybe they're calling a warning, but by then it's too late.

The relic has me, Lem thinks as he realises he's let Yam out of his sight.

"William," the bald man says.

Lem stops and looks across his car bonnet. He hears the clumsy footfalls behind him, then feels something sharp pressed into his back.

"I'll take that," Yam says, reaching down to Lem's hand. He

tries to prize the wad of notes from his closed fist. Lem grips harder. "I said—"

"You ever stabbed anyone?" Lem asks. He already knows the answer to that. Yam is a petty criminal, probably guilty of theft a hundred times over to feed his habit, breaking and entering, perhaps even an assault here and there. But Lem knows the look of someone who has killed, because he sees it on those rare occasions when he chooses to look into a mirror. He can smell it, a scent of bad memories. It's like an aura that hangs around someone, the ghosts of the people they've killed clinging on as if to clasp on to life. The only aura surrounding Yam is one of desperation and need.

"I've got a—" Yam says, and Lem takes a step backwards, feeling the pressure of the knife growing against his back... and then easing again as Yam also steps back. At the same time Lem hears the gentle *rip!* of brown paper as Roth's finger presses through, and he knows he has only a second or two. Yam might not be a killer, but this man – Lem thinks he's probably the junkie's dad, or maybe his uncle – might well do anything to save the wretched fuck.

Lem drops the money, spins and elbows Yam in the face, reaches down with his other hand and grabs his wrist, keeps turning, brings Yam around in front of him, and turns his arm up behind his back until he feels and hears the crunch of shoulder muscles and tendons.

Yam cries out and Lem rips the knife from his hand.

Roth points the paper-wrapped package that might be just a chunk of wood, but is probably a sawn-off shotgun. "Let him go!" he shouts.

Lem presses the blade against Yam's throat and pulls tight.

"I said let him go!"

"He your son?" Lem asks.

The man nods. It's not clear whether he's furious or crying, and Lem guesses he often experiences a combination of the two when it comes to Yam.

"You want to see him bleeding out?"

Roth shakes his head. He's still pointing the package, and Lem can now see the shade of dark metal where it's torn in several places.

"Neither do I. So I hope you've got what I came here to buy. I'll still pay you the five hundred we agreed. Fair trade."

"You fucking asshole," the man says, and it's directed at Yam.

"OK, David, it's you and me," Lem says. "Let's ignore your son for now, yeah? I deal with you, you deal with me."

Roth nods. He still doesn't lower the shotgun. Lem is in control, and it's a position he's used to. *Almost let it slip there*, he thinks, and he sees his father glaring at him, a wry smile pulling up one corner of his mouth. It's a smile that says, *I'd have beaten you to within an inch of your life if you'd let yourself get shot.*

"Get the antique."

Roth holds the shotgun one-handed, still pointed at Lem and Yam, and reaches into the car. This time what he brings out is what Lem came here for. The dusky air seems to brighten and warm, catching on the dark wood of the long, thin relic. Lem feels his heartbeat quicken, just a little.

"Gun down. Put that—"

"No way," Roth says. Lem sighs, but his eyes are on the relic in Roth's left hand, and despite everything he knows and has already been through, its gravity draws his attention just a little too much.

Yam slams his head backwards into Lem's chin, then folds his knees and drops. Lem pulls on the knife and feels it catch across Yam's cheek and ear, then there's an explosion of sound and light and he's punched in the chest, pushed back, tripping over his heels and falling, falling, and even as he hits cracked concrete and the raw cold numbness across his body starts to give way to pain, his attention is still on the artifact that he can no longer see.

Then dusk falls quickly, and the words that accompany him down from an impossible distance are part of a lie that will soon bring him awake once more.

"He's done, he's dead…"

And maybe he is, because Lem meets his father on a long winding path across a landscape he recognises. This might be his first time here, or maybe it's the last. Everything happens at once here. Tomorrow is yesterday, and now is forever.

Further ahead, past the blazing sunset smeared across inviting hills, maybe he'll find the true peace he has been seeking for so long.

His father is the only one fully there. Other shadows and shades stand around, and Lem thinks perhaps he'd know them, if only he took time to make himself known. But his father does not allow that. He comes at Lem, furious and scarred and mutilated. Without moving his lips he shouts, *What the fuck are you doing here, boy?*

You're not meant to be here!

Get your sorry arse back where you belong!

And beneath the shouts and rage, Lem hears something else in his father's voice. It's a whispered plea, as if the shouting and swearing are there only to cover up the thing he really needs Lem to hear.

You haven't finished yet.

When Lem wakes the sun is down and the stars are out and he is on fire. The flames prick and speckle all across his torso, from neck down to stomach. Deeper inside is more pain, hotter, so hot that it feels like ice embedded in him. His heart, perhaps. He's always known he was fire and ice, and nothing in between.

He made me that way, he thinks, and in his mind's eye his father sneers and turns away from him, walking towards that distant light but never arriving.

Lem rolls onto his side and butts against his car. He raises his head and looks around, sees that the Mazda has gone. He doesn't know how much time has passed since he was shot, but he knows that he should be dead.

They won't let me.

His wounds are bleeding, sticking his shirt to his chest. He touches them, wincing as the fiery agonies flame at the contact. The ground beneath him might be dark with blood, but he can't see enough to tell.

They won't let me die.

He sits up slowly, back against the car. The half-moon hangs high, silvering the scene, and as he levels his breathing he sees another vehicle creep through the overgrown entrance and into the car park. He tenses, wondering if they've come to finish him off. But no. Yam and his father already think he's dead.

The car drifts to the far corner of the car park and stops. The interior light comes on briefly, and he can just make out the shifting shapes in there, the baring of flesh, and then the lights flicker out.

Pain is his companion as he hears his father's voice echoing, again and again, *You haven't finished yet*.

※

It takes Lem several days to recover enough to go after Yam and his scheming father. His thick leather jacket has saved him, and he's done his best to pluck out the shotgun pellets from his chest, left shoulder and throat, cleaning and dressing the wounds. He has no wish to visit a hospital and attract the inevitable attention a shotgun wound would draw. The holes are still scabbed and weeping when he finds out where David Roth lives. He goes in that night, forcing the back door and killing the small dog that starts yapping in the kitchen. Roth is crashed out on the sofa and virtually unconscious, an empty whiskey bottle on the coffee table beside him. Lem checks the rest of the house and Yam isn't there. It doesn't take him long to find the relic; it calls to him, guides him, lures him upstairs and through a rubbish-filled room to the eaves storage cubby, and as he holds it in his hands everything feels right. The pain across his chest fades. Those wounds making him stronger.

Downstairs, the sleeping man doesn't even have a chance to wake. Lem slits his throat and bloods the relic, then spends some time spreading Roth around the house, making sure he coats the walls and leaves him here, there, in places where it will take his son days or weeks to find him.

He leaves just before dawn, already looking ahead to what comes next. He's a long way from the rest of the relics that he's already collected, and once this one is in place he'll rest, recover, and then smother his new wounds with another tattoo before recommencing his search. He doesn't know exactly how many parts there are to the whole, but he is bringing them slowly back together. Maybe there are half a dozen left to find and gather, maybe fewer. It keeps Lem going. It keeps him alive.

It doesn't trouble him that Yam was not there. Lem's purpose is too clearly defined to hold a grudge.

Maybe it's a rib.

Lem has long-ago stopped trying to make sense of the things he spends much of his life looking for, finding, gathering, at least when it comes to physical shapes. *It's not really a witch trapped in a tree,* he sometimes thinks. *I mean, that would be crazy.*

And yet there's the different shades and textures showing at the ends of the relics, the broken or cut ends, as if this hard wood has grown around bone, replacing flesh and blood, sinew and skin. The idea of an old family curse often feels foolish and distant, and yet it has steered Lem's route through life since his father died. Witches and trees, trees and witches.

Or maybe it's a leg, he thinks. *Her shin, perhaps.*

He drives, conscious of the relic safe on the seat beside him and yet still reaching out every few minutes to touch it, just to make sure. He enjoys the warmth. It's as if the drunken man's blood is still flowing through the relic's petrified capillaries, giving it new life. The blood on the surface has dried now, and it's darker than it was when he found it in the man's house, and somehow heavier. It can't just be from the blood. Perhaps taking it closer to its companion pieces is bestowing a gravity of need and belonging.

Lem drives through the day. He stops several times, in lay-bys and narrow country lanes, waiting to see if anyone is following him. He also cuts across-country from one road to another, checking his atlas to make sure he's heading the right way. He's spent his whole life travelling, so he has a good sense of direction.

He doesn't believe he's being followed at all, and he took care to ensure no one saw him arriving at Roth's house, or leaving. But Lem has lived like this for a long time. Being cautious means he can still do what he's doing. It's for him, yes, but it's mainly for the rest of his dead, tortured family – his aunt, his father and grandfather, his dear mother, and others. They need him to do this so that they can take the final step and disappear into the light. When it's done, he will be content to join them all.

As he nears the place where he has been keeping the relics gathered by him and his father before him, the object on the passenger seat feels even warmer, even heavier. It knows that it is coming home.

Lem found this place when he was just a kid, and each time he's approached since then he's had the niggling worry that someone might have discovered it. *What would they think?* he wonders. *How could they even begin to understand?* But he is also quite confident that this place is so well hidden that no one will ever find it.

And if they do, they'll suffer.

He parks the car in an off-road, shaded parking area he's used before, one that's difficult to stumble upon unless you know it's there. There's one other car, an old Fiesta. He sits in his vehicle for a while, watching, but no one seems to be around. Probably a dog walker. He's eager to go but knows he has to be careful, and safe, so he opens the door and gets out, stretches, cricking the muscles in his back. Taking his time. He's been driving for two hours, and the wounds healing across his chest are sore. They itch but he doesn't want to scratch, in case he knocks off the scabs and sets them weeping again. The sooner the shotgun wounds heal, the sooner he can tattoo them into the story of his past.

It's good to feel the sun on his face. The heat always sets his burn scars afire again, and that reminds him of Wayne and Jodi, the crashed van, and what Lem gained from that experience. Soon he'll be somewhere dark, but it's a good hour's walk yet, and he's looking forward to it. He hopes the tide is out so he doesn't have to wait. He sets off, the package in a rucksack that might simply contain a packed lunch and a drink. Lem knows how important appearances are. He can't do anything about his scarred face and head other than to try and hide behind glasses, a beard and a hat. He cannot change his haunted eyes; they're as much a part of his story as his growing number of scars and the tattoos that cover them. But he can dress so that curious eyes slide from him. He's a walker in the sun, that's all. He hasn't just murdered a sleeping man in cold blood.

Soon he's off the beaten track, deep into the woods and forcing his way past banks of brambles and high ferns. There's no path through here, and that's another reason it feels safe. He could have gone another way, following a rough farming track down to the coastal path then along the clifftops. But even walking, it's best to hide his tracks.

Soon he's out of the woodland and heading down a sloping field towards a tattered barbed-wire fence. He climbs over, wincing as his wounds stretch and open again beneath the strain. Ten minutes along the coastal path, and then he reaches the steep scramble down onto the rocky beach. He's sweating now, the sun playing hide and seek behind scattered clouds, and he pauses on the beach to wipe his brow, take a drink of water, and use the moment to scan for anyone watching him. There's no one else on the beach. He can see no walkers on the path atop the cliffs rising to either side.

The tide is out. The rough causeway is revealed, and he knows that people often make the trip out to the small island a couple of hundred yards off the coast. Anyone seeing him walking out there would believe that he's just a curious hiker. He's keen to get there, to make sure the relics are safe.

They are, he thinks. *I'd know if they weren't. I'd sense it. I wouldn't feel so... settled, being here again.*

His mother and father were still alive when he came here for the first time. They were camping on a site a couple of miles along the coast, and his mother sent him packing with lunch, a drink and strict instructions to be home by four o'clock. His father watched him go with a nod, and then Lem spent the day on his own, hiking the coastal path, scrambling up and down cliffs, discovering small beaches, exploring caves. He was still a young kid, maybe ten years old, and he had yet to accept what his father really was. He'd seen things, of course. But he was still possessed of a sweet childhood innocence that papered over the violent cracks of his reality.

As Lem walks out onto the raised walkway – eroded by the relentless sea, slippery with seaweed and barnacles – he tries to remember what he was like when he came here for the first time. Try as he might, he can't dream back that far. The surroundings are the same, the sea just as calm and timeless, the sky just as blue. But for Lem innocence is years in the past. His father is dead, and before his mother went as well she left him with a present and future that scarred him as much as the knife, the shotgun blast, the fire.

As he approaches the end of the causeway that is only exposed at low tide, he thinks of the small structure on the island's far side. He found it back when he was that kid, the tumbled remains of an old building whose purpose was lost to the sea-haze of time. Even back then there was hardly anything visible aboveground – just a low wall and hints of other tumbled stones – but it was down below where he found somewhere fun to explore. So much fun that he arrived back at their campsite an hour late, and his father gave him a clip around the ear and asked him what the fuck did he think he was doing, scaring his mother like that. The sinkhole close to the ruined building's thickest wall, from the depths of which he could hear the ebb and flow of the sea, the endless breaking waves marking the heartbeat of the land. The tangle of brambles hiding the hole's entrance and preventing anyone from entering, but Lem wasn't just anyone. The scratches and cuts he gathered as he pushed through, climbed down, using the little torch he always took with him in his pack to light the way.

Later, in his late teens, he returned to that place with the box of relics his dead father had spent the last years of his life recovering, and the first one Lem had found and blooded.

Much more recently, he brought something else.

Now he remembers the smell of that place, like secrets and long-forgotten dead things. In the wall of that sinkhole, halfway down towards where the sea roars and crashes in the open cave below, a small opening leads to a larger space beyond, obviously man-made and yet surrendered to nature, to the dark, generations before. He's excited to climb down, take in that smell, see those relics and what sustains them. Every time he comes here he pretends he's that kid again, not yet the man of scars.

He reaches the end of the causeway and continues up onto the rocky slope of the place he calls Crow Island.

It is a fitting resting place for a witch.

ELASTICITY

SEPTEMBER 2024

CROWBAR

METAL ON METAL

MATT

As they jogged along the riverbank towards where they hoped the dredging barge might still be moored, Matt knew that they were running away from responsibility. They could not stay ahead of it for long. With every blink he saw his old friend being put down beside the river, and felt BB's dead weight slipping from his hands. He saw the waters washing around his feet, and in death BB held the same magnetism that he'd had in life. He tugged Matt back towards him even as they put down distance away from him. Eventually that draw would reach its modulus of aching grief-filled elasticity, and Matt would be hauled back into his orbit. He silently swore that he would not leave BB on his own for long, and that he would face up to his responsibilities. For now, though, Jodi led the way, and however fucked up it might seem, Matt felt safer with her.

Besides, she had the means to end this. That strange thing was still tucked into the side pocket of her leggings, and she regularly touched it to make sure it was still there.

If Matt took it, arranged to meet Lem, maybe he could negotiate some sort of exchange. Lem's admission to Rash's murder for the relic. Would that be enough to clear his name? Matt didn't know. His interaction with police up to now had been two speeding tickets and a drunken fight in the street when he was sixteen. He knew nothing about murder.

Maybe if he managed to steal the relic from Jodi and took it to meet Lem, he could even have him arrested.

It was too much to hope for. Too much planning. Matt was just an electrician, someone BB had once accused of existing within his own bubble. He'd been calling him boring, though his friend would have never used that word.

And Jodi wouldn't let him just take it. She was guarding it, keeping it close, because for her this weird object could bring what she wanted. Revenge, for sure, and now perhaps the truth about what had happened to her father. The fact that Matt didn't give a fuck about her past didn't make any of this any easier. There was no revenge that he wanted, against Lem or anyone else. As far as he was concerned it was Jodi who had caused BB's death.

He'd have to watch for the right moment. And if the right moment didn't come, maybe he could force it.

I don't know her, he thought, staring at the running woman ahead of him, and he realised what BB had meant when he'd said she was haunted. If only BB had asked what haunted her. Perhaps she would have opened her past up to him, and it would not have remained a dormant, deadly threat.

She'd displayed grief at the death of the man she professed to love, but he was a man that Matt loved too. She seemed all too capable of functioning with that death on her mind. Matt only wanted to stop running, curl up, and try to come to terms with what had happened. In truth he was still numbed, feeling no stress in his legs from running, no breathlessness from exertion. It was as if his body and mind were detached, his mind floating and adrift and screaming, his body going through its robotic motions.

And still BB's presence drew him back, not just to his body tangled with a dead tree on the riverbank miles upriver from here, but back to the decision they'd taken to break into Morgan Manor, the evening BB had introduced Matt to Jodi, and the times they'd spent together before that, when Matt was still married and BB moved from fling to fling looking for the one. Jodi was the one, he'd told Matt. Even then Matt had worried, because BB had only known her for a short while, and she'd seemed closed to him. Not unfriendly or even cool, but closed off by a protective distance that hung around her like a moat. Matt had sensed secrets, and though everyone carried them, part of him had always known that Jodi's were more troubling than most.

I just don't know her.

Jodi touched the object in her pocket again, then skidded to a halt. Matt ran into her, hands on her shoulders, and they stumbled forwards a few steps together.

"Dog," Jodi said.

"Huh?"

She pointed at a small brown and white dog sniffing around some trees close to the riverbank ahead of them. It was the sort of mutt BB had called a yapper, and pretty soon it would see them and possibly bark their presence to its owners, wherever they were.

"We can't be seen. Come on." Jodi pushed into the bank of undergrowth to her right and Matt followed, shoving through tall ferns, nettles and brambles, wincing at stings and the stabbing of thorns.

The dog barked. A voice called out to it, too far away to discern its name.

Jodi fell through into a field and rolled, looking back as Matt followed her. He kept his footing as he tugged free of the undergrowth, then she was on her feet, grabbing his arm and pointing along this side of the natural hedge. They jogged, and Matt crouched low as he went. Voices came louder as they closed on the couple walking on the other side.

The little dog growled.

"Oh Ziggy, give it a rest," a man's voice said.

"Got a rabbit, boy?" a woman asked.

Jodi hunkered down and froze. Matt did the same. The growling turned into a chomping slurp as one of the owners gave Ziggy a treat, and then they walked on.

Jodi nodded and they continued on their way, skirting the edge of the field where corn grew almost to their heads.

A few minutes later they reached a gate leading from the field back to the riverbank path. Jodi peered over and looked both ways.

"Popular place?" he asked.

"Yeah, there's a path here, but the dredger's a bit further on past the car park," Jodi said. "Let's risk it."

They ran on, keeping alert, and soon Jodi let Matt take over as he led them past the small, gravelled Moon Bridge car park. Beyond, the path became much rougher and more overgrown, the terrain more difficult to negotiate, especially at the height of summer with heavy undergrowth and deep banks of nettles beneath overhanging trees.

Matt ran right through, feeling the warm tingling stings on his exposed hands and arms. He didn't mind. A small, spiteful part of him hoped it hurt Jodi more than him.

After a few more minutes they emerged from the cover of trees onto the overgrown riverbank, and the dredger was still there. It had been a while since Matt had seen it from the river when he and BB had taken a couple of canoes out for the day. He didn't recall it looking this old and rusted. Its green paint was mostly gone, the deep open hold speckled with new plants growing from the muck left in its base. It was moored close to shore, tied to two thick wooden stakes with heavy ropes, and it tilted ten degrees towards the river. Its keel must have been grounded close to the bank.

"Looks OK," Jodi said. She climbed aboard and the vessel didn't even move. There was a small windowless cabin at one end, the door padlocked shut through two thick metal eyes. Jodi shrugged off her pack, one hand going down to touch the thing in her trouser pocket again.

I could just snatch it and go, Matt thought, but he knew that Jodi would chase him down. She was faster than him.

Jodi took out the crowbar and worked at the padlock, trying not to break the metal eyes attached to the door. As she strained, Matt looked around. It was quiet but for the whisper of a breeze through the trees and a mother duck and several chicks hurrying somewhere across the river's surface. He tried to imagine BB and him paddling past, their ripples still striking shore.

A crack, and they were in. Jodi hauled the door open and took a look inside. She propped the crowbar beside the door before stepping in, turning at the door.

"Coming?"

"We're staying here?"

"Ten minutes," she said. "Catch our breath. Hide that thing." She nodded at the rucksack of stolen goods he was still carrying, then disappeared inside.

Matt boarded the barge and glanced at the river flowing slowly by. BB had brought a couple of four-packs of beer, dragging them behind his boat on a small pink unicorn float he'd bought from the supermarket to keep them cool. He'd tipped Matt in, of course, but then he'd capsized himself, attempting an kayak roll before coming up spluttering and laughing. Four hours together that were imprinted on Matt's mind, and it was the sort of memory he wanted to grab on to forever.

Not BB bleeding to death in the back of his van.

Not Lem butchering that poor thug in his house.

"What?" Jodi asked from the darkness.

"Nothing. What's in there?"

"Fuck all."

As he heard her rooting around inside, Matt checked out the broken padlock, and the metal eyes on the door and frame that were only bent a little out of shape. To one side of the door was an old toolbox, lid rusted half open, several screwdrivers and a hammer stuck inside. He kicked the box and the tools rattled loose.

"OK?" Jodi called as she half-emerged, crouched in the open doorway.

"OK," Matt said.

OK.

He unshouldered the rucksack and flexed his arms, then held it out to her. "Take this for me?"

Jodi reached out and grasped one of the rucksack straps, then turned in the doorway to head back inside.

Matt leaned down and forwards and grabbed at the relic tucked tight in her running leggings' pocket. As his fingers closed around it a sudden, deep feeling of sickness and dread churned his guts. Dizziness struck him. If he hadn't been crouched down he might have fallen.

It's been so close to her, he thought, and it felt so warm. But as he pulled hard and the relic ripped her pocket and probably scratched her leg on the way out, he wondered whether that sick warmth was all its own.

"Matt!" Jodi said, her panicked voice muffled by the cabin's interior.

Matt pushed against her lower back and sent her sprawling. She grunted, and he heard a metallic jangle as she landed on the rucksack.

He pulled back and dropped the relic to the barge's deck. He had a few seconds, he knew. Maybe not even that long. He could see her scrambling in the shadows, trying to gain her feet and turn around, and she was silent now. She already knew what he was doing. She knew she could not change his mind.

Only by force.

Matt slammed the door closed and leaned hard against it, propping his work boots against the deck. He reached for the toolbox, grabbed a screwdriver, and as he went to shove it through the locking eye, Jodi crashed against the door from inside.

Matt jarred back, but only a little. He was heavier than her, and with his feet braced against the deck there was no way she'd be able to—

She hit the door again, and as it shifted an inch in its frame she shoved a thin wooden object through, blocking it open. Matt recognised it as something they'd brought with them from Morgan Manor, an oak panel with what might have been gold inlaid in an extravagant tree pattern.

He shoved back and the door bit in, splintering the wood's surface.

"Don't be so fucking stupid!" Jodi shouted.

Matt waited, and when he felt the pressure against the door ease as Jodi pulled back to hit it again, he also relaxed, allowing the wooden block to fall. He kicked it back through the opening, leaned against the door, and thrust the screwdriver through the locking eyes.

He let out a breath, but still kept pressure on the door as Jodi hit it again, again. *That's not going to hold.* The screwdriver was shaking with every impact, and it wouldn't take long for Jodi to either bend it in half or work it loose.

The locking eyes were at least an inch in diameter. He needed something else.

Down at his feet, the crowbar she'd leaned against the cabin's exterior clattered to the deck.

Matt snatched it up and held it close to the locking eyes, other hand on screwdriver's handle. He'd have to be quick with this, and smart. He measured by eye, pretty sure the end of the crowbar would pass through.

If it doesn't and she gets out, what's the worst that happens? he wondered. Adrenalin flowing, thoughts racing, there was no certainty at all to his answer. Maybe she'd just berate him and snatch back the relic.

Maybe she'd want to make sure he couldn't try anything like this again.

She still has that gun.

The thought shocked him and he caught his breath. Jodi kicked at the door, and a moment later he slipped the screwdriver out and pushed the crowbar through. It fit, just. He shoved it all the way, metal squealing against metal, and then turned it so that the curved end hung through the eyes.

Then he stepped back and picked up the relic. It was still warm, like rough knotted flesh. It was disgusting.

"Matt, don't be so fucking stupid!" Jodi shouted. Her voice was dull, echoey, and he looked around at the peaceful river surroundings. It was as if he was hearing things.

He closed his eyes and breathed deeply, then turned to go. He'd been thinking about the old trainline that ran along a ridge close by, a place he and BB used to come cycling when they were kids. It was mostly overgrown and forgotten now, but it took the most direct route back to town, and he'd be unlikely to see anyone else up there.

Even if Jodi knew about it he could get a good head start, and she had no idea where he might be going.

A loud metallic clanging startled him. Jodi was attacking the door, probably with something else from the rucksack. It struck and rang out, metal on metal, but the eyes holding the crowbar looked sturdy enough.

For now, he thought. *But she'll find a way.* He put one foot up onto the gunwale ready to jump back onto the bank.

"Matt!" Jodi shouted. "You don't know him like I do. You can't negotiate with him."

"I know him about as well as I know you," Matt said. "And this is just going to get worse until someone makes it better."

"This isn't the way to make it better!"

Matt went to say more but decided against it. She'd sway him. He had always been easily persuaded, jumping from one side of an argument to another depending on who he was listening to.

This was his decision, and it was the right one.

He slipped the screwdriver into his pocket, grabbed the weird warm relic in his other hand, and jumped across to the bank.

As he ran, Jodi's voice faded behind him, shouting that he was doing the wrong thing, he was a fool, he would end up…

And then she stopped shouting and he heard nothing, save for the frantic impacts of metal on metal.

Not long till she gets out, Matt thought.

But he didn't need very long at all.

LEM

Lem knew that it was pointless calling Matt Shorey again. Jodi had taken control of his phone and sent him that teasing message, and she thought she was in control. He had to let her believe that. He was struggling not to believe it himself—

Pull yourself together, idiot, his father grumbled in the background of his thoughts.

—but he had to play this right. Everything relied on what he did next. So he drank his coffee and waited for fate to catch up with him.

Sometimes Lem felt as if the world did not recognise him, and that he was a wraith passing within and through without leaving any trace or disturbance behind. Like a black swan gliding across a reservoir leaving no ripples in its wake, seen by no one. Other times, he believed that this whole world was built for him. He was the focus, the central pivot around which everyone and everything hinged. His was the prime aim and anyone he met, and all the places he travelled to, were bit players in his life.

But now, searching for what he was convinced was the final relic, he knew that neither was true. He was the extra, and Mary Webster was the star. That broken down and scattered tree was the core around which his world orbited, and each part had exerted its gravity upon him ever since he was a child. Lem's supposed free will was the dead witch's will, drawing him this way and that as he gathered her dried withered parts, blooded them, and brought them together again.

Now this final part was the heaviest, its gravity the most profound. He could feel his cells vibrating at its pull, his hair almost standing on end, and if only he could close his eyes and let it draw him directly to it.

If only he could do that.

But even though it was not working that way – such magic would have made it all too easy, after all – Lem did believe that his future was set. He would retrieve the stolen object from Jodi, give it the blood it sought and craved, and then it would be time to make his final journey to Crow Island.

Even Lem's usually calm heart sped up a little at that prospect.

"Finished up?" The spotty kid reached for Lem's coffee cup, and Lem looked up and caught his eye. The half-smile fell from the kid's face, and Lem tried to lighten his eyes.

"Thanks, it was nice," Lem said. "Good coffee. Thanks."

The kid nodded, looking anywhere but at Lem as he took the cup and hurried away towards the counter. He dropped a spoon. Ignored it.

Lem stood and left the café, beanie pulled tight over his

head and long-sleeved shirt covering his tattooed scars despite the warm day. He'd spent some time scraping dried blood from beneath his fingernails in the café's bathroom, and examining himself in the mirror to make sure there was none ground into the scarred landscape of his face. He was as presentable as could be.

It was strange looking at himself in a mirror. It wasn't something he did very often. His father stared back at him.

Outside, the late afternoon sun beat down. Mariton was quiet, peaceful and not yet abuzz with whispers of murder. That was good. He knew that Rash might be found at any time, but without murder on the air, being a stranger in a town of this size meant he blended into the background. Once the murder was known, he'd be noticed. He didn't care much either way, because he knew that his route from here to the end of his task was prescribed. His preference, though, was for his quest to be over soon. Today.

Killing Rash had shown Jodi, and more so her unfortunate companion Matt, how serious he was. It had taken away one potential place of safety for them. It had also made them run, but that had been a balanced decision on his part. He knew that mention of her father would draw Jodi back to him. All he had to do was wait.

He checked his phone to make sure it was still on and charged, then dropped it into his pocket. He'd hear it ring, feel it vibrate, and when she called to offer him a chance to swap the final relic for information about her father, that would be the beginning of the end.

He walked along the shadowed side of a street, slipping into a bakery to buy some food. Sandwich and a drink in hand, he weaved his way between buildings until he found the town's park. Kids played in the sun close to a climbing frame and a set of swings. Parents sat on the grass chatting while their sprogs shouted and screamed. Lem avoided the play area and found a sheltered spot beneath some trees. He sat on a bench dedicated to a dead man and started to eat.

Everything Lem did was passing time, counting minutes, and preparing for what he was certain would come next. He was a patient man. Even so, he breathed a sigh of relief when his phone rang almost an hour later.

He answered and said, "I'll tell you about your father, but only face to face."

"It's not Jodi," a voice said.

Lem raised his eyebrows. "Where is she?"

"This needs to be done quickly," Matt said, ignoring the question. "I have it. And you can have it, but for a price."

"What price?" Lem asked.

"You leave us the fuck alone."

"Of course. My concern isn't with either of you."

"And you admit to the murder in my house."

Lem shrugged. "No problem."

"You will?"

"Sure. Give it to me, I'll be long gone. I'll call the cops, tell them who he is and where they can find his ear, his nose and what the symbol is carved into his stomach. And I'll say where they can find me. They won't, of course."

"Why the hell would you..." Matt trailed off, sounding nauseous.

"Are you in town?" Lem asked. No reply. "Whatever. Meet me at—"

"No," Matt said. There was a *tap tap* of something against the phone. "I have that disgusting thing you want, and I'm in charge. Meet me at the pub by the river, the King's Arms. In the beer garden. Seven o'clock this evening."

"If you don't bring it—"

"I want you out of my life," Matt said. "I want you fucking *gone*. Of course I'm going to bring it."

"Wise move," Lem said. He glanced at the phone, saw it was almost six-thirty. So Matt was in town, probably quite close. "Where is she?"

"She's not involved," Matt said. "By the time she finds me, it'll all be over and you'll be gone."

Lem saw the waves boiling across the causeway to Crow Island, a light mist rolling in over the sea, and the island silhouetted against the setting sun. If he hurried, he might be there tonight.

JODI

Jodi's shoulders ached, she'd pulled a muscle in her thigh, and the bottom of her right foot hurt from where she'd been kicking against the door, again and again. But the slice of light between metal door and frame was wider with each impact as the eye lock bent and deformed.

Sweating, shaking with effort, she kicked out at the door one more time. Metal tore as the latch broke away and it burst open. It ground on grit and jammed, and Jodi crouched and shoved her whole weight against the door, emerging at last into sunlight.

She wiped sweat from her face and flicked it away, and took in a few deep breaths. Thirsty, shaking and sore from her escape efforts, the sun and daylight felt good against her skin. The relic had scratched her leg when Matt ripped it out of her pocket, and in the daylight she could see through the rip in her running leggings to where blood bubbled along the scratch. It hurt more than it should have for such a small cut.

In her other pocket was the bulky gun.

It was over half an hour since Matt had locked her in and gone, and he would be too far away to catch now, even if she knew the direction he was headed. She'd been thinking about this as she kicked and shouldered the door, and the only guess she had about his ultimate destination was the King's Arms. He'd mentioned meeting Lem there, and it made sense. There would be lots of people on such a warm summer's evening, and Matt probably believed that such a public place would protect him.

"You fucking idiot!" she muttered. Angry at him, fearing for him. She couldn't lose him as well. The idea of Lem killing Matt, because of her... she tried to shake it from her head. But every time she blinked she saw Lem's callous face, his heartless eyes, and a knife in his hands stained with Matt's blood.

Jodi delved into the small running backpack she'd dropped before trying to batter down the door and pulled out two phones, hers and BB's. She dialled Matt on her phone and it went straight to voicemail. She hung up and tried calling him with WhatsApp, then Messenger. No answer. He must have turned his phone off.

"Fuck!" she shouted. She considered tucking the crowbar into her small backpack, but it would only bounce around and cause her discomfort. She had to run as fast as she could. She snatched up a small chisel from the rusted toolbox instead, slipped it into her waistband, pulled on the backpack. She sucked on the water pipe but the bladder was empty. Damn, when had she last had a drink? She was parched from the heat, the exertion, and for a second she was tempted to dip her hand into the water and drink.

Then she remembered placing BB by the riverbank upstream, and decided she'd go thirsty.

She jumped across to solid ground and started running, following the course of the river back towards Mariton. Matt had probably called Lem already and arranged a meeting. Her heart hammered at the thought of that happening without her there to protect her friend.

Without her there to face that bastard Lem.

And deep down, though she tried to deny it because it shamed her and made her selfishness so much obvious, was the idea that if Lem took the relic from Matt, or was somehow fooled and caught by police, or if anything else happened to him, she would not be able to question him about her dad.

But I saved him, Lem had said.

Her leg and shoulder hurt, her feet hurt, and she hadn't had a drink in hours. But she ran as fast as she could, because every minute counted now, every second brought Matt closer to making a terrible mistake.

It has to be the pub, she thought. And it absolutely did have to be, because if Matt had arranged to meet Lem anywhere else, she'd never find out and get there in time.

The river turned slowly to the left and she followed the path worn into the land by decades of hikers. She'd never run this way with BB, because he'd loved pounding the roads rather than negotiating rough trails, but she had ventured out this far on her own a few times. Mariton was a good five miles distant. She watched for other people, trying to settle into a rhythm and not look panicked, though on the inside that panic was eating away at her soul.

There might have been a faster way to town along the narrow country lanes. She'd also heard Matt talking about an old railway line somewhere around here, unused for decades but sometimes frequented by off-road cyclists or runners. She had an inkling that it might have provided a more direct route back to Mariton, but if she went searching for it she might get lost, lose time, and that was one thing she could not risk. It was the trails she knew well, so she made the decision to keep to the river path.

BB is in there, she thought as she glanced to her right. The water flowed smooth and slow, rippled here and there by insects skimming its surface. A kingfisher streaked neon ahead of her. Ripples spread as a fish splashed, and a heron stood utterly motionless close to the opposite bank, watching for dinner. Insects buzzed, birds chattered. It was beautiful. It was thriving with life.

"I'm sorry, baby," she said, her voice hitching as she ran, breath stalling.

I'm sorry, Matt, she thought.

The more she tried to shut out the pain of bringing him into such a situation, the worse the things she imagined happening to him.

Jodi ignored her tiredness and the pain in her muscles, and ran as fast as she could.

LEM

Lem was used to scoping the ground and getting the lie of the land, and ten minutes after approaching the King's Arms pub he was on the opposite side of the river, sitting in the shadows of an old oak tree at the edge of a car park, watching the bustling pub garden across the water. He'd parked and circled around from the other side first, but beyond the pub was a tangle of old scattered houses and lanes, some of them cobbled, all narrow and with stone walls on either side. He might have been able to keep a good watch on the pub's entrances and garden if he'd gained entry to one of the several houses bordering it on that side, but that would have meant ensuring they were empty, or incapacitating anyone within. Lem was a violent man, but only when it was necessary.

It would be necessary again soon, but the time was not now. He was calm and content in the way things were going. He was following fate into this warm summer evening, and by midnight his life would have changed.

And then what? he thought.

"Huh." He was startled by the idea. And then what? He'd never thought much past achieving his aims, bringing the relics back together, and lifting the curse on his family. Beyond that was a blankness, and he frowned when he tried to think of it.

Perhaps after this would be that soft light he sometimes saw in his dreams, the final destination that his family were denied. If that was the case, Lem would welcome it. He never thought much in terms of life and death, only of being in pain and at peace. Lem had not been at peace since the death of his father, and the day his mother had told him he had this journey to continue in his father's footsteps.

Trees and witches, witches and trees.

He looked across the river at the pub garden, scanning the benches and the kids' playground, the groups of people sitting on the grass, and the sloping riverbank where the pub owners had cut in heavy wooden sleepers for customers to sit on. He looked back and forth, and still he could not see Matt.

But Lem thought he was close. The air had changed. He felt alive and alight, his senses spiked and alert. His skin itched beneath the tattoos that covered the scars he had gathered on his quest. Most of all he felt that pull inside, the drawing of his living flesh to that dead flesh and bone contained within the final relic. He'd felt this before, but never like this. Never so strong, so vital.

So final.

Lem resisted the temptation to stand. He had to be patient. The man was not here yet, but he would be soon.

"Not long," he muttered, and between blinks he saw his grizzled old grandfather in his woollen burial suit, his sad mother with her deformed head, and his father, stern and hard and scarred by his violent death, and still frightening even after so many years gone.

Too long gone, he hears his father saying in accusatory tones.

"I've done my best."

No answer this time.

"I've always done my best," Lem said again.

Across the river a group of drinkers laughed, lifting and clinking glasses. Children screamed in the playground. Parents sat on benches watching. This had never been Lem's world, but soon he would have to cross the bridge and become part of it again, just for a little while longer.

"Not long now," he said again.

He waited. He watched. A few minutes later a figure entered the pub garden from inside the building, and even among the revellers and the children and the couples out on dates or stopping for a drink on their way home from weekend work, this person stood out.

He wore a wide-brimmed hat and a plain white shirt, and he walked slowly like an older man, but it was Matt.

Lem stood and stretched the stiffness from his limbs. He waited until Matt had negotiated his way across the garden to a bench close to the riverbank and taken a seat. Matt sipped at a drink, looked at his watch, and looked around the garden. Never still. Nervous.

Looking for him.

Lem kept to the shadows beneath trees as he approached the road bridge that crossed the river, and every step took him closer to his destination.

MATT

Matt stood just inside the pub's double back doors for ten minutes, scanning the garden for any sign of Lem. He could not see him.

It was fifteen minutes to seven.

He went into the disabled toilet and locked the door behind him. He put down his pint of cider and pulled out his phone. It was on silent, and there were various missed messages and calls from Jodi. He ignored them, and instead tapped in *999*. He paused for only a few seconds before dialling.

Once he was put through to the police, Matt said, "I'd like to report a murder."

"Could I take your name and—"

"Just listen to me. King's Arms pub in Mariton. In the garden. I'm wearing a white shirt and a sun hat. The man with me is a murderer, he's very dangerous, and he's fearless. I'm afraid but..."

"Sir, if you're afraid please let me know if you're being coerced or feel that you're in danger—"

"In danger?" Matt actually laughed. His heart was beating so hard that his voice quivered. "Yes, I'm in danger."

"Do you feel—"

"King's Arms garden, now."

He hung up.

Fuck, will they come? Will they think it's a joke? Will they get here too soon and scare him off?

He looked at his watch. It was ten minutes before seven, and he was certain that Lem would already be here, watching and waiting. What Matt carried tucked into his belt beneath the long shirt was something that man had been seeking for years, something he'd killed for and would kill for again. He would not be late.

Matt reached for the door. His heart was beating so hard and fast that his vision blurred. Fuck, this wasn't him. But he had to go through with this now. This was the only way to end things, and he and Jodi would have to accept whatever consequences arose from the things they'd done.

With Lem in prison, accepting those consequences would feel almost welcome.

He held the handle and suddenly imagined Lem standing outside, so close that his mad mop of hair and his nose touched the other side of the door. Matt cursed himself for his stupidity. This was all about being visible, being among so many people that Lem would never dream of doing anything stupid. And now he'd gone and shut himself in the fucking toilet.

He waited, listening at the door, and then kneeled and pressed his face to the floor, trying to look beneath. There were no shadows outside, no indication that anyone was standing there. He stood again, grabbed the handle and opened it. No one there. He walked quickly out into the heat and bustle of the garden, keeping his head down but glancing left and right, looking for Lem. There was no sign, but that meant nothing. He saw an elderly couple he'd done some work for, and looked the other way. He saw a young man who he'd given a quote to just a fortnight ago, caught his eye, looked down at his feet again. Matt didn't think the guy had recognised him, and if he had it had caused no reaction. No sudden, *Holy shit that's the nutter who cut someone up in his house!* The hat he'd stolen from outside a second-hand shop shaded his eyes. The shirt he'd plucked from a washing line was two sizes too big, plenty roomy enough to hide the relic tucked into his belt. That thing was sickeningly warm against his skin. Intimate, like an unwelcome hand touching him close to his thigh. It made him want to puke.

A kid ran across his path and he stopped, spilling some cider.

"Careful, Danny!" his mother scolded.

"It's fine," Matt said, voice high and broken, and he wondered just what he sounded like. A man on his own in a family pub garden, they'd all be looking at him, wearing a bright blue sun hat and a too-large shirt, walking with his head lowered.

Good, he thought. *I want them to see me, notice me, know that I'm here... but not just yet.*

He'd heard no whispers of murder on his way back into town, and seen no police, but that didn't mean that the body in his house had not been found. The police might be covertly watching the roads into and out of town right now. He didn't fool himself that the hat would work for long – he knew plenty of people here, and lots of people knew him – but it only had to work for long enough.

Just long enough for this to work.

He saw an empty bench down close to the river, at the far edge of the pub garden, and he headed that way and sat down. He looked across the river and wished he could enjoy the view, but it reminded him of BB and the last time they'd been here with Jodi, and tears blurred his vision. He put his pint on the bench and wiped his eyes, and when he looked up he saw a young boy watching him from his father's lap.

Matt smiled, then looked away and picked up his drink. He took a sip and looked across the river again at the car park on the other side, and the huge old oak tree that had grown there since before the town was just a church and a few outlying buildings. He turned in his seat and glanced around the garden, and he had never felt so alone and exposed among so many people.

There were no sirens in the distance yet, but perhaps they would come silently. He didn't know how the police worked in such situations. He didn't know anything.

This is not my world, Matt thought, but the idea sat bitter and harsh, because he realised that now it really, really was. His whole life had changed since this morning, and what he was doing now was an attempt to halt that change before it went too far.

He picked up his drink and sipped again, not enjoying the taste. The bench flexed a little as someone else sat down.

A chill went through him, as if a shadow had fallen across the sun. He held the glass two inches from his mouth. Even the river seemed to pause in its flow, waiting to see what came next.

"Not long now," a voice said. "Not long and it'll all be over."

Matt turned and looked at the man. This close he seemed bigger, older, more scarred. More terrifying. Lem wasn't looking at him, but out over the river, as if he was talking to the old oak tree on the other side. In profile he looked almost handsome, the weight of his years and experience giving him gravitas.

"I give it to you and you go," Matt said.

"Where's your friend?"

"I left her behind."

Lem looked right at him. His eyes seemed darker than they should, sunken beneath his beanie, as if they bore the weight of his heavy history.

"She's not your friend," Lem said. "I mean the other one."

"He... he's somewhere else," Matt said.

"Uh-huh." Lem stared at him. A small nod. "Ah. Right. Well, that one isn't on me."

Matt didn't know what to say. He was afraid that if he started talking about BB his breath might hitch, his eyes mist, and he would not do that in front of this man. This murderer.

Lem looked him up and down, and his gaze settled on Matt's large shirt where it gathered in his lap.

"I give it to you and you go," Matt said again. He tried to sound in control, but his voice felt feeble.

"Guess you think you're safe, meeting me here," Lem said.

Matt's breath froze. He opened his mouth.

"Good move," Lem said. "I mean, I'm not going to do anything stupid here, am I? Only a fool would do that. Or someone desperate." His mouth cracked into the semblance of a smile, then he picked up Matt's drink and took a deep swig of the cider. "Are you desperate, Matt?"

"Only to have this over with," Matt said. "To go back to my life."

"No one goes back. We only go forwards. Until there's nowhere left to go."

Where are they? Matt thought. He glanced over Lem's shoulder at the rear of the pub, and at the large garden where people were having a good time. He wished he could be like those people, with BB, and even with Jodi. Before they'd made that stupid, fateful decision, steered by her, to get themselves embroiled in all this. *Where the fuck are they?*

"Expecting someone?" Lem asked. "Only you arrived here alone, and I believe you when you say you left her behind."

"No one," Matt said. *Will they use their sirens? Will they even take me seriously?*

Lem's eyebrows rose a little, then he nodded slowly and said, "Ahhhhh. I get it. OK, then. Best give it to me before the law arrives, yes?"

"I give it to you and you—"

"Because if they get here and I'm still here, I'll take it off you and murder one of these brats running around. You'd like that, Matt? Maybe the little shit who made you spill your drink. How would that sit with you? How would you carry the sight of my braining a little kid in front of its parents?"

Matt could not answer.

Lem leaned back on the bench. "So, let's not make a scene." Casual, enjoying the evening, he reached out one scarred and tattooed hand.

JODI

Jodi had never run so far so fast. Her legs ached, her lungs burned, she was sweating and dehydrated and exhausted, and with every step she became more and more terrified that Matt and Lem would be meeting somewhere else. Approaching town she stayed close to the river, because she knew that path led eventually to the warren of narrow residential lanes behind the King's Arms. It was a warm, fine summer evening and she started to see people walking their dogs, strolling with kids or running, and she kept her eyes averted and her head down. She tried to put on an exercise face – a concentrated frown, panting with effort – rather than looking afraid.

Passing the first buildings on the edge of Mariton, she soon heard the growing sound of kids' laughter and the low susurration of conversation from the pub garden. She came to a halt by a high stone wall. Behind the wall were several expensive houses fronting onto the river. To her left was a row of semi-detached houses. The narrow road curved as it followed the course of the river, and up ahead she could just see the pub roof.

Breathing hard, walking slowly instead of running fast, Jodi took a moment to prepare herself. She touched the gun in her pocket, hoping she would not have to take it out. It gave her little real comfort.

All the way here she'd been running scenarios through her mind, desperately trying to imagine them all ending in the same way – with Matt safe. She couldn't face anything else. Even if it meant Lem gone and taking the relic with him, and her losing her last chance of finding out the truth about her father.

Matt's safety came first.

As she headed along the road towards the King's Arms, she froze.

There was a truck reversed into a narrow lane leading to a small patch of allotments. She thought it was the one Lem had been driving – same model she'd seen at Morgan Manor, bumps and scrapes on the bodywork, and the small stepladder was still propped in the back and tied to the roof bar. The front driver's side wheel that she'd slashed with her knife had been replaced, the new tyre black and clean with sharp tread.

Jodi reached into her pocket for the gun, hand around the handle, finger resting on the trigger guard. She took a couple of steps across the road towards the lane. It wound between two sets of houses, opening into the allotments, and it was wide enough for allotment-owners to park on one side.

Sun glinted from chrome and glass, and she could not see through the windscreen. It had been reversed in, nose out ready to leave. If Lem was in the cab he'd be staring right at her.

Jodi thought he was not there. *I'd feel him*, she thought. *I'd feel his eyes on my skin*. She had sensed that before, recently and also long ago when things were less complicated, and she would never forget the sensation. Like spiders on her bare skin.

She went a few paces along the road, then stopped. She looked around to make sure no one was watching her, then strolled towards the truck, casual but fast. As she approached she tightened her grip on the gun, but the cab was empty.

She looked into the truck's open bed. It was dirty with sun-dried mud, a few lengths of sawn wood were scattered around, and the punctured wheel was there too. There was also a small toolbox fixed to the rear of the cab, its lid open several inches.

There, she thought. *That's how I find him. That's how I fucking beat him.*

She shrugged the pack from her shoulders and opened it, pulled out BB's phone, checked the charge and made sure it had reception, turned it to silent, went on tiptoes, and slipped the phone carefully into the toolbox. She made sure it was hidden away, pushing it towards the back.

Then she paused, looking around to make sure no one had seen her, and thinking through what she had done. *It'll work*, she thought. *It has to work.*

Heart still thundering even though she had finally stopped running, Jodi headed along the road towards the King's Arms.

LEM

Matt took the relic out of his waistband and held it close to his side on the bench.

"That's it," Lem said. "Quickly now, before they get here. What, you're watching for them? Waiting for them to come screeching into the car park, all sirens and SWAT team?"

Matt looked at him. The bastard was fucking terrified. Good. Lem could use that.

"Give it here and I'm gone, and it's all over. I'll call the law, tell them all about what I did to Rash. They'll believe me. I'll say where I left his right hand, in your downstairs sink. His head in your spare bed. His top lip stuck on the cactus on your kitchen table."

Steady, you fool, he heard his father say. *Don't gloat in what you are. Don't fucking* preen.

Matt had grown pale. He looked down at the relic again, and Lem felt its draw in his gut. Felt *her*.

"Just fucking give it to me," he said softer, quieter. He could take it in seconds, and his patience was failing.

"I'm not sure I've done the right thing," Matt said. "If I get up and run you won't be able—"

"Matt!" The voice was swallowed among others in the pub garden, talking and laughing, kids screeching on the climbing frames, and Lem took a casual look around, knowing she was somewhere in the distance. There. Across the garden, just coming through a side gate from the lane where Lem had parked his truck.

"Come on, son," Lem said. "Give the thing to me and live the rest of your life—"

"Matt, no! Don't give it to him! He'll—"

As Matt looked up in surprise at Jodi's voice, Lem lunged at him, one hand gripping his shoulder, fingers digging in hard enough to grind bone. With his other hand he grasped the relic, the last one, the object that would fulfil his quest and save his family.

"*No!*" Jodi shouted, and she was running across the garden, drawing attention from the adults, most kids still in their own worlds and ignoring her. She sprinted between tables, leaped over a couple lying on a blanket, kicked over a glass, focussed totally on Lem and what he was doing.

Matt made a small, feeble attempt to push him off and Lem squeezed harder, digging his thumb into Matt's shoulder so hard that he screamed.

"Leave him alone!" Jodi shouted.

Lem tugged the relic from his grasp and pushed back, standing up and holding it in both hands. It drew him, exerting its irresistible gravity. But it was also cold and hard and—

Dead, his father said, *of course it's fucking dead. But you know what to do to bring her back to life.*

From behind him Lem heard an engine's roar as a car powered across the road bridge, another following close behind. No sirens, but he knew what he was hearing. He could almost see the police cars reflected in Matt's eyes.

Jodi was close now. She had one hand in her pocket but she hadn't drawn the gun, because they were in a pub garden packed with cheerily pissed adults and sweaty kids, and she knew that nothing would go down here. Matt did too, and that was why he'd chosen this place to meet. It made him feel safe.

They were both so wrong.

Lem lifted the relic in both hands and brought it down onto Matt's head. Once, hard, its end striking him above the left ear, bone crunching, skin breaking, flesh tearing, and blood…

Blood pouring.

Lem followed him down as he slipped from the bench, pressing the relic to the terrible bleeding wound so that it felt the warm blood, and as he heard shouts and screams erupting around him he smiled, because he was now close to the very end.

Every part of his life had been moving towards this.

People ran, parents called for their kids, kids screamed, and then Jodi was standing behind the bench with the gun drawn and pointed at his face. She only glanced down at Matt, then she was focussed on Lem.

She didn't want to see what he'd done to her friend.

"Touch him again and I'll fucking kill you," she hissed.

"In front of all these nice people?" Lem didn't look at her. He held the relic up to the sun so that blood ran down from its tip, soaking into the surface before ever reaching his hand. Being absorbed, sucked in. "No need. I think this will do fine."

Jodi stepped around the bench, and though she looked scared she was also filled with determination and hate. For just a second Lem felt a quiver of something he was not used to. For a moment, he was afraid of her.

She pressed the gun to his chest and kept walking, forcing him to take two steps back.

"Inside, inside!" a woman shouted. Behind Jodi, the garden was emptying. The pub drew the people in as readily as the relic sucked in Matt's blood.

The police cars were coming closer, out of sight but almost there, in the car park at the front of the pub. He didn't have very long.

"Shoot me now and you'll never know the truth about sad old Wayne," Lem said.

"I've grown up not knowing," she said. But her need was obvious.

"And yet he sustains," Lem said. He stepped to the side, gun barrel scraping across his chest. Then he started walking away. An itch began between his shoulder blades. *That's where she'll shoot me*, he thought, and he wondered just how he would dodge this death. He gripped the relic, warm and vital in his hand, and no bullet came. People remaining hunkered down in the garden looked at him with fear, but most of their attention was on Jodi and her gun now, and that helped him. He walked with head held high, moving towards his destiny faster than ever before.

When he reached the gate out into the lane and looked back he saw Jodi kneeling beside Matt. Maybe he was dead, but Lem hoped not. If he was still alive, she'd stay with him a few moments longer.

A few moments were all he needed.

JODI

Oh shit oh fuck oh shit oh fuck!

She kneeled by Matt's side. There was so much blood.

She didn't have much time.

"Matt…"

She reached for him where he lay in front of the bench but there was *so much blood*. The side of his head above his left ear looked deformed, a fold of skin and flesh hanging over the top of his ear. Bone was exposed. She'd heard a *crack!* and maybe it had been the relic breaking, but she thought not. She thought it had been Matt.

Dear, sweet, uncomplicated Matt.

His eyes were open wide, mouth agape, tongue lolling. There was a discarded cigarette butt stuck to his lip from where he'd hit the ground. It was a mere detail but she fixated on it, because he should be able to feel it, taste it. He should pick it off. But he was not moving, other than a slow, grotesque squirm back and forth, like injured roadkill slowly winding down.

"Matt," she said, kneeing beside him.

His left eye rolled to the side to look up at her. Some veins had burst across his eyeball, flushing it pink.

"... kayak..." he said.

Jodi shook her head, frowning.

"Me and BB... he tipped me out..."

"You're OK. You're OK." She looked over her shoulder towards the rear of the pub. Reflected through windows from the front parking lot she could see the blue flicker of a police light, and she realised what Matt had been trying to do. Maybe it would have worked, *maybe*, if he'd truly had any understanding of just how brutal Lem could be.

They'd enter the pub first. Assess the situation. Then they'd come for her. The mad woman with the gun.

She looked back to Matt. "You're OK," she said, but she really didn't know if he was. Either way, the police were here now, and soon there would be an ambulance. She could do nothing for him.

And if they arrested her, it was all over. She'd never see Lem again, and he would have won, and she'd never know the awful sick truth about her father – *And yet he sustains* – and every second that ticked by was a moment that could change her life forever. She felt the inexorable flow of time passing like never before.

"I have to go," she said. She didn't know if Matt could hear through the blood and the ruin of his ear. *Something's broken in there*, she thought. "I have to catch him to clear your name. Our names. I have to go, Matt."

She thought she saw him nod. Maybe she'd just imagined it.

She pressed her hand to his chest and felt his heart beating fast, much too fast, pumping the adrenalin of shock through his veins.

"You understand?" she asked.

Perhaps he nodded again. But as she stood and ran across the garden after Lem, she knew that she was only fooling herself.

They'd call him an ambulance. She could do nothing for him that police and paramedics and a hospital could not do better.

Telling herself these lies, hating herself, but knowing nothing else, she sprinted after Lem, through the gate and along the lane, rounding the bend just in time to see the rear of his truck as it passed out of sight further along the road.

Jodi sprinted, tired muscles complaining as she demanded more of them, passing the high stone wall on her left and the row of houses on her right, and every second held value now, that flow of time leading towards her failure. Every moment took Lem further from her and made him harder to follow, and eventually she would not be able to follow him at all.

Her mind sprinted as well. She needed a vehicle. Matt's van was out of action, hidden away in the woods. BB's car was parked outside his house, but his keys would be inside. Her car was there too, but he lived over a mile from here on the other side of Mariton. Too far. Much too far.

Still running, Jodi thought of BB now, still tangled in a fallen tree at the side of the river. Or maybe the gentle flow had worked him loose and pulled him downriver, further away from town and her. Bodies sank, didn't they?

Maybe she'd lost him forever.

The lane turned to the right and followed the river. The tall wall ended and the view opened up, the river to her left and the scattered houses and fields at the edge of town beyond. On her right were detached houses and bungalows, all neat gardens and sun-drenched patios set up to take in the view. She couldn't just start trying car doors. News of the incident at the pub would likely travel across the small town faster than she could sprint.

And sprinting, Jodi was running out of time.

She passed an old house on her right that was being refurbished, its shell gutted, stone walls encased with scaffold. It didn't appear that anyone was living there while the work was done, and she'd seen this place a few times. Whoever owned it was working slowly.

She took a risk and dashed up the short gravelly drive. The house itself was protected by wire mesh fencing, so she headed around the side and ducked down behind a pile of building blocks.

Panting, she pulled out her phone.

Please let this work please please please—

She opened the Find My Phone app and waited for the devices to load up. There was her phone, and hers alone.

"Oh, no."

She stared at the screen, willing BB's phone to appear, and just as she was about to shut it down, his device suddenly flickered on. It was moving slowly away from her as Lem negotiated the narrow residential streets cobwebbing this side of the river at the edge of town.

"Oh, thank fuck!" she said. She watched for a few more seconds, then clicked the screen off and pocketed the phone.

Jodi had a chisel in her pocket, a knife in her backpack, and as she stood and started running again she tried to settle her mind. Matt was badly hurt but he'd be taken care of, and however fucking shitty she felt for fleeing and leaving him there, she knew that staying behind would not have helped him one bit. Still, the guilt bit in, at everything she'd done to lead BB and Matt into her own messed-up world.

Worse was the thought that in some way this was what she'd wanted. Now that Lem had the final relic he would be racing towards wherever he kept them, and if her father was still alive – unlikely, but still possible – she thought that he'd be there too. She'd been trying to plan how to let Lem have the relic so that she could follow him, but she had wanted to act without Matt being involved.

He'd surprised her. He'd forced her hand. Now she had to make the most out of how things had turned out.

Thinking about her dad recalled a memory that shocked her with its intensity. It was one of those weird, meaningless moments that had meant little at the time, but which somehow came to mind at the strangest of moments. They were standing in a queue together outside a cinema. She was maybe thirteen, and her dad was trying to get them in to see a 15-certificate film together. It was a cool winter's evening, they were wrapped up warm, and he'd bought them both big cups of coffee before they'd started queuing. She held hers in both hands close to her face and breathed in the steam, and he told her a really bad dad-joke that set him laughing and snorting. And that was it. Her father, relaxed and comfortable and at ease with Jodi, who he loved so much. And Jodi, so trusting of her dad, even though she knew he had his own deep problems. So set on fulfilling her promise to her mother that she would look after him. So confident that he would be there forever.

Jodi ran, silently promising that she would find out the truth about her father. The chance of him still being alive must surely be remote, and she almost hoped he was not. If he was, and Lem was keeping him prisoner somewhere in some sick fantasy to feed those weird fucking relics, Jodi wasn't sure she would be able to handle that.

Either way, she had to find out. And in that moment another memory came – her dad showing her how to hot-wire a car after he'd lost his keys to an old banged-out Mini he owned.

And she knew what she had to do.

She found the car ten minutes later, parked in a lay-by on a lane leading out of Mariton. She'd come this way with BB on a bike ride a few times, and knew that the lane eventually led to a nice country pub called the Bell. She didn't think they'd ever ridden here without stopping for a drink in the pub on their way back home.

Close to the lay-by was a rundown house, its render cracked and crumbling, windows smashed and boarded over. The garden was an overgrown wonderland of old vehicles, a rotting caravan and the prehistoric remains of a giant JCB slowly rusting into history. The old guy who lived there was known to everyone as Dodge. Rumour had it he'd never sold a vehicle, but he just kept buying them.

Some of them he still used. And one of them was an old Ford Capri, its shell a patchwork of different coloured panels. BB had joked a few times about buying the car from Dodge and doing it up, though he'd never claimed any mechanical knowledge. *That's more Matt's bag*, he'd said.

Jodi slowed to a walk as she passed the dilapidated house, facing ahead but glancing to her left, trying to make out whether anyone was at home. The Capri was parked off the road just past the garden, and as she reached it she paused and looked around.

There was no sign of Dodge. The space behind the Capri was obviously somewhere he used to park another vehicle – there was churned mud and old oil stains – but it was empty right now. Maybe for once, luck was on her side.

Jodi took off her backpack and dug around until she found her folding knife. She shouldered the pack again, flicked open the blade, and approached the car.

She knew that the police would be looking for her by now. People would have seen her fleeing through the gate and out into the lane, and plenty had watched her toting the gun and pointing it at Lem. They couldn't even begin to guess at what was going on, but by now the police and probably half the town knew that there were two extremely dangerous people at large.

Armed response would be on their way, if not in Mariton already.

Jodi didn't have long.

She went around to the Capri's passenger side and found a low, tumbled brick wall covered in weeds. She stayed on that side, thinking that if she heard a motor approaching she'd have time to duck down and hide. She hefted a brick, placed the point of the knife against the corner of the passenger window, and gave it a good hit. It bit through the window, leaving a small hole, and she struck the cracked glass a few times with the brick until it shattered. She knocked it from the frame and reached in to pop up the old-style lock.

She was inside. All was quiet.

Calm, calm, she thought, and as she opened the door she took a few seconds to take in a long, slow breath.

There was a quick way and a more complex way to hot-wire an old car like this. Once inside, she tried the quick way first, with no real expectations. And she was right. Pounding the chisel from the dredging barge into the ignition slot succeeded only in snapping the chisel, cracking the steering wheel housing and breaking the ignition.

"Yeah, it follows," she muttered.

Plan two.

Crouching down in the driver's seat, she tugged out the nest of wires from beneath the steering column and sorted through them, selecting what she hoped were the correct wires. She stripped them with her knife, wound the bare ends together, and tried the radio. Some inane DJ told her that it was another hot one so here were Oasis to make her evening cool. Good, that meant power was flowing.

A spark, another, and then the engine coughed over and caught.

She sat up in the driver's seat and revved the motor. Checked the mirrors. Looked all around. No one rushed out of the house behind her, no one dashed along the road. If Dodge was at home, he hadn't noticed that someone was stealing one of his collection.

Surprised at how easy it had been, Jodi eased the car forwards, bouncing onto the road and almost driving straight into the opposite hedge before she realised there was no power steering. This was genuinely old-school, and the engine chuckled and roared as if laughing at her surprise.

The road twisted down a hill, and when she was far enough away from Dodge's place she pulled to the side and propped her phone on the dash. The Find My Phone app still showed BB's phone moving away from her, faster now, and she started to follow.

If anyone local saw the Capri they'd think it was Dodge. Jodi was pretty certain she hadn't seen another of these old classics in years, certainly not around Mariton, and the patchwork painted body was distinctive. If she had a hat she might have been able to hide herself, but instead she lowered the sun visor and sat upright. That was as much as she could do.

The old car growled along the country lanes, heavy yet responsive. Whatever horrors she was leaving behind – BB dead in the river, Matt badly injured or worse in that sunny pub garden – Jodi could not help thinking whatever she was driving towards would be worse.

LEM

The further he drove into the setting sun, the more Lem started to believe he was being followed.

He'd been nervous leaving Mariton, worried that the police presence would have expanded far and fast enough to cover many of the roads in and out. While he had left bodies in his wake over the years, he had always succeeded in keeping to the shadows, existing off-grid and working his own way through life. Making his own decisions. Mixing with those who might be of use to him, but never, *never* making friends. Even so, he'd always been prepared to fight his way through and away if the police ever did come calling.

He was ready for that now.

But not so close to the end, he thought. It was a silent prayer to no one but himself. He was not used to uncertainty and doubt, but this was not that. It was more a statement of intent. Nothing would stop him from finishing the task set for him by his mother, and by those dead family members who whispered in his dreams and haunted his waking hours.

Anyone who followed or stopped him, police or not, would not live to regret their actions.

After twenty miles and almost an hour of changing direction, passing along barely used tracks, and working his way north-east away from town, he began to feel comfortable that he had slipped away without drawing attention to his truck. Plenty of people had seen what he'd done in the warm pub garden. He didn't think anyone had seen him jump into the vehicle and leave.

Whoever might be following him was not the police. He thought it was her.

He'd always liked Jodi. That first time he'd met her in a different pub garden over fifteen years ago with her old man, he'd noticed the fight in her, and the sense of responsibility she'd held over her dad. Wayne hadn't really acknowledged it, and therein lay her power, and her strength. She was just a kid back then, but somehow that kid had allowed her father to believe he was the one looking after her, when it was plainly the other way around.

Seeing her at Morgan Manor had been a surprise, but not really a shock. After Lem had smashed up her old man and blooded the relic, and the van crashed, he'd always suspected that they might cross paths again. She had left him to burn, but he knew that she would keep the fire of vengeance simmering.

A child no more, she had come back at last to avenge the father she believed to be dead. It seemed appropriate that it was happening now, with the weight of the last relic lying between them. In a way it was inevitable that the two of them would collide after orbiting each other for so long.

He had the relic resting on his lap. It was warm, heavy, like someone's arm and hand settled across his thighs. There was something intimate about it. It was closeness, almost tenderness, and Lem briefly imagined the comforting touch of his mother. A lump came to his throat, a tear to his eye. The emotion surprised him, and he wiped his eyes hard. He glanced in the rearview mirror and caught sight of himself. Even beneath his hat, the scars on his face and the side of his head looked worse than usual. Fresher.

Get a fucking grip, he thought, and this was in his own voice, not that of his father. Maybe he'd been thinking of his mother because this was close to being over. She had set him on this task, dictating the ragged course of his life like few mothers ever could, but he did not blame her for that. Only rarely had he ever doubted his fate, and he'd never railed against it. He was the centre of his family, and other than a few bastards whose trails were cold, he was the only one still alive. He was useful and taking action. They were relying on him. He could save them all and give them peace, and perhaps in doing so he would save himself.

If Jodi was following him, it was because he'd let slip the idea that Wayne was still alive. She didn't care about this relic anymore, heavy and warm with the blood of the friend she had fooled and betrayed. This was all about finding her father, and seeing him one more time.

Lem would see him first.

GULLS

JULY 2011

RUMOURS OF TEETH

HE SUSTAINS

LEM

Lem is on Crow Island, and his slaying of David Roth is already mostly forgotten.

The strong sun is making Lem sweat, and that causes the shotgun wounds to itch even more beneath the long-sleeved shirt he wears to cover them. *I've been injured worse*, he thinks. Once, he almost crawled along the storm-lashed causeway to place a relic he'd recently retrieved, a knife wound in his gut pouting and promising to spill his insides like sick secrets.

Even though he knows he's alone, he waits until he's scrambled around to the seaward side of the small island before stripping off his shirt. He has to put the relic down to do so—

Yes, I think it really might be a rib, broken off, shortened like Mary Webster's life.

—but the feel of sunlight on his scarred, tattooed torso is soothing and sweet. These wounds still trouble him, and he probably won't sleep well for a few more nights, but they're not dangerous. So long as he keeps them clean they will become just another scattering of scars.

He thinks about what he might have tattooed across these new scars. They form the story of his body and the map of his life, and while no one who views them would really be able to translate that story into any sort of sense, that does not concern Lem. They are all for him.

Seagulls cry out where they're roosting on the sheer cliffs that form the seaward side of the island, and Lem smiles. That's what the new tattoos will be. The gulls of Crow Island.

He walks along the low clifftop and looks down at where the sea meets the land thirty feet below. Waves break in ebullient violence, and he feels the spray even this high up. The sea surges and swells, battering itself against the island as if striving to abrade it to nothing. Perhaps to scour away whatever unnatural thing the island hides at its heart.

Shirt tied around his waist, relic clasped in his left hand, he finds the tumbled remains of the old building. He's never been able to glean what this building might have been constructed for, nor its true age. It could have been fifty years old and built as something to do with the natural sinkhole that its thickest wall skirts. Or maybe it was five hundred years old, a lookout hide or a smugglers' den of some sort, and that sinkhole might have been forged by human hands. He liked to imagine pirates or wreckers clambering up the hole from the sea down below, bags over their shoulders filled with loot from ships they had pillaged or lured onto the rocks.

In truth, Lem does not care. This place is his now, and his

family's. And once he has placed this next relic, it will belong more and more to the memory of Mary Webster.

He kicks around the base of the walls until he finds where the sinkhole begins. The brambles are thicker than ever – it has been a couple of years since he recovered the last relic, brought it here, and put it carefully in place – and he tries kicking them aside with his boots. His laces tangle, and barbs scratch against his skin.

He could pull the undergrowth away, tear it right back, but that will expose the hole. He prefers it like this. So instead he sits and pushes his feet in, moving them around to form a big enough hole for him to lower himself into. Thorns snag against his clothing and skin and hair, and the pain is sharp and sweet, like an echo of the lead shot peppering his shoulder and chest. He winces but lets his bodyweight pull him down, and the brambles and thorns cannot bear him up. Instead, they lodge in his skin and then rip out again, tearing, tearing, and by the time he is beneath the bramble branches with his feet lodged against the sides of the vertical vent, he bears a hundred more tiny wounds.

Blood flows. He pauses, motionless, but he cannot hear its dripping against the clash and roar of the waves striking the bottom of the sinkhole far below. Still clasping the relic – he would sooner fall rather than drop it and lose it to the sea – he starts climbing down.

It's dark. The undergrowth above shields the hole from the sun, and any weak light from below ebbs and flows with the pulse of the ocean. But Lem has made his way down here before, often bearing a heavier load. He has the climbing route imprinted in his mind. A foothold, a crack in the wall, a ledge to rest on a dozen feet down from the surface.

And then the darkness in one wall of the sinkhole becomes even darker, because there is nothing there.

Lem takes a penlight from his back pocket and flicks it on, holding the small torch in his mouth. He directs the light beam at the opening, turning his head slightly from side to side. It's a narrow fit, but Lem is lean and strong, and he soon winnows his way inside.

Something tickles at his mind. A flicker of disquiet. His heartbeat has increased, he can feel it fluttering in his chest just as he shifts and moves in this narrow underground space. Lem is never afraid, not even when he visits that stark place in his dreams and his dead relatives berate him, and his father's presence towers over them all.

Not afraid, no. But he knows what he is about to see, and understands that it is not natural.

He wriggles his way through the short tunnel and emerges into the larger space beyond. It's the size of a small bathroom, not quite big enough for him to stand upright, and so well defined that he cannot believe it is anything other than manmade. Those pirates or smugglers again, he guesses.

It is home now to a different kind of loot.

The relic in his hand is warm and almost vibrating with its need to be placed.

Lem stands half-crouched, torch now held in his right hand. Its light is enough to fill the space, but shadows still shimmer and dance as he moves, as if they're flitting in an attempt to keep out of sight. He has the feeling that there is something just behind him, however fast he turns his head or shifts his body to look. Always there, always just out of sight.

He takes a long, low inhalation, and as he breathes out his breath is echoed by another.

Settled at last, excited as well as nervous, Lem shines the light into the far corner of that small cave.

The remains of the man shift beneath the light, and not only from shadows slinking away. Lem holds the beam true and still and the figure in the corner still moves, shifting, flexing, dried skin brushing against dried skin like old leather, joints crackling, tired bones creaking. Arranged around the body – behind, beneath, *within* – are the relics Lem has spent his adult life retrieving, and those found by his father before him. Some of them are attached like barnacles to the unfortunate man's skin. Others are ingrown, as if the skin and flesh matured and grew around them. That's not the case, Lem knows. It's more likely that certain relics have penetrated the meat of the body. Part of the left thigh is the heavy relic he took from the gallery in Hay-on-Wye. On his upper right chest, two ribs encased in polished wood have taken the place of the man's pectoral muscle.

"Wayne," Lem says. "You're looking well."

The body's head lifts. Only a little, but enough for Lem to make out his face. His cheeks are sunken. The eyes are pale orbs in too-large sockets. The nose is a broken mess of skin and cartilage. His mouth protrudes from beneath the withered nose, top jaw home to half a dozen yellowed teeth. The lower jaw is missing, fallen away long ago to make room for the knotted round shape held there. In this shape, beneath the rough wood encasing it, Lem also sees the rumour of teeth, and the rough yellow curve of a skull.

"No, it's OK, don't get up," Lem says. His bad jokes are to protect himself, bind him to the world he thinks he understands, because this…

This is something he cannot understand. Something that

should not be. And yet Wayne is here, and he sustains. The relics draw sustenance from him, and in return they allow him to persist. Unfed, unwatered, more corpse-like than all the dead people Lem has seen, he rests slumped into the corner of this strange cavern, alive and somehow horribly aware, and the remains of Mary Webster are slowly becoming a part of him.

The old oak tree that encased the murdered witch, and whose wood protected the remnants of her dismembered body, suckles on his blood. Wood and flesh become one. Trees and witches, witches and trees.

Wayne's dried and hollowed throat emits a long, rasping rattle. It starts low, almost sub-audible. Then it grows, filling the small cavern, an exhalation of pure hopelessness that sets Lem's skin on edge. As Wayne's shrivelled head lowers and that other smaller skull rests against his sunken chest once more, Lem wields the relic and steps forwards. He offers it out. Wayne's body and the remains of the old dead witch that possesses it suck it in, almost tugging it from his hands. There's a dry whispering sound, and then a single wet sigh, like the oldest person alive smacking their lips.

Ah, yes, Lem thinks, *a rib for sure.*

As he releases the relic and steps back, Wayne's voice rises one more time in pure pain, as if he has healthy lungs to draw air. As if his throat is rich, not raw. As if he has a mouth to scream.

The relic sinks into his chest and starts suckling on his meagre blood.

"He sustains," Lem says. He takes another step back, and before turning away to leave he scans the torch up, down and around Wayne's tortured body, and sees just how much work he still has left to complete.

BEING SEEN

SEPTEMBER 2024

REFUEL

THE STORM

JODI

Almost two hours after leaving Mariton, with night falling and BB's phone a steady quarter of a mile ahead of her, Jodi noticed that the fuel in the Capri was dangerously low. When she'd started out the tank was almost full, so either the indicator was lying or there was a leak in one of the fuel lines.

She couldn't risk leaving it to chance. She also hated the idea of stopping at a petrol station. The violent incident in the King's Arms garden would almost certainly have made the news, and there was a fair chance that one of the shocked patrons had recorded or photographed her, Matt and Lem on their phones. She'd be a wanted woman now. Armed and dangerous. Approach with caution.

Jodi also suspected that Kojak might have reported finding BB's body by now. Through talking to townsfolk, it would not take long for the police to link him to her and Matt, and his death would only add to the seriousness of what was occurring. If they'd also found Rash's body in Matt's house, the whole of Mariton would be in lockdown. She'd tried the radio in the Capri, but reception kept cutting in and out, and she wasn't able to find any local stations. The story had not yet hit the national news, but it was only a matter of time.

All of this, a matter of time ticking down.

She wished she'd been forward-thinking enough to procure a change of clothes somewhere. But everything that had happened, and was still happening, was occurring moment by moment. Since Morgan Manor that morning, the day had been staggering onwards from one panicked instant to another, with very little concrete planning in between.

It was also likely that Dodge had noticed the Capri was missing. Would he call the police? She had to assume yes. If so, they'd almost certainly link the theft with the pub garden incident.

She slammed the steering wheel, looked again at the fuel gauge. As if to taunt her, the warning light winked on, off, on again.

"Fuck it!" She glanced at her phone wedged on the dashboard. For the first thirty minutes out of Mariton, Lem had taken a dozen random turnings, changing direction at every opportunity. But now he was settled, heading a steady north-east towards the coast.

In the top right-hand corner of her phone screen, the battery indicator turned red.

"Oh for fucking *fuck's* sake!"

They were on a dual carriageway, traffic flitting past in both directions. She drove in the slow lane, keeping pace with Lem and resisting the temptation to put her foot down and draw in closer. If he began to suspect he was being tailed, he'd have to wonder how, and he was not a stupid man. He'd figure it out. That, or he'd set a trap for her. Draw her in, attack her. Or he'd swap his truck for another vehicle to prevent her from following him anymore.

She saw a junction approaching, and up on a small rise the familiar orange sign of a Sainsbury's superstore. The idea of something to eat set her stomach churning, and she could also buy some new clothes. But she couldn't risk entering the brightly lit store. She was sweaty, dirty, scratched, her running leggings torn by brambles, and she still had BB's blood drying on the backs of her hands and blackening her fingernails.

But the petrol stations in these places sometimes allowed you to pay at the pump.

She checked Lem's direction and speed. It was steady.

Making a quick decision, she turned off and drove up the exit ramp. She needed to pee too, but there wouldn't be a toilet in the petrol station.

Another reason to go into the main superstore, she thought.

"Stupid. Stupid."

She could piss by the side of the road.

The petrol station was not too busy and she drove straight beside a pump. She parked the car and reached into her backpack, which she'd placed on the passenger seat. She rooted around inside and found her debit card. When she turned to open the door, a man was standing right outside.

She jumped, banging her head on the low ceiling. The man put both hands out and took a couple of steps back, mouthing, *Sorry!* He was middle aged, bald, looked after himself. He wasn't acting as if he'd recognised her from some news report.

Jodi paused, staring at him. She could start the car and drive away without getting any fuel, but that would look strange. And she'd still have to stop at the next garage to top up.

Reaching for the door handle, she glanced back and down and saw the gun resting in front of the gearstick. She dragged the backpack across to cover it and wondered if the guy had seen it, and if that was why he was backing away with his hands held up.

"What a fucking mess I am," Jodi muttered, and she opened the door.

"Sorry, didn't mean to startle you," the guy said, "it's just I haven't seen a Capri on the road in years. What is it – two litre?"

"Er, yeah," Jodi said. She had no clue.

The guy edged around and looked at the back of the car. "Holy shit, it's a two-point-eight!"

"Yeah, yeah."

"I had one of these when I was a teenager, just a sixteen-hundred, you know, loved that car, it was matt black, really felt like you were driving something, you know?"

"It really is something," Jodi said. She was aware of her mud-covered and torn running tights and T-shirt, and the dried blood on her hands. Crispy, dark beneath the artificial lights of the petrol station, it could have been mud.

"You had the car long?"

Couple of hours. "Six months. My husband bought it to do it up, and didn't."

"Awesome!" He was looking at the car, not her. That was good.

Jodi inserted her debit card, tapped in the number, then started fuelling.

Holy shit can they trace my card? she thought. Panic sent a chill through her. The pump had accepted the card, but that didn't mean anything.

She glanced at the illuminated window of the station's store. The two people behind the counter weren't paying her any attention.

As the litres ticked over and the guy strolled around the car making admiring noises and grunts, she tried to hide her growing nervousness. The pressure from her bladder increased, and she tipped from foot to foot.

Looking up again, she saw that the man and woman behind the counter in the store were now staring at her. Her heart stuttered. She smiled, and the woman gave a thumbs up with her eyebrows raised. Jodi nodded and returned the gesture, realising what was happening. They were making sure she wasn't being bothered.

Every moment here, she was being seen and remembered.

"Gotta dash," she said. "I heard the road heading east is choked because of a crash."

"Right, yeah," the guy said, almost as if he'd forgotten she was there. "Nice motor. Tell your husband to treat her with love." And he turned and walked away.

Jodi paused for a second after she'd screwed the petrol cap back on. Inside the petrol station's shop she might be able to buy a mobile charger, though she wasn't certain a modern one would work in an old car's cigarette lighter. And she could get some food and water.

Time was not on her side. Every moment took Lem further away. Every heartbeat brought her closer to being recognised and caught. It was a risk.

But if her phone ran out, she'd lose him for good.

She jogged to the shop and opened the door, going straight to the small section of car gadgets. There were several phone chargers, most of them USB, but she found one with a multi-adaptor that promised to work with a cigarette lighter point. She also grabbed some random bags of crisps and biscuits and a couple of bottles of water.

As she approached the counter, the guy was looking at her strangely.

"Had a tumble?" he asked.

"Eh, yeah, been running." She held up her purchases. "Refuel."

"Nice car."

"So I'm told." She smiled again, trying not to project her nervousness.

As the man scanned her purchases, Jodi looked for the woman. She'd moved into the small stock room at the side of the counter, and Jodi could hear her voice, low and fast.

"Card or cash?" the man asked.

"Er, card please." Jodi leaned forwards, looking through the half-open doorway. She could just see the woman's phone in her hand as she talked, and on the screen of a small desktop computer was a page from the BBC News website.

Even from this distance, Jodi could see her own face in a frozen image from the King's Arms garden.

She grabbed the charger and as much of the food as she could in one sweep, turned, and ran for the door.

"Hey, you can't just do that!" the man shouted.

"Rob, that's her, that's the woman from the—"

Jodi heard no more as she rushed out of the door and across the forecourt. The guy who'd been admiring the Capri watched her go, standing beside his own vehicle dispensing fuel. His smile slipped.

Jodi tugged open the door, dropping half of the food but ensuring she still had hold of the charger. She threw everything into the passenger seat and slid behind the wheel. Twisting the wires, hearing the car roar to life, she looked straight ahead at the shop.

The man and woman stood together behind the counter, watching her. The woman was still holding the phone in front of her as she talked to whoever was on the other end.

The police, she knew.

She pulled away with a screech of tyres, and she uttered a high, hysterical laugh as she thought, *I bet Bald Guy loved that.*

Two minutes later she was back on the dual carriageway. She hoped that if and when the police arrived, the guy would mention about her saying she was heading east.

But she knew how rare and distinctive her ride was.

She wouldn't be able to do this for very long.

Lem was almost five miles ahead of her now. She put her foot down and accelerated fast, the engine grumbled, the car shook, and she drove towards a beautiful autumnal dusk settling across the western hills.

Darkness brought the storm.

It came out of nowhere and spattered fat raindrops across the windscreen. Jodi waited for the wipers to flick on then realised they wouldn't be automatic in a car this old. She used the indicators first, then hit the arm on the other side of the steering wheel.

For a few moments nothing happened, and she began to panic. It was almost full-dark now, and if the rain came down heavy and the wipers were screwed, so was she. Then they stuttered to life and swept the windscreen clear.

Well done, Dodge, you've kept her well, she thought. The old Capri could do with a paint job, but mechanically it felt ready to rock.

The rain came heavier, and she felt the first heavy swipe as a gust of wind hit the car. She held the wheel straight. Something dazzled across the windscreen, either a burst of lightning or a full-beam flash from a vehicle moving in the opposite lane.

She glanced in her mirrors, watching for a flashing blue light.

A few minutes after the downpour began, she noticed Lem slow and turn off the main road up ahead. She breathed a heavy sigh of relief and followed, putting her foot down to draw closer to him. Once off the dual carriageway, he could easily lose himself, and her, in a maze of country lanes. The Find My Phone app was only so accurate, and one wrong turn might mean losing him forever.

Her mind went back to Matt. She remembered the bloody mess to his head, bone showing through, and she felt a flush of hatred for Lem. So casual in his assault of her friend. So uncaring. Matt had lured him there in the belief that he'd do nothing violent in front of so many people, but Lem had acted as if nothing bothered him.

And it didn't, Jodi realised. *It's just him and that last relic. He's almost done. And that's good.*

Maybe being so close to the end of his weird quest would make him careless.

She'd seen his face as he lifted the relic and brought it down on Matt's head. There was no glee there, no triumph, no expression at all. Not even a glimmer of satisfaction that his was almost a job well done. If he even experienced emotions he kept them buried, giving away nothing to the outside world and taking nothing in. He'd walked across the pub garden with that thing in his hand, dripping Matt's blood across dry grass and the scattered coats of those who'd fled before him, not giving a single fuck about the phones probably pointed his way and the fingers tapping out 999.

For Lem, nothing about the future mattered other than reaching wherever it was he'd been hiding those relics over the years.

"And you might be there too, Dad," Jodi said.

Verbalising that idea, solidifying it in voice and sound, made her realise how ridiculous it was. She'd seen Lem smash her father across the face with the relic. Seen her dad impaled on the tree after having been thrown through the windscreen, flames already crawling and clawing up his clothes. The idea of him having survived the assault, the accident, the blazing van and the subsequent fifteen years was crazy.

A crash of thunder exploded above her. The car was filled with a burst of lightning so bright that she slammed on the brakes. The car slewed to the right, and she turned the wheel that way to feed the skid. If anything had been coming from the opposite direction she'd have ended this day in a car wreck.

The Capri stalled. She started it again and crawled away, checking the phone. They were close to the coast. Lem was still ahead, perhaps a quarter of a mile now.

Where the hell is he going?

Another flash of lightning, followed a second later by a crack of thunder that rocked the car. She maintained control this time.

And where the fuck did this storm come from?

It had been a warm few days, but dry and light, not heavy and humid. There had been no talk of an impending storm. And in truth, this didn't feel like a typical summer storm at all. Heavy rain fell in a deluge that put the old car's wipers to the test. Stark lightning lit up her surroundings, freezing waving trees and thrashing bushes along the roadside in violent snapshots. She felt the thumping thunder through her feet on the pedals, up her spine, in her chest.

It felt like she had driven from one world into another.

LEM

She knows I'm bringing her home, Lem thought. Mary Webster is waking up.

He'd spent so many years on his journey, but in all that time he'd hardly considered the subject of his obsession at all. Despite the nightmare visions of deceased family members held in eternal torment, and the strange attraction drawing him towards the relics scattered across the country, their true nature was something that he'd not spent much time considering.

He thought perhaps that was the logical part of him having trouble accepting the truth. He had a task and he went with it, because it was his driving force, and his only purpose in life.

It was only during those time when he visited Crow Island – the relic he had retrieved heavier with blood, warmer with unnatural heat – that he thought about the reality of what he was doing. When he went down into that cavern. When he saw those relics coming together, like estranged siblings sharing sick bloody warmth for the first time in a long, long while.

It always took him days after such a visit to shake himself back into the real world. Sometimes he did so by sleeping or drinking, but mostly it was the long periods on a tattooist's chair that became something of a meditation for him. It was a different tattoo artist every time, but he always made clear that he was not paying them for their casual chatter. He sat or lay, absorbing the pain and allowing it to flood and clear his mind.

Now he was approaching his final visit, and he had no real idea what to expect. The idea of the murdered witch was stronger in his mind than ever before, and the relic on the passenger seat beside him seemed still to be drawing him with a dreadful blood-red gravity. He kept glancing at it as he drove, until he almost put the truck into a ditch when a gust of wind jarred the wheel against his hands.

He breathed deeply, gripping the wheel harder. "Let me concentrate, Mary," he said. "Or you'll lose yourself just as you're about to find yourself again."

The storm had come out of nowhere, but it did not surprise him. Crow Island was a wild place. It had always seemed just outside reality to him, and it wasn't just Wayne's impossibly blood-drenched corpse and the relics making him their parasitic home that fed that perception. The place was parted from the mainland in the same way that it held its own space in the world, connected by a fragile, thin thread of land that was not always visible. He thought maybe he was another link between Crow Island and the rest of the world.

He wondered what would become of that link, and him, once

he had achieved his purpose and finished his task. Would Mary Webster live again? Or would she find true eternity at last, brought back together to rest in endless peace? It was a luxury that had been denied her by his ancestors. He hoped that his efforts would put things right.

His own fate in this story was of little concern. He had lived a life, many times over. He could count at least five times that he should have died, five times that he had approached that strange light and been turned around and sent back by his tortured family dwelling in that purgatory. Maybe soon they would also be at peace, and he would finally be able to keep on walking.

Lem had rarely thought hard enough about his own existence to identify the pain he carried with him. His ego was small, his presence a narrow function rather than a wide, full rich life. But now he thought the idea of peace, and an ending, would actually be quite pleasant.

The storm raged outside, illuminating the inside of the truck's cab. Each blast of lightning seemed to land on the relic and bring it alight, and Lem finally reached for it and placed it carefully down into the passenger footwell.

Rain swamped the windows, thunder roared like the laughter of amused gods. He was close to the coast now, and he was preparing for the walk through the woods that would bring him to the cliffs and beach adjacent to Crow Island. He'd started to worry about getting across the causeway – even if it was low tide, the sea would be whipped into a frenzy by the storm.

But he didn't concern himself too much. There was something about this weather that brought comfort, not doubt.

"Mary's having a happy day," he said. The idea that a woman

dead these past two centuries could conjure a storm was ridiculous, but it also set his mind at rest. There was no point worrying about something until it happened, and when it did he would confront the problem then.

Fuck it, if he had to swim the couple of hundred feet to Crow Island through tumultuous seas, he would. He would not die. He *could* not die until his work was done. He truly believed that, and over the years several people had tried to prove him wrong.

Lightning flashed again, and the light remained with him for a while afterwards, a pure white light he had seen before in his dreams. He slowed the truck and blinked several times, but he still saw afterimages of his father, his mother and other family members where they stood eternally striving for the light as yet denied them. He blinked again and the shadows on his mind's eye began to fade, but not before he saw their pain. He had seen it before, but it never failed to make him ache with sadness.

"Soon," he said, and he wiped moisture from his eyes. Too much blinking. That was all.

Another flash caught his eye. This one left no afterimage, and he waited for the thunder. But this had been different. Level light, and low down. He looked in the rearview mirror and saw nothing, but he frowned and kept glancing back. He turned off the truck's lights and stopped in the middle of the winding country lane, the engine turning off, rain hammering its natural jazz on the bodywork. He waited for any vehicle following him to catch up. If it did, he'd go into reverse and ram it off the road, get out, kill whoever was inside.

Jodi, he thought, but that was crazy. He'd left her behind hours ago, fawning over her fallen friend. Even if she had been selfish enough to leave him bleeding into the grass in the pub garden, she would not have been able to follow him. He'd done his best to shake anyone on his tail, turning and stopping and doubling back several times until he was sure he was on his own.

"Imagining stuff," he said. His breath condensed on the windscreen. Above the passenger seat the window was also steamed, as if the relic had sighed.

He tried driving again without lights, but after almost dumping the truck into the hedge he flicked them on again, low beam. He was almost there. He'd arrived at Crow Island during the night only once before, and that time the weather had been cool and calm, his walk across to the island lit by a single flashlight. The closest he could park was half a mile from the coastal path and the scramble down to the beach, and he already knew he would not wait unless he absolutely had to. He had no idea of tide times, but as long as the causeway was visible, he would make his way across it.

He stopped again, lights off, looking in his rearview. No more lights from behind. He must have imagined it. Either that, or it had been lightning reflected from a sign back along the road. Yet still the feeling persisted that he was not alone here.

"Come on, Lem," he said. "Nothing to worry about. Everything is fine. Everything's going to plan." He was not a man prone to talking to himself, but here in the truck's cab, with the relic four feet from him and the unnatural storm stirring up hell outside, his own voice gave him comfort.

Lem was never afraid, but anticipation sang along his nerves and tingled up his spine. Everything was coming to an end.

JODI

When Lem's truck stopped moving Jodi turned off the Capri's headlights and crept forwards another two hundred metres. She'd steadily closed the gap when she saw the coast looming on the phone map. Now with him apparently having reached his destination, she didn't want to give herself away, but a sense of urgency bit in. If she lost him once he left the truck, finding him again would all be down to chance. It was more than three hours since they'd left Mariton, and the unseasonal storm meant that the night was truly dark.

She stopped the car in a field gateway, grabbed her phone and backpack, held on to the gun in her pocket, and got out. Rain soaked through her running kit in moments, and the raging wind buffeted her from all sides and ripped her breath away. She was glad it was a summer storm and so not too cold, but she also knew she had to get moving to keep warm. Sitting in the car for three hours hadn't helped. As she shrugged on the backpack, she wondered what might have changed in her life by the time she returned here to drive away.

Jodi edged in front of the car and looked along the lane ahead. She couldn't see much, but despite the heavy clouds she could just make out the shape of the stone walls on either side. Keen to move on, she took a moment to crouch in front of the car to empty her bladder. It had been screaming for the last hour, but she hadn't dared stop again.

Feeling lighter and better, she headed off. She kept her phone in her left hand and drew the gun in her right.

Lightning clashed and grounded far to her right, briefly illuminating a low line of hills. The thunder rolled a few seconds later, rattling her core. The storm had been raging for over an hour now, and it was like no summer storm she'd ever experienced. There was something frightening about it, and it wasn't the darkness, and it wasn't that Lem might be anywhere ahead of her. The storm sounded angry.

She started jogging along the lane, squinting, wiping rain from her eyes with the back of one hand. She hoped she still had Lem at a disadvantage. She'd been careful not to be seen following him, she had a gun and he didn't, and she hoped he would be focussed on his task. If he'd found BB's phone he'd have thrown it from the truck. She risked a glance at her phone, shielding the light with her body, and his signal was still static. She estimated about three hundred metres ahead, as the crow flies.

Jodi pocketed the phone and moved even faster, the thought that Lem had dumped BB's phone driving her on. Soon she saw a glint of metal up ahead, and she stopped and crouched down beside a stone wall. Breathing hard, she scanned around her. Darkness, driving rain, thrashing trees. Even if Lem was close, she'd never see him.

Swearing softly, she ran in a crouch towards Lem's truck. It was parked in a small, gravelled area that also marked the end of the narrow lane. It was the only vehicle there. She circled around to the driver's side, staying ten metres away, gun aimed at the side window. She couldn't see inside. The doors were shut, though, and if he was in there he wouldn't be able to see her through the water streaming across the glass.

Keep him safe and close if you can, Wildflower.

Her mother's words rang in her mind, louder and stronger that the pounding rain and reverberating thunder. She'd lived her adult life knowing that she'd failed her father. If he really was close by, rescuing him would not put things right. But it might give them both some peace.

"Fuck it," she whispered at the storm, and she edged towards the side of the truck. She reached the vehicle and crouched down, gun still pointed at the driver's door. Moving slowly, keeping as low as she could, Jodi took in a deep breath and switched on her phone torch. In one fluid movement she stood and pressed the phone to the window, touching the gun barrel to the glass beside it.

The truck's cab was empty. She leaned in close, just to make sure Lem wasn't crouched in the rear seats. Then she flicked the torch off and squatted down again, allowing her eyes a moment to re-adjust to the night.

She reached up and touched the bonnet, and even in the rain it was still warm. It can't have been more than ten minutes since the truck had stopped, but that was still a good head start. And she had no idea where he was heading.

Constantly panicked at the prospect of losing him, she shielded her phone as much as she could with her body and opened the map app. They were half a mile from the coast, maybe closer. There didn't appear to be any buildings nearby, only open land and forest, and the coast showed a couple of narrow beaches. There was also a small island just off one of the beaches. And wending from the car park towards the shore, a public footpath.

Jodi pocketed the phone and dashed past the truck towards a wall of undergrowth. She moved back and forth, searching for an opening that might indicate a footpath, gripping the gun, feeling Lem and her father getting further and further from her with every heartbeat. Shrubs and trees waved back and forth in front of her, dancing in delight at her frustration.

Lightning sheeted across the sky, pulsing and fading for at least three seconds. In that time, Jodi saw something on the ground to her right.

A series of water-filled depressions.

Thunder slammed at her, shaking her bones, and she pulled the phone again and kneeled down. Definitely boot prints in the soft ground, filled with water, heading towards...

And there, just before her, a narrow opening in the foliage that had been hidden by thrashing plants.

She pushed through, arms held up to ward off the branches, and started stalking ahead. She resisted the temptation to move too quickly, afraid that she'd collide with a tree or break an ankle, or even wander from the path and become lost. The route was heading towards the coast, and she wondered what might be there. Some old building? A cave?

Maybe something on the island.

She tucked the phone in her pocket and probed ahead with both hands, still gripping the gun in her right hand, pushing aside vegetation heavy with water, feeling her way through the darkness, and her mother's voice was with her again now.

You're a wildflower. You're there because the world wants you there, and you're strong enough to always just be yourself.

Was she really strong? Jodi wasn't sure. She'd bided her time to seek revenge on Lem for what had happened to her father, never considering violence, always knowing that disrupting his mad quest would hurt him more. Even so she'd ended up hurting other people, and losing the man she loved. That wasn't strength. It was selfishness.

She forged ahead, moving faster now, driven by confidence or rashness, or a combination of the two. She was soaked to the skin, tired, aching. Branches whipped at her face, ragged fingers seeking her eyes. Lightning continued to flash. Thunder rolled almost instantaneously, as if the storm had circled back to clash directly over her. It sought to slow her, crush her, drive her down into the mud, but she would not succumb. Not after so much had happened. Not so close to the end. She was unstoppable.

That was when she ran into something immovable.

The impact was huge, ringing through her head and critching her neck. She grunted, her legs flipped out from beneath her and she fell onto her back. The muddy wet ground softened the impact, but the breath was still knocked from her.

That'll be Lem, she thought, and she rolled to the right.

Something slapped into the mud where she'd just been lying. Someone grunted.

Jodi kicked out her right foot in that direction and it struck something softer, with more give.

Another grunt, and she saw the shadow stagger back and then fall to the ground.

For a moment she lay there dazed, waiting for sensation to return to her arms and legs. Her head rang like a bell echoing inside a hollow, forgotten cathedral.

The figure was standing again and Jodi thought, *If I dropped the gun and he found it, then he'll probably kill me right now.* The idea did not seem as frightening as it should have.

She felt nothing in her hands. Her arms were numb. Her senses juggled, roiled. She fisted her hand and a gunshot rang out.

The report brought her back.

Trying not to groan – not wishing to portray any weakness that Lem might fall upon – Jodi lifted her hand and pointed the gun at his shadow in the darkness. Seeing the faint object in her hand made it seem more solid, and the weight of metal gave her comfort.

"I'll shoot you the second you move, you fucking bastard," she said. Her voice felt weak but sounded strong in the night, despite the pouring rain and rumblings of thunder conspiring to steal it away.

"Do that and you'll never find your dad," Lem said.

"Where is he?"

"I haven't finished with him yet. Neither has the thing in there with him. The thing he feeds."

"Shut up," Jodi said. "I *will* shoot you."

"No, you won't."

She shifted the gun a fraction to the left and pulled the trigger.

She thought she saw the shadow shift a little in the brief flash, but the loud crack stole away any grunt or shout of pain.

"You won't kill your last chance," Lem said. If the bullet had caught him, his voice sounded no different.

"I'll look as long as I have to," Jodi said. She stood slowly, testing her footing. She was slightly dizzy from where he'd punched her in the head, but her feet planted strong in the mud, her gun hand stayed firm. "I'll search for any buildings close by. A hole in the ground. The caves along the coast."

Lem chuckled. To Jodi, it was louder than the thunder.

"Maybe the island," she said, and Jodi was sure she heard a reaction from Lem. Not a noise, but an absence of sound. A held breath.

So it is the island, she thought. But she could not be sure, and she didn't want to shoot Lem, maybe kill him, unless she absolutely had to. Alive, he could still lead her to wherever her father might be.

"You can't kill me," he said. "Shoot however much you like. You'll miss. Or it won't hurt me enough. You can't kill me."

Jodi frowned at the certainty in his voice, and with lightning arcing across the landscape, thunder shaking the ground, and rain attempting to drown them in unseasonal torrents, his words chilled her to the core.

Can I kill him even if I wanted to? she thought. *Those scars he has, all over his body... he should have been dead ten times over.*

In the end, Lem forced her hand. He came for her, strolling across the few metres separating them, and as he closed the distance another flash of lightning lit the trees and plants above and around them, a thousand reflections glimmering from wet leaves.

She saw his face. And his raised arm, holding the relic high above his right shoulder.

Darkness fell again.

Jodi ducked to the left and pulled the trigger.

In the same instant she felt a jarring, white-hot impact against the junction of her neck and right shoulder. Pain arced up into her head and down across her shoulder and arm, and the world pulled away from her. She pulled the trigger again, but the gun made no sound. She realised that she'd dropped it.

Feeling weightless, drifting, Jodi started to fall, and she put her head down and ran with it, feeling the world tip onto its side as her legs worked, trees scraping across her face, branches grasping at her arms and hands as they struggled to hold her fast, and the darkness of this unnatural stormy night was nothing compared to the pitch black that pulled her down.

LEM

Lem knew that he should go after her and finish her off. He took two steps and then pain kicked in, a blazing bloom in his left hip that sent him to his knees. He grunted as he hit the ground, then pressed his hand to the pain and brought it to his face. It was black with blood. The rain washed it away. His hip felt hot and cold.

He looked around, and already he'd lost track of where Jodi had gone. Left, back along the trail towards the car park? Ahead, through the wall of undergrowth and into the forest? If it was daylight he might have been able to go after her. He had walked this way in good weather and foul, in light and dark, but never when the heavens were raging like this, and the ground seemed to absorb and echo their fury.

Mary Webster is urging me on, he thought, and a crack of lightning was his reply. It struck somewhere close by, so close that the shockwave punched the bullet wound in his side, his hair stood on end, and he smelled the harsh tang of burning air.

"I'm coming," he said. He pushed up slowly, experimenting with putting weight down through his hip. He didn't know how badly she'd winged him, but it could *not* be bad. It can't have taken out his hip bone, or shattered his femur, or nicked his artery. That just was not possible.

The pain roared in, finding home in his bones, knotting his muscles, singing along his nerves and exploding in his brain. He winced and stood there for a few seconds with his hand still pressed to the wound.

Walking was going to hurt like hell. But everything he did hurt. His life was a place of pain, and he had always confronted it head-on. Now would be no different.

Lem looked around for a moment, then took his first steps and kicked through the plants and mud, looking for the gun. He'd seen Jodi drop it, but now it was gone. If she'd picked it up he would have seen her... or maybe not.

Maybe she'd picked it up and was watching him even now. Hiding in the dark, observing from the shadows, waiting for him to move so that she could follow.

"You can't kill me," Lem said. The shadows did not respond.

He started walking. He carried the pain well. His hip was working, his leg did not fold and spill him to the ground. The damage was superficial. He was still bleeding, but the rain washed that away as if to make him forget.

In his right hand, the relic was warm and soft, as if out of sight in the storm it had changed into something else. He squeezed and felt give in the wood. It grew even warmer, as if it was enjoying his touch.

He pushed through undergrowth hanging over the path and heavy with water, keeping the relic low against his leg. His other leg obeyed, despite the damage done to it, despite the pain. Lem had experienced worse.

He blinked water from his eyes and saw his family, shadows within shadows because he was not actually there with them, not yet. If he had been they would have turned him back once more.

But they were watching, for sure. He felt his mother's sad, gentle gaze on the back of his neck, her face deformed by the wall that had crushed the wretched life from her. He sensed his father close by, scowling through scars as Lem limped forwards, always forwards. Perhaps soon his father might smile.

That made Lem wonder once more whether he would die this night. The thought was not unpleasant.

The storm strengthened even more, lightning sheeting in the sky above the ocean ahead of him, occasional strikes hammering down closer by. Thunder rumbled and rolled back and forth, blurring his vision and hurting the bullet wound in his hip each time it roared. The ground was soaked, and so dry from the recent hot weather that water flowed across its surface as well as soaking in. He kicked through mud almost up to his ankles.

Everything was movement and noise. Water ran down his back and diluted the blood seeping from his wound. He smelled summer rain and mud and lightning scorching the air. He wondered where Jodi was. He didn't think she could ever find the sinkhole and the small cavern hollowed out of its wall, but still he moved faster, just in case. He could not risk anything going wrong now.

Soon he reached the edge of the wooded area and emerged onto the coastal path above the crescent beach, and he took a moment to absorb the view. Sheet lightning danced across the ocean, marking the nebulous horizon between sea and sky. Closer, Crow Island loomed as a huge shadow away from the beach. Waves broke around its bulk and roared onto the beach beneath the cliffs, filling the air with the deafening grind of a billion pebbles ebbing and flowing with each impact. The sky, the water and the land were alight with violence.

He could just make out the causeway that led out to the island from the waves smashing across it, foaming white as they came apart over the rocks.

Lem would have to walk out across that natural bridge between beach and island. He felt a tickle of fear at the prospect. *Of course this last time wouldn't be easy.* He tucked the relic into his trousers, feeling it warm and comfortable against his uninjured leg, and started along the path.

He remembered where the scrambling descent to the beach began, but even so he approached it carefully, not wanting to miss it in the storm. Once there he paused and looked around, turning in a slow circle as he scanned back and forth along the coast path for Jodi. There was no sign. He tried to see back into the woods that ended close to the coast, but they were dark, wild trees dancing in the wind and waving him on.

Thriving on pain from his injury, Lem started his final descent towards the beach, drawn onwards by a sense of purpose that could never entertain failure.

JODI

Something was broken in Jodi. Whenever she moved her head or lifted her right arm the pain screeched in, exquisite and hot. She thought it was her collarbone. It felt like her whole right side was on fire, from her face down her neck and shoulder, and into her chest. Someone had filled her with acid. Someone else had scorched her with invisible flame.

All she could do was fight the pain, try to shut it out of her mind, because she knew that the damage was already done. She crouched and ran, tripped, and crawled through the agony washing over her, and eventually she burst out into the open and stumbled over a fallen wire fence. She grunted as she hit the ground, then rolled down a small slope and splashed into a mucky puddle. On her back, she stared up at the sky as another burst of lightning seared the scene onto her mind. Rain lanced down around her like a million silvery spears.

She rolled onto her left side and sat up, and realised that she was very close to a cliff edge. If she'd rolled one more time she might have gone over. *Always so close to death*, she thought, and she remembered BB's quizzical smile when he realised a simple accident had wounded him so badly that he was bleeding out.

Jodi stood and looked along the coast path in both directions. Out here in the open she could see more, even though the moon and starlight was mostly blocked by storm clouds. She was alone. She leaned over and looked down towards the ocean, where the dark mass of an island hunkered away from the beach, violent waters breaking onto its rocky shores. She scanned the beach, but could not make out any detail.

She frowned. What was that? Waves broke past the island and foamed white across a long, narrow rocky structure between mainland and island. Another flash of lightning imprinted the image on her mind of the windswept and foam-covered beach, the stark island shadowed against the sea, and the causeway linking the two.

And at the beach end of the causeway, a lone figure that had to be Lem.

Ignoring the pain, Jodi hurried along the path above the beach. There must have been an easy way down, but perhaps the dark hid it from her. She paused at every point where the undergrowth might open up into a steep scramble down the cliff, moving on when it looked unsafe, and eventually she found what looked like the beginning of a descending route. She leaned out and looked down again, but this time the lightning did not illuminate the scene for her.

She sat and probed forwards with her feet, finding a footing before easing her weight downward. She gripped onto plants and rocks, struggling to ignore the agony in her shoulder that threatened to consume her. She wanted to move fast, but she also had to hold on, testing each step before committing. Water flowed down the cliff face around her, a constant deluge of mud washing past her hands and feet and behind. Her limbs began to shake where they were tensed against the ground, and she turned around so that she was facing the cliff and looking down between her feet. She moved faster that way.

She slipped and cried out, gripping on with her good left hand and wedging her right hand behind a thick plant stem. Her feet kicked in open air, then found footholds again. The route was steep but not sheer, and she started moving again with slow, methodical steps. Foot, hand, foot, hand, moving down, down, and glancing between her feet again she could see that the beach was close.

Jodi leaned into the cliff and took a deep breath. It was worth the pause to compose herself. *Don't slip now, Wildflower,* she imagined her mother saying. *You've come so far.*

"I'm coming, Dad," she said. In this violent stormy darkness, the image of him still being kept alive somewhere by Lem seemed very real. "I'll be with you again soon."

She scrambled down the final descent to the beach, then turned and tripped over a rock. She landed on her face, the wind knocked from her. A chipped tooth was grit on her tongue. Blood filled her mouth. She spat it out.

Jodi stood and hurried across the pebble beach, heading for where the causeway out to the island began. She could not make out any detail, and assumed that Lem was already making his way across. She had to catch up with him. She had to see where he was going, and only then could she risk being seen.

She picked up several large pebbles and shoved them in her leggings pockets, taking up the space where the relic had been until Matt snatched it away from her.

Jodi shook her head, groaning at the pain it brought. She was dizzy, and the ground seemed as fluid and flexing as the sea, juggling her senses. She bent with her hands on her knees, then stood again and looked out towards the island.

Lightning flashed somewhere inland. She saw Lem's shadow frozen out along the causeway, breaking waves static around him, and the island was a vast shadow beyond.

As her eyes adjusted to the darkness again and thunder shook the world, she started out along the pebbles that quickly became larger rocks, piled together to form a path out to the island. She couldn't tell if it was a natural umbilical from island to land, or if these rocks had been placed here sometime in the distant past. Either way the sea conspired to spill her from them. She slipped on seaweed and went down, cutting her hands and knees on sharp limpets. Standing again, the sea roared as a wave smashed along the causeway, breaking closer to the island and then sweeping along the surface. She tensed, holding herself fast as the water smashed into her, jarring her backwards.

On her hands and knees, Jodi could no longer make out Lem against the island's mass. She stood and hurried on, crouching down when waves hit, moving forwards between the swells. The causeway was uneven, and the next wave threw her onto her back. She shifted onto her knees and hands again, feeling her way forwards while trying to keep her weight off her injured right shoulder. Her hands passed through a spread of thick seaweed, and as a larger wave reached across the rocks she crouched down and held on tight. The harsh tang of seawater made her gag and stung her eyes.

She crawled on, and soon the rock beneath her grew wider, protected from the sea by the mass of the island. She stood again, legs shaking.

How the fuck didn't I just drown? If she'd been swept into the sea, she would have. Even if her shoulder wasn't broken there was no way she'd be able to swim to safety in that. Jodi was a good swimmer, but the storm, the waves and the rocks would have colluded to batter her to death.

She hurried on until she was clambering over a pile of larger boulders, and then her feet crunched down into a spread of thick, gritty sand. She was on the island.

After looking around to make sure she was on her own, Jodi took off her running pack and took out her knife. She almost discarded the pack, but slipped it back on and secured the front clip.

Holding the knife in her left hand, she started up a rocky slope towards the top of the island.

Another flash of lightning lit the landscape around her. She looked quickly for Lem and saw nothing.

Moving forwards again she tried to stay quiet, climbing the slope, holding her left arm out for balance and keeping her right pressed across her stomach. As she approached what she thought might be the top of the small island a flash of lightning froze the scene again, and she scanned quickly left to right.

She saw what she thought was Lem, a bedraggled figure caught half-stagger maybe fifty metres ahead of her. She continued on, crouched down now in case he was looking back. When the next burst of lightning came she wanted to be a rock, a shadow, a fold in the island.

If he knew she was following he might just turn and face her. She *had* to see where he was going. She *had* to know.

Only then would come the fight.

The elements battered her, the wind even harsher than it had been across the clifftop, the rain lashing in at an angle and stinging her exposed skin. Water spray stung her eyes and foam from breaking waves flitted across her vision like shattered ghosts. She hurried on and found herself edging downwards again, towards the seaward side of the island.

A break in the clouds allowed weak moonlight through, barely touching the stormy chaos. In that light she saw Lem.

He was standing close to what appeared to be a low wall, bending down and feeling around by his feet with his right hand. He held on to the wall as he did so, and his left foot was held up from the ground.

I winged him! Jodi hefted the knife in her left hand, wincing against the pain as she tugged a fist-sized pebble from her pocket with her right. She held it down by her side, the added weight aggravating her broken shoulder. *It's only pain*, she thought. She had to fight it, ignore it. She would need both hands to fight Lem.

And the fight was now. He had reached his destination. He was looking at something on the ground, perhaps a hatch or a tunnel, or a route into a cave.

Jodi closed her eyes and took in a deep breath, and a harsh truth hit home. She'd been avoiding it since leaving Mariton, turning her gaze from the idea because it was not comfortable. It was not something she wanted to deal with.

But now she had to.

If she wanted to find out what had happened to her father, she would have to fight Lem. And to defeat him in a fight, she had to kill him.

As she stood and ran, her dead mother's voice whispered in disappointment.

Oh, Wildflower.

LEM

I can sense her down there, Lem thought. *She's eager for the last relic warm in my belt, growing warmer, warmer. She wants to be made whole again. This is where I've been heading all my life. This is the end.*

"I'm coming," he said. The storm stole his words, keeping them close. "I'll be there soon." He sat on the wet ground and felt around, fingers spiked by cruel thorns, until his hand scraped across rock beneath the brambles and he felt open space.

There it is.

He turned slightly to position himself beside the bramble-covered sinkhole. Mary called him, her voice quiet and old but insistent. She whistled him closer. Her hiss was a compulsion. And he could smell Wayne, just a stale hint on the warm sickly breath coming up out of the hole like a wretched exhalation.

"I'm coming," he said. He started to lower himself, and grunted as his left hip twisted.

As he flinched at the pain he saw the figure coming at him. He scrambled, trying to make his feet, and the shadow leaped.

Lem lifted his left arm, hand fisted, and felt it connect with Jodi's shoulder. She let out a loud cry of pain and her hand swung into his face. He felt something slice along his chin and jaw, opening his skin, scouring against bone. He punched again, unable to pivot and bring his right fist around, trying to claw his fingers into her hair.

Jodi was on her knees now, right hand held across her chest, jabbing forwards with whatever she held in her left hand.

Lem knocked it aside and felt the kiss of something sharp across his palm. He welcomed the pain. It was bright and warm and it focussed his perception, lightened the darkness.

"Hurt you, did I?" Lem asked, and he rolled on to his left side, groaning loud at the agony in his hip and then turning his groan into a loud laugh as he kicked at her right shoulder.

Jodi twisted to one side and grabbed at his foot, but missed. She gained her feet and stepped to the side, launching a kick into Lem's hip. It connected hard and he couldn't hold in the cry of pain.

"Hurt you, did I?" she shouted. "Hurt you?!" She kicked again but he was ready this time, grabbing her foot with both hands and twisting, hard. If she hadn't turned with the twist he might have broken her ankle.

Jodi fell onto her front, rolled, stood again and came for Lem.

He was back on his feet now, advancing on her. He felt blood flowing from his lower face, diluted by the rain. He glanced at his hand and saw blood there, too. More fresh injuries, more tattoos. His body would soon be one big work of art.

He tugged the relic from his belt and wielded it, feeling its warmth and eagerness.

"You can't win," he said. "You were a fool to follow me. If you think you can—"

She came at him low and fast, feinting towards his wounded side. He half-turned to protect himself and brought the relic around, but it only glanced from her back as she slammed her left hand against his right thigh. He felt the impact and knew that he'd been stabbed, but there was no pain yet, just a cool flush through his muscles. He raised the relic to bring it down on her head.

Jodi pushed. Twisting the thing in his leg, griding its point against bone. Shoving him off balance.

She swung her right hand and only at the last moment did he see the rock clasped in her fist. It slammed against his wounded hip and he shouted, smashing the relic down onto her back.

She continued pushing and Lem staggered back, doing his best to veer away from the covered sinkhole. If he fell down there he'd be broken, smashed and left at the sea's mercy. He tried to stand firm but she hit his hip again, and as his legs crumpled he struck the wall.

Jodi kept pushing.

Lem reached back with one hand and grasped open air.

At the last second he knew that he should drop the relic and grab on to her, use her weight to hold him back, stop him from falling.

But he could not release the relic. His hand was tight around its warm solidity, and even though he willed his fingers to open they stayed gripped, grasped, as if his skin was grafted onto the old wooden surface and the witch's old bone contained within.

He tilted back over the wall, and Jodi's roar of triumph accompanied him as he fell towards the sea.

JODI

He's gone.

Jodi leaned against the low wall and peered over the top. The drop on the other side was almost sheer, with just a few shadowy rocks protruding from the cliff wall. It was fifteen metres, maybe even more.

He's gone.

The sea smashed and boiled against the rocks, drawing out, crashing in again, back and forth in a violent onslaught, and she thought for a second or two she caught a glimpse of Lem's body caught in the sea's jaws. He was facedown and his limbs were splayed, rising and falling between one wave and the next.

He's fucking gone!

She felt nothing. No regret at having killed someone. No sense of relief. A few memories of Lem flashed through her mind, her subconscious drawing a line. The first time she'd met him, sitting on a bench beside her father on that long, hot afternoon in the Longship's garden, when she'd emerged from the pub with drinks for her and her dad. Later, when her father was becoming more involved with a man whom Jodi just knew was trouble, but whom her father seemed to hold in some high regard. Sitting in the front of the van after they'd stolen a relic, listening as her dad talked, and then Lem swinging the blocky wooden object into his face.

Standing in the road, on fire.

Now he was gone, a man who had haunted her life for a decade and a half without ever being a part of it.

She wondered if his death would haunt her also, and she thought not.

Jodi pushed away from the wall and stood, swaying when a flush of dizziness turned the world this way and that. The storm was lessening a little, clouds parting here and there to reveal patches of starry sky. The rain still fell, but when lightning flashed somewhere far behind her it took a long time for the distant thunder to roll in. The sea still boiled, and she could hear a strange intermittent hooting sound as waves smashed against the island.

She went to where Lem had been rooting around on the ground and took out her phone, hoping it hadn't been damaged in the brief bout of violence. Its screen opened and she clicked on the torch.

Dizziness hit her again and she went to her knees. Pain washed through her and she tried to ward it off, but her shoulder felt all wrong, bone grinding against bone.

A little while longer, she thought. She took deep breaths and fought down nausea. She realised that she hadn't eaten all day. The last time had been a brief breakfast with BB before they'd gone on their dawn run along the river towards Morgan Manor. She'd been too intent on driving, too focussed on following Lem, to eat anything she'd stolen from the petrol station. Her stomach rumbled. She felt weak.

Just a little while longer.

BB came to her again, and all she could remember was his smile, his voice, his laughter giving theme to a warm summer evening. She had no idea what he would say to her now, or what he'd think of what she was doing. The Jodi of today was someone he would never know.

"I'm sorry, baby," she said. His absence squeezed her heart.

Nursing the phone gently in her right hand, she aimed it at the undergrowth and felt around with her left. Soon she found the hollow beneath the bushes, and that strange hooting sound began to make more sense. It was some kind of sinkhole leading down to the ocean, perhaps caused by millennia of erosion.

She shoved the bushes aside as well as she could, and then leaned in and shone the phone light inside. The walls were uneven, the hole narrow, and she could just see the boiling white of breaking waves far below.

What the hell? Maybe he'd known that she would follow and he'd been rooting around here to lead her off the scent. A flutter of panic settled in her gut.

But Jodi could not give in. Not now, not after—

I killed a man.

Even that thought felt flat and unimportant. Lem had hardly been a man. He'd been a monster in a man's clothing.

She eased herself into the hole, using both legs and her good left hand. It was narrow enough for her to prop her back against one side, legs against the other, and once she'd pushed past the bushes and been scratched and cut in the process, she started down.

She soon came to a deep, dark opening in the wall. Even the phone light could not penetrate far. It was as if the darkness held weight.

"Dad?" Jodi asked. She breathed in deeply and smelled only age and must, and the warm, rank tang of decay from the ocean. Waves crashed below, echoing up through the sinkhole. "Dad!" Her voice did not echo.

She crawled into the opening, pulling herself with her left arm, pushing with her feet, and soon the moving light hinted at a larger chamber beyond. Her breath was harsh, light. Her heart hammered fast.

No way he's here, she thought, crawling forwards. *There's just no way, don't be stupid, just get in there and see what Lem's been doing and then you can—*

The short tunnel opened up into a wider hollow, maybe the size and shape of her childhood bedroom. She found her feet and stood, her head just brushing the ceiling. It smelled in here, something dry, old. It reminded her of the basement in Morgan Manor.

Jodi took three steps to the centre of the space and swept her phone light around in a slow circle.

And then she saw her father.

LEM

Treading water as well as he could, kicking with both injured legs, keeping hold of the relic as though his hand were welded to it, Lem tried to judge where the opening at the bottom of the sinkhole fed out into the sea.

He knew that he was badly hurt. After toppling over the wall his left foot had struck the cliff face, flipping him out into the open air. That shattering pressure on his already wounded leg had probably saved him from scraping and sliding down the exposed rock wall. But striking the sea so close to the cliff base had put him at the mercy of the waves, and he'd been battered into the rocks three times, four, maybe more. Each impact broke a different part of him, until his exhaustion pulled him down.

Beneath the waves, he had swum for his life.

Now blood filled his mouth, everything hurt, and Lem wondered if he was finally dying.

There was no light, though. No stern looks from his dead family. Only the waves lifting and dropping him and breaking over his head, the looming shadowy bulk of Crow Island trying to draw him in again to scrape and tear and dash him to pieces against its sharp uncaring shore…

And Jodi.

He had to get back up to the place where he was bringing Mary Webster back together. Making her whole. Easing her curse. Because Jodi had seen him starting to descend, and she had come for her father.

Lem could not let her reach him.

He kicked for the rocks, shouting out as pain rocked his whole body. He stroked with both arms, and each time his hand splashed down holding the relic it seemed to draw him on, hauling him closer to those others he had found and blooded and brought here over the years.

The sounds of crashing waves was deafening, even when they drove him down beneath the surface. He kicked and swam for the point in the cliff where they did not break white, hoping that was where the opening into the sinkhole lay. And as he kicked and floated and spluttered closer, weakening with every stroke, swallowing water and gagging and puking it back up, he heard the echoing impact of the sea surging into the hollow at the base of the sinkhole. He aimed for that place, leading with his hand holding the relic.

The sea drew him in.

Lem braced himself. He knew this was going to hurt, but he also knew that he could not tread water for much longer. He was weakening. His throat and eyes and nose burned from the saltwater, both legs were blocks of pain, but the relic sought to keep him afloat. A wave scooped him up and dragged him towards Crow Island's rugged shore, and he could only let himself be carried.

He struck a submerged rock and span around, facing out to sea as another wave broke over his head. Dragged under, blinded, Lem felt a sudden acceleration as he was drawn through a narrow gap. This time when he hit rocks he attempted to hold on, slipping on slick seaweed, skinning his knees as he tried to scrabble up and away from the water.

Waves boomed through this hollow space, and he knew he was at the base of the sinkhole. It was almost pitch black, and he could only work by feel as he tried to climb from the water.

Another wave smashed in, lifting him and depositing him on a slick ledge. He slammed the relic against the wall and it jammed in a crack, his cold hand still gripped around its wooden exterior.

Climb, he thought. *Climb or you die, however hard to kill you think you are, however much you think those who've died before you keep pushing you back.*

Lem climbed. Out of the freezing water, his wounds sang in again – the bullet in his left hip; the stab wound in his right thigh; his split cheek and chin, open to the bone. And there were cuts and bruises, scrapes and torn muscles from where the sea had welcomed him in and spat him back out. He climbed in the darkness, ignoring the pain because he was a man of many wounds, and these too would heal into rugged scars, and he would cover them with tattoos that continued to tell his story.

A crow perhaps, to signify the island.

A broken tree, formed together once again.

Soon the waters were below him, though their booming, hooting impacts still filled the darkness and splashed him with spray. He pulled himself higher, fighting the weakness in his arms and legs as they shook and shivered. He climbed, and climbed, and wondered if he was dead and would be climbing forever when he smelled a familiar musty scent.

I'm here, he thought. *I'm here.*

He listened for any sounds that might indicate that Jodi was also in the cavern. He could see no lights. He heaved himself into the short, narrow tunnel and just lay there for a while, breathing hard and allowing his shaking body to slump down. Muscles cramped and knotted. He smelled blood. Groaning, he started edging forwards, knowing that there would be no rest until this was over.

If she was in there, if she heard him coming, she would be ready. But that did not faze Lem. His path was set, his purpose unchangeable.

As he felt the space open up before him, he frowned.

Something was different. Everything was wrong.

The relic in his left hand suddenly felt light and dead, instead of heavy and warm with rich bloody life.

"I'm here," he said. "I'm here with the last of you."

His words were muffled and without echoes. The darkness swallowed them whole.

He heard nothing, sensed no movement or paused breaths. Either Jodi had not found her way down here, or—

Or she had been and gone.

Lem felt panic tickle his senses, settling them alight.

He rolled into the chamber and went left, hand spidering back and forth across the floor searching for the small flashlight he kept tucked away. He found it and flicked it on.

Even though the batteries were low, the weak light hurt his eyes. He blinked several times, then stood and aimed it into the far corner.

He let go of the relic. It dropped to the ground with a dull *crack!*

"No," Lem whispered. "No. No."

What remained of Wayne was tied to the wall in the corner of the cavern, as he always had been. But he was shrivelled and dry now, not wet and heavy with blood. An echo of what he once was, staring at Lem from hollow sockets as if he had been dead for many, many years.

From within him and without, the relics of Mary Webster were gone.

"Nooooo!" Lem shouted, and this time his voice was not muffled. It filled the chamber, filled the whole world, echoing back and forth so that a thousand voices left him and returned again, screaming from every desperate hour and day and year he had spent finding the remnants of the old witch to bring her back together. Now she was gone once more, because Jodi had come and stolen the relics away.

Lem felt a cool tingle on the back of his neck, like stick fingers running their chipped nails across his wretched flesh.

He turned and crawled, pain forgotten. All he had was fury and rage. It made his heart sprint, his blood pump and flow, greasing his way back through the short tunnel. His hands became slick with it, his knees and elbows open and raw. It stole his caution. He reached across the sinkhole and slipped, grabbed on, then plummeted, bouncing and twisting from the uneven walls. He felt and heard bones breaking, skin being torn, flesh ripped as he smashed into the rocks below, sinking into the waves, and true darkness closed around him one more time.

Screaming and crying inside, the threat of defeat scorching through his veins and venting through countless wounds, he prepared for his dead family to deny him peace and send him back one more time.

Lem's grandfather is there, smartly dressed as ever, hobbled by the lifetime of pain he has given out and been subjected to in return. Beside him is Lem's mother, crouched low as waves of agony wash over her, deforming her head again and again. Further away is his Aunt May, pressing her hands to her face and crying blood.

Beyond them all is his father, standing upright and proud. A hard man who will not look upon his failure of a son.

But this time something is different; they all have their backs turned on Lem, and they're moving away. Walking, maybe. Or perhaps it's simply that the distance between them is growing, stretching out so that he might never touch them or be with them for real.

Wait, Lem tries to say, *I've done my best, and I can go back and do it all again*. But his open mouth is flooded and full, and the words will not come.

He notices that the blazing sunset – that promise of peace and comfort that he and his family have always been denied – is no longer there. There's no landscape, no discernible terrain at all. Just the vague memory of his dead relatives, and they have nothing to say now that his failure is so obvious. As they move away from him they start to fade until they are no longer there at all.

It's as if they never were.

Lem tries to call after them again, but everything is growing dark.

I tried, he thinks. As the dead people he used to know disappear forever, and his vision fades to black, he realises that everything he has done, all his efforts, have been stolen away. His family are long-dead, long-gone. A deep lonely darkness is all that awaits him.

And as his thoughts fade to nothing, it's a darkness that he welcomes.

JODI

The skull was the worst.

The other relics were mostly thin, straight, sometimes gnarly, the longest the length of Jodi's thigh. Some wooden objects were carved with designs of varying intricacy and quality, others were scarred and knotted from whatever they had been through since their—

Growth?

—creation. Their broken ends all looked similar. Wood around the outside, something different within. The wood might be cracked. The yellowed thing inside, fractured and splintered. Sometimes worn smooth.

Jodi did everything she could to believe they were not the remnants of bones, but the skull told her otherwise. It was also subsumed within a large knot of wood, almost completely buried save for a sharp, curved section that protruded at one edge. If it weren't for the three yellowed teeth embedded in that portion of jaw, she might have believed it to be just another piece of old preserved oak.

Her backpack wasn't big enough for all of them, so the skull-shaped relic and a few others sat on the passenger seat as she drove the Capri towards the dawn.

Every time she blinked she saw the remains of her dead father with those relics surrounding him, some piled at his feet, others tied into his open ribs with frayed string or fixed against his exposed thigh bones as if to become part of him. Lem had returned there again and again, believing that withered, mummified body might give those strange objects some kind of sustenance. It was this blind belief that disturbed Jodi the most.

She'd known the body was her father, even though there was very little left but dirty yellowed bones, swathes of leathery skin and a few scraps of old clothing. Mostly it was the hair. Much of it had fallen away from the dried scalp clasped close to his skull, but the ponytail was still there, and she recognised the leather bangle that secured it in a tangled knot. It had once been hers, and she'd given it to him when she was fifteen years old.

"Nice bangle, Wildflower," he'd said. He'd hardly ever used her mother's name for her, but sometimes when the mood was low and the lighting lower, and he was in one of his funks, he'd breathe it as if to bring his wife back. Jodi had never particularly liked her dad using the name. It was something precious, one of the few things she really remembered about her mum. But right then, she didn't mind.

She'd handed him the bangle, of course. He'd worn it ever since, of course.

Now he would wear it forever.

Jodi had left her dad where he was. The idea of moving him after so long felt so strange, and with Lem gone into the sea, she'd made sure he would be left in peace at last. She'd wondered whether she should say something, but in the end she'd waited with him in silence, just for a while. There was nothing she hadn't said already, while she lay awake in the dark unable to sleep after nightmares about that day.

Stepping in close, she'd been able to see the multiple fractures across his face from where Lem had smashed him with the relic – the smashed eye sockets, ruptured nasal bones, cracks radiating around the skull. She hoped he had not still been clinging on to meagre life when Lem had tied him up in that wretched fucking hole. But she would never know.

She disposed of the skull first. She tried smashing it up to begin with, but it didn't break, and she hated the feel of it in her hands. And she'd already decided that scattering these wretched relics was more appropriate, more poetic.

And doing so gave her time to think.

The skull went into a small lake a couple of miles inland from the coast. The sun was up by then, and it cast a beautiful haze through the post-storm mist hanging above the water. A small splash, and Jodi stood and watched the ripples reach every shore. It sank, and she was glad. She stayed there until the ripples had died away and the lake was still once more.

A long relic – forearm or thigh bone, perhaps – went into the excavated foundations of a farm building. She made sure there was no one on the site, then lobbed it over a fence into a trench. There were excavators and concrete mixers standing ready. She did not wait to see them working.

A pond in a small woodland. A marina on a local canal. A river, weighed down in a plastic bag from the car's boot with the big pebbles she still carried in her pockets. An old well in the ruins of a country home, its cover rotted and fallen away. She drove haphazardly, never in a straight line, sometimes with a mile between relics, sometimes twenty. And she did not remember where she left them. Once gone, she would not be able to bring these things back.

She never once felt safe with the things in the backpack on the seat beside her. Heart fluttering in her chest, fear scraping at the inside of her skull, she drove at random, and was always relieved when she threw or buried or dropped another one of the horrible objects. She was lifting a weight from her own shoulders, the good one and the broken.

The last relic went into the river close to Mariton. In her tired, befuddled state she couldn't quite make out whether it was upriver or downriver from where they'd left her dear beloved BB.

After making sure there were no scraps of anything left in the backpack, she got back in the old Capri and waited for the relief, or the tears, or the grief. None came. Only emptiness.

She abandoned the car in an old dead-end lane a couple of miles outside town, a place she knew was used by lovers in the evening and dog walkers in the morning. Then she went for a stroll. She found a fallen tree away from any footpath and sat against it, head resting back on the rough bark. She closed her eyes but could not sleep. She opened them, but could not cry.

AT LAST

OCTOBER 2024

SETTING SUN

SAY SOMETHING

MATT

At last, there she was.

"Took you long enough," Matt said.

Jodi jumped in surprise and turned to face him. She was trying to smile. He saw in that moment that she was changed. The air of mystery about her was gone, and in its place was a deep sadness that seemed to subdue the changing early autumn colours around them.

Still the river flowed, fuller than it had been the last time they were here together and just as indifferent.

"How did you know I'd come here?" Jodi said.

"I've been waiting."

"Every day?"

"Since I got out of hospital." He was sitting on a slope among a spread of wild undergrowth. Not quite hiding, but keeping himself out of the sun. He nodded over his shoulder. "Got a little tent back there."

"You've been sleeping out here?"

"Not at night." He didn't elaborate. He didn't have to explain himself to Jodi. He was doing his own thing now.

"Oh, Matt," she said, and she started towards him.

Matt stood and held his hand out. *Keep back*. He wasn't afraid of her – not *really* – but he didn't want to be close. Events had changed him. Being smashed over the head and almost murdered had changed him, too. After coming around, his stay in hospital, and following his release he'd been rebuilding himself again. It was like a slow-motion awakening from a deep sleep, and he was gathering the scattered parts of himself back in, rediscovering what it was like to be Matt Shorey.

He was quite OK with what he was finding. He didn't need Jodi's contact or her pitying touch to muddy the waters.

"You've come for that," he said, nodding at the rusting dredging barge.

She looked that way, then back at him. "I waited till things had cooled down a bit. But yes, I've come for—"

"I got rid of it," Matt said. "All of it. There was nothing in there I wanted. Nothing of use. And all of it was stained with BB's blood."

Jodi went to say something, paused, smiled. "Probably for the best." She nodded to the overgrown bank behind him. "Want to sit and chill, talk about—?"

"No. Stay away from me." He remained standing, right hand close to his pocket where he had a folding knife. It only had a short blade, but it was enough to make him feel just a little bit safer. Danger haunted him now, and sometimes his heart raced and the world seemed to be closing in ready to crush him. He was working on that. Jodi being here wouldn't help.

Jodi turned her back to him and looked at the river and dredger. He didn't think she was a threat to him, but he couldn't be certain. He would never be sure about her again. She probably believed that he'd dumped the loot, but she might also be desperate and demand he took her to where he'd ditched it.

Matt wanted this over with, now and forever. That was why that first day out of the hospital, still delicate and weak from his injuries, he'd gone inside the rusted cabin, retrieved the hidden rucksack and then emptied it into the river a mile downstream. He'd opened it up and thrown the contents as far as he could across a wider part of the river. He didn't hesitate. Getting rid of the loot from the old house had felt like shedding part of that terrible time, an early funeral for BB. They still hadn't released his body. It was something that happened in murder cases, he'd been told. He felt in a constant state of limbo with BB's funeral hanging over him, and disposing of the stolen goods had felt like taking action.

He'd set up the little tent where he sometimes took a midday nap, and he always brought lunch, a flask and a book. He'd come to know this part of the river and its daily rhythms very well. A kingfisher flitted by sometimes, and once or twice he'd seen it fishing. A heron often stood in the water close to the opposite bank. He would sit as still as the bird until it caught its lunch and flew off. A few times people had walked past. He'd heard their approach and retreated into the undergrowth, watching them pass him by, his heart beating faster even though he knew that Lem was dead. But it didn't happen that often. This place was off the beaten track.

"I did the same with the relics," she said. "Threw them all away."

"I don't care."

Jodi turned around again, but didn't come any closer. "So are you OK?"

"OK?" he asked in disbelief. He left the word hanging. As if he could ever be OK again. After a moment he chuckled, changed the subject. "You look like a criminal trying not to get caught."

"Well, I am." Jodi's hair was cut short and dyed blonde, and she wore a baseball cap and dark glasses. "So you're not being watched?"

"What, you're worried I'm important enough to be under full-time surveillance? Afraid I'll shout out, 'Here, she's over here, come and arrest her'?" He realised she was nervous, and it had nothing to do with the idea of being arrested. She was afraid of him. "You came for the loot."

"Yeah." She shrugged. "I've got some cash, and a place to stay in the Welsh hills, but—"

"Don't care," Matt said again.

Jodi shrugged, and when she went to speak again, Matt really began to say what he wanted to say.

"I blame you for everything. All of it. I blame you myself, and I've told the police you're to blame too, for bringing that psychopath into our lives. BB, that thug Lem murdered in my house, it's all on you. One of my neighbours saw the two of them breaking in, and Lem leaving on his own. And they found his body washed up on that beach, and took his prints and whatever else they do."

Jodi's eyes closed briefly at that, then opened again as she went to say something.

"I don't... want... to know," he said. "Whatever went on between you and him, whatever fucking horror and violence, I have no interest. But at least I'm off the hook, mostly. Though my house is still the murder house. That's what kids in the town call it now, you know – I heard them in the street. Two nights ago I went there to get some stuff and there were three kids looking in the front window."

"So where are you staying when you're not…?" She nodded behind him, in the vague direction of his tent.

"A friend's. Until I can rent somewhere else."

Jodi looked out across the river again, sighed, and said, "It's true I am to blame. All true."

"Kojak stuck to his word, bless him," Matt said. "But they know BB was dead before we put him down by the river. They found my van covered in his blood. I've persuaded them it was all Lem, coming after you because of something to do with your past. It tracks, you know. You're such a cold fish, everyone in town says so. So it all makes a weird sort of sense. I blamed it all on you."

"How are you?" she asked. She looked directly at him at last, her gaze going to the shaved scar above his ear.

"Hairline fracture. Headaches like a motherfucker. Had plastic surgery to reattach my ear." Matt blinked a couple of times, then closed his eyes. He could remember nothing about Lem attacking him. His last memory was the big man sitting on the bench beside him in the pub garden, and the next thing he knew it was a day later and he was in hospital.

"I'm sorry," she said.

"Don't… you… fucking dare," Matt muttered.

"Well, I am."

Matt snorted and looked past her at the river. He could still remember paddling past this place with BB, but for the life of him he couldn't recall what they'd talked about that day. Probably just friendly banter, the sort of stuff that two good friends fill their time with, countless words of no importance that fed the day and were therefore more important than ever. He felt sad that he couldn't remember, but BB was a warm place within him, a comfort. That warmth and comfort would be with him forever.

"I tried to come after you," he said.

"Huh?"

"In the hospital. When I woke up, I tried to get up, wanted to help you because I knew you'd gone after him. I fell, ripped the drip from my arm. Blood everywhere, apparently. And that's all because BB would have wanted me to."

Jodi looked a little shocked.

"They had to sedate me."

"I'm glad you're OK," she said.

"Huh." *I'm not interested*, he thought. *I really don't want to know.* But there were parts of Jodi's story that he knew he would never be able to ask about after today. "Your dad?"

"Dead," Jodi said. "Dead a very long time ago. Of course."

"You seem different. Quieter. Or maybe... calmer." *She's not like Jodi anymore*, Matt thought, and then he realised that he'd never known her. Not really.

"Sadder," she said. "Matt, I can't stay long."

"They're releasing his body soon. Funeral's in ten days."

"I wish I could be there," she said.

"Yeah, I get that. But you can't."

She lowered her eyes, rubbed her right shoulder with her left hand.

"I've lost my best friend," Matt said. "I know you loved him, and he worshipped you. I mean, you were the one. And I know you're cut up about it all, but… he was my other half, Jodi. We grew up together. Scrumped apples, rode bikes around town. He had the first girlfriend, of course. Got laid first, too, and never let me forget that. Our first drink, he stole four beers from his dad and shared them with me, down by the river close to where… close. He left town and I stayed here, but he came back. I loved him. I still do love him. And now he's gone."

Jodi nodded. Through his tears, Matt could see her own.

"I blame you, but I can't hate you. Part of me *wants* to hate you, but I can't and won't, because BB just wouldn't want that. But please stay away from me, and from here. Please."

"One condition," Jodi said, and before he could object she said, "Say something over his grave for me." He'd never heard her sounding so hollow.

"Yeah. Of course. What do you want me to say?"

She told him. Then Jodi smiled at Matt, turned and started walking away along the riverbank. He sat down again and watched her go, and even after she disappeared into the undergrowth along the overgrown path he kept watching for a while. But she never came back.

"There she goes, BB," Matt said to the river and the cooling autumn air. "The woman who calmed you down." He decided to stay for a little while longer to watch the setting sun.

THE END

ACKNOWLEDGEMENTS

Thanks as ever to my agent and friend Howard Morhaim for his wisdom and guiding hand. Big thanks also to Chris Golden for title discussions. And as ever, a shout out to the whole Titan crew, especially my editor on this novel Fenton Coulthurst.

ABOUT THE AUTHOR

Tim Lebbon is the *New York Times* bestselling author of *Eden, Coldbrook, The Silence,* and the Relics trilogy. He has also written many successful movie novelizations and tie-ins for *Alien* and *Firefly*. Tim has won a World Fantasy Award, four British Fantasy Awards, a Bram Stoker Award®, a Shocker, a Tombstone and been a finalist for the International Horror Guild and World Fantasy Awards. *The Silence* is now a gripping Netflix movie starring Stanley Tucci and Kiernan Shipka.

For more fantastic fiction, author events,
exclusive excerpts, competitions, limited editions and more

VISIT OUR WEBSITE
titanbooks.com

LIKE US ON FACEBOOK
facebook.com/titanbooks

FOLLOW US ON TWITTER AND INSTAGRAM
@TitanBooks

EMAIL US
readerfeedback@titanemail.com